Paris EVER AFTER

A NOVEL

K.S.R. BURNS

velvet morning
press

Published by Velvet Morning Press

ISBN-13: 978-0-9977676-5-0
ISBN-10: 0-9977676-5-0

Cover design by Ellen Meyer and Vicki Lesage
Author photo by Anne Lindsay

Adventure awaits

THE K.S.R. BURNS COLLECTION

Find out about new releases and deals
by signing up for Karen's newsletter:
https://bit.ly/Parisaholic

(She'll even send you *You Don't Want to Know* for free!)

Everything I write is for Steve

previously…

LAST APRIL—grieving the death of her best friend, unsure of what her future should be—Amy Brodie set off for Paris. Just for a few days. No one needed to know, not even her husband, William. But Will is not a fool, after all. Even though he was out of town at the time, he discovered Amy's absence and followed her to France. They argued. He returned to Arizona. After a short delay (not her fault), Amy went after him. Then they had another fight. A big one. Taking the gamble of her life, Amy set off alone a second time to Paris, where she's been living all summer long. It's now early September.

There. That should get you started.

one

WHATEVER HAPPENS, he must not see me. Not yet. Not like this.

I sprint to the opposite side of the street, barely avoiding a speeding purple Peugeot, and duck into the shadowy recesses of a nearby doorway. From here I can see without being seen.

Unbelievable. I pass the Hôtel du Cheval Blanc almost every day. But today—on my "special day," as Margaret has been calling it, when I feel particularly at ease and happy and hopeful and just plain good—William appears.

Checking into my former hotel.

William.

At least I think that's him, hunched over the cluttered reception desk, writing in the old-fashioned registration book.

I creep forward a few feet. The street is very narrow, and the hotel lobby is brightly lit so I have an excellent view.

Yeah, that's him all right. His hair is shorter and he has one of those hipster stubble beards and I think he's gained weight, but it's unmistakably William. As tall, as grave, and—I have to admit—as beautiful as ever.

Oh no. He can't see me. Not today, not yet. I'm not ready.

And though he doesn't know it, he's not ready either, because I haven't had a chance to tell him my big news. I study his profile as he extracts a blue American passport from the inside pocket of his jacket and hands it to the deskman. Seeing William again shouldn't come as a complete surprise. We are still married after all.

My scalp prickles. The last time I talked to William—about four months ago—he was furious at me for taking off to France for a week without telling him first. OK, I see now how this reaction could be understandable. Yet at the time, I was so freaked out. So mad. And so sad. All I wanted was a break—from my life, from my past and present and future. When I returned to Arizona and tried to apologize, he didn't accept that apology.

Nope, he informed me he never wanted to see my face again. Boom. Just like that.

So, feeling I had little to lose, I turned right around and came back to Paris. Just like that. Now it's September (already), and as crazy as it might sound, I haven't had a single reason to regret my rash move. Not so far.

The deskman holds up a key, which William accepts with a polite nod. In addition to it being weird for William to show up in Paris with no warning, it's weird he would opt to stay in the dumpy little Hôtel du Cheval Blanc, where the beds sag, Wi-Fi is not included, and the rooms lock with massive brass keys instead of compact twenty-first-century digital key cards.

It's also a major clue that he isn't here on some kind of company business. Absolutely. A cheapie hotel is all the confirmation I need that William is paying his own way. And that can mean only one thing: He's come to Paris to look for me.

I admire the straightness of his nose and the curve of his neck. Maybe he wants to get back together. Maybe he's lonely. In our four years of marriage, I've noticed he has no friends other than work friends and no family other than his granddad, who lives in Minnesota and only visits Phoenix at Christmas. William is a guy with many fine qualities that I've always admired, but he can be cool, aloof, stern. Withdrawn even. He may be coming to a realization that, in an important way, he needs me.

It's been hard to tell sometimes. On my wedding day I believed I loved him and he loved me. Simple. But it rapidly became more complicated. I know I haven't met his expectations, and I'm not sure he's met mine.

One thing I'm absolutely sure of, however, is that he has no idea I'm in possession of the wildest of wild cards. He doesn't know about Catherine.

I tuck the *baguette* I'm carrying under one arm and cup my melon-sized belly with both hands. Yes. There she is, as always, growing every minute. Surprise, William. You may be Mr. Science Guy, but this time I'm the one with the superior facts and data.

Not that I planned it this way. It's you who's been shunning me, remember? If you'd seen fit to respond to any of the many emails, voicemails, texts, and even postcards I sent you over the summer, I'd have told you about my pregnancy, about Catherine.

But you didn't. And so I couldn't. I wasn't about to leave my big news in a voicemail or write it on the back of a postcard. Who does that? No one. Telling someone he's going to be a father is major news, the kind of announcement you want to make face to face—or at least ear to ear. In real time.

Meanwhile, real time has slipped by like river water. I can't believe I've spent an entire summer in Paris. An entire intimidating, astonishing, exhilarating, and divine French summer.

The deskman points to a wooden staircase at the rear of the lobby. William picks up his carry-on and turns his back to me, jump-starting my heart into a wild gallop. I forgot how splendidly he moves. I forgot how good his butt looks in jeans.

Oh William.

I step out of my doorway hiding place as a woman about my age strolls past. I smile at her because though she has one child by the hand and another on the way, her pink ballet flats perfectly complement her fuchsia flowered top. She glances at my modest baby bump and smiles back. We're members of the same sisterhood, the smile says. Even her little one—a boy, judging by his blue cap—favors me with a toothless grin. I again place my hands around the satisfying roundness and firmness of my belly.

Catherine. My little stowaway. When I came to Paris—terrified because I'd rarely even been outside the state of Arizona—my unborn child came along with me, unafraid, unworried, unhesitant.

I had no clue back then. If I had known I was pregnant, I wouldn't have dared to come. But even before I received confirmation that she was growing inside me, I'm convinced it's

Catherine who gave me the courage to create my new Parisian life. Together we've discovered how to decipher the Métro map, repel street hustlers, tie a silk scarf a half-dozen different deceivingly casual ways, jaywalk without being run over by a bus, and slice through throngs of pedestrians without jostling a single elbow. Together we've learned the perfect French words to use to keep the bakery girl from selling us a half-burnt *baguette* and to charm the produce man into giving us the ripest melon. We can order in a restaurant. We can hail a cab. Paris is ours, baby. We own it.

When my phone jingles, I brace myself for the sight of William's handsome face grinning up at me from the touchscreen. It's happening. It's time. Despite myself, I can hardly wait. It's been so long since I've felt his, or anyone's, arms around me.

But my caller isn't William. It's Margaret, my excellent landlady-slash-confidante. She's probably wondering why I'm not back yet, even though it was she who sent me to fetch our dinner bread from the distant "superior bakery," the one with a sign in the window announcing that three years ago it was awarded a mayor's commendation for best *baguette* in Paris.

"Only the very finest for your special day, my darling girl," she said as she handed me the butter-soft leather jacket I've come to think of as my own. "Besides," she added, winking, "the fresh air and exercise will do both you and baby a world of good. Off you go!"

Off I went. Margaret came to Paris in her mid-twenties and has lived here for more than forty years, but she still sounds like the born and bred English lady she is.

"Amy dear, good job I've caught you," she says now. "I've just realized we haven't a morsel of Comté in the house. We can't very well do a proper cheese course without Comté, now can we? Would you mind terribly popping over to the cheesemonger's on your way home?"

I smile at the word "cheesemonger." It's classic Margaretspeak. "Comté. No problem. From our favorite place, right?"

Margaret and I have not only a preferred bakery but a preferred cheese shop. We're super organized. Our life together, unlikely and untenable as it may seem, is cozy and predictable and safe and relaxed. It's good for me and for Catherine. And even for Margaret. After all, I save her from loneliness, and she saves me from living under a bridge. Perfect.

She laughs. "But of course, my darling. Not more than two hundred grams, mind."

"Yes, I know."

"I'm so looking forward to our *soirée* tonight," she adds before I can thank her (again) for hosting tonight's dinner. Her voice is eager yet shaky. Not long after settling into Margaret's spare bedroom—at her insistence—I realized she's much more frail than she seemed when we first met, on only the second day of my original Paris trip. Lately she seems to have been getting frailer. Sometimes she even gives me the feeling she's about to slip through my fingers, like a snapped strand of antique pearls. "We've much to celebrate," she adds.

We do. Well, I do. Today I am not only officially five months pregnant, I am turning thirty years old.

Thirty.

I say goodbye, drop the phone into my tote bag, and gaze up at the sooty façade of the building across the street. The good-old-if-somewhat-crappy Hôtel du Cheval Blanc was my first landing place in France. In fact, there, on the third floor, is the window of my old room. From this very window, I studied and admired and lusted after Paris—fearful, guilty, exultant, grieving, thrilled. I dreamed of staying here forever.

Don't laugh. That's all it was at first. Just a crazy dream. I had no intention of leaving Arizona, and William, and my so-called life for good. No. I never meant for William to find out about my brief adventure. I never meant for him to get hurt.

But, oh, he did find out, and he did get hurt. For which I was and remain truly sorry. For which I owe him, in ways I can't articulate and have been doing a pretty good job at avoiding.

Catherine tickles me from the inside. Sweet girl. She's happy, uncomplicated, safe. She has no idea that her father is estranged from her mother and that said mother hasn't gotten everything together yet.

I'm trying. Now that I'm thirty, I need to try a lot harder.

For at least the trillionth time I wonder if I should've just left

Paris the second I found out for sure I was pregnant. It's what a lot of people might have done. No doubt most people. I often think the smartest, sanest, safest thing I could do is go back to Phoenix and try to work things out with William. But then I remember that William ignoring every single one of my attempts to get in touch with him probably means he really, truly doesn't want to see me and that I really, truly need to get busy on building a life as a single mother.

Now he's here in Paris. It's a little frightening, a lot confusing, and a tad titillating. No wonder I'm swinging back and forth like a birthday piñata, knowing only that whatever I do—or don't do—it needs to be the right thing for Catherine.

The tricky part will be figuring out what that right thing is.

two

"YOU KNOW AMY, I am of the opinion you have arrived at a crossroads," Margaret says as she reaches her cheese knife toward the Comté.

Hervé nods. "*Absolument.* Agreed."

Manu takes a sip of wine and says nothing.

We are near the end of my special birthday dinner. No one here can possibly know William showed up in Paris today, unannounced and unanticipated. I haven't even confided in Manu, who is usually the first person I tell about anything. I've been working hard to act completely normal all throughout the lavish meal, from the asparagus with Hollandaise sauce to the *confit de canard* to Margaret's famous *Pommes Anna* to now, the cheese course.

I look from Manu to Margaret to Hervé and back to Manu again. These are my three friends in Paris. "What do you mean?"

Margaret flutters her eyelashes at me as she positions a sliver of Comté on a shred of superior *baguette*. "Today marks your fifth month," she says.

"Right. Yes. I know."

Of course I know. And it seems incredible to me that I'm more than halfway through, but this is because my pregnancy was confirmed rather late. Oh yes. I was in denial for quite some time and didn't heed Margaret's entreaties to visit a doctor until mid-

July, when I was more than three months along.

Her green eyes sparkle. "A woman in your condition, my dear girl, needs to start taking far better care of herself."

"Margaret." I put down my fork. "What are you talking about? You think I'm not taking care of myself? You can't be serious!"

She laughs at me. Margaret's great gift is that she accepts people for who and what they are. But at the same time, she loves to stage direct the humans in her life. She thinks she knows best, and often, she's right.

Hervé waggles his forefinger at me. "Nevertheless, you cannot, *chère* Amy, continue to go on as you have been."

I sigh. Margaret and I met Hervé at a wine tasting not long ago. He approached us bearing flutes of champagne and a story about Margaret's late husband, whom he claimed to know from a business acquaintance. Now he's a frequent visitor to the apartment. He is charming, normally, but in every discussion, no matter the topic, he always takes Margaret's side. Sometimes I wonder why.

"Quite right, *monsieur*!" Margaret says. As she reaches across the table to squeeze my wrist, her elbow hops, and I worry she's going to knock over her wine. She's only sixty-five, but she isn't one of those hale and hearty oldsters who sails around the world solo or hikes the Pacific Crest Trail. She drinks more wine than maybe she should and takes a huge number of pills, red ones and blue ones and white ones and pink ones. I don't think even she knows what they're all for.

I ignore Hervé, wink at Manu, and smile at her. "Margaret. You don't have to worry. I'm fine. Catherine is fine. Really. No one needs to worry about anything."

Well, that may not be a hundred percent true. Even as we speak, William is somewhere out there in Paris, walking off his jetlag or eating his dinner or sleeping in his room at the Hôtel du Cheval Blanc, not far from this very spot.

Manu snorts. "*Aimée* is right. She must do as she pleases."

Everyone turns to stare at him because these are his first words since the asparagus course. "She is well. Strong. Happy. Is that not all we can wish for her?"

He pours himself another glass of the Saint-Émilion he

opened to go with the cheese. All evening, Manu has been quieter than normal, I think because Hervé is here. Manu doesn't like Hervé, and Hervé has little use for Manu. It was crazy of Margaret to invite them both, but she insisted. "We'll make it a party!" she said.

"Gentlemen! I think everyone can agree that we all have Amy's best interests at heart," she says now, and right hand still gripping my wrist, clamps her left around Manu's shoulder. His scowl fades, and for a moment it's like the sun has come out. All thoughts of William are erased from my mind. I feel lighter.

"Certainly, *madame.*" He reaches up to give her arm a squeeze. "You are correct."

Margaret and Manu remind me a little of William and his granddad. Best buddies. Mutual admiration society. Last April, when she first introduced him to me, explaining that "Manu" is the nickname for "Emmanuel," she called him her "young friend" and made it clear she thought the world of him. As well she should. He is good to her. They became acquainted when Manu dated Margaret's daughter, then stayed friends after the break-up, and grew closer after the daughter mysteriously disappeared. Which was two, maybe three, years ago. Way before I came to France. I don't know all the details, but I've always assumed the loss of her child is one of the reasons Margaret takes a multitude of pills.

"But Amy!" Hervé is practically bouncing up and down in his chair. He never likes to be left out of the loop too long. "I believe Margaret is trying to tell you it is time to stop your job."

I stare at him. "Stop my job? What? But no. I love it."

Just like that, the scowl on Manu's face is back. He knows, and I know, that by "job" Hervé is referring to the heavy crates filled with sandwiches and salads that Manu and I heft out of his delivery van every day and lug upstairs to third- and fourth-floor offices, often without the aid of an elevator. The lunchtime catering gig is the bigger of Manu's two income streams—the other one is freelance tech support.

"Nevertheless," Hervé persists, "you must guard the health of your child." He lifts his chin in triumph, proud of his ability to pull off the tricky pronunciation of an English word like "health," normally a no-go for French people. The man loves to show off his English, what can I say, and insists on speaking it whenever we're together. Manu is the opposite. He is all about me perfecting my French. I am too. But, let's face it. English is much easier. And it is my special day, after all.

"Hey, give me some credit for having a brain." I help myself to a hunk of bread, tear it in two, and try to think of a way to disagree without sounding disagreeable. "The exercise is great for me. And for Catherine."

"*Mon Dieu*, Amy!" Hervé arches his eyebrows into peaks and tilts his coiffed head. His grooming is impeccable. Maybe too impeccable. "You should be napping two hours every afternoon. You must avoid—"

"Two hours? Are you kidding me?"

Hervé ignores my interruption and continues to enumerate his points on perfectly manicured fingers. "You must avoid the lifting of heavy objects. For exercise, you should be making the promenades with me in the gardens at Luxembourg. You should register for new mother classes. You should drink plenty of water. Finally, you should eat less bread and more meat." He places his cheese knife at a precise forty-five-degree angle across the top of his plate and sits back in his chair, as if waiting for applause.

"Wow. Sounds like you've been googling tips for prenatal care." It's kind of a strain to be polite here because Hervé, as a newfound friend, shouldn't be passing judgment on what I do or don't do. "I appreciate your concern, Hervé. I really do," I add. "But, as a matter of fact, I have more energy than I've had in my entire life. Tons more. And people ought to work, right? Even mothers-to-be are allowed to work. Also, it's a lot more fun than my old career."

Which was human resources. Which I don't miss one tiny bit. I'd much, much rather work with food—buying it, cooking it, thinking about it, talking about it. Eating it. I even blog about it.

Now would be an ideal time for Manu to speak up again, but he's busy glowering at Hervé, who is frowning at Margaret, who is cutting herself a second helping of cheese. This is actually breaking a rule.

Yes, in France the cheese course comes with rules. It's hilarious. Women are served first. Older people are served before younger people. If a cheese is round you carve out a wedge. If a cheese is rectangular you cut an even slice across the short side. Your pieces should be no bigger than the size of your pinkie finger. Do not take more than three varieties of cheese, and, whatever you do, serve yourself only once.

I love stuff like this.

Margaret lobs the illicit cheese into her mouth and chews thoughtfully. Hervé shakes his head. I take advantage of the distraction to check my phone, which throughout the meal has been resting on my knee like a snoozing kitten, in flagrant violation of Margaret's strict no-electronic-devices-at-dinner rule. William should have contacted me by now. Before now, actually. As best as I can calculate, he's been in Paris for six hours.

Assuming that was him I saw at the hotel.

Because, who knows, maybe I was seeing things. Even before my pregnancy was confirmed, I stewed over why he was being so unreachable, and how he could have erased me from his life so completely. I obsessed. I cyberstalked him. I considered contacting Granddad, then rejected the idea, not wanting to bring him into it. Hell, maybe my hormonal brain just conjured up a William-shaped hallucination.

Hervé, still watching Margaret, glances at me, his nostrils flaring. "Nevertheless, Amy, you cannot go on like this forever."

Margaret bobs her head in wholehearted approval. "Just so, *monsieur*," she says. "Just so. Amy is in fine fettle now. But in a month or two—who knows? All we are trying to say is that our little Catherine deserves the best start in life, do you not agree?"

I rise to the bait. "Yes, of course I agree. That is my feeling exactly."

But I could have saved my breath because Margaret isn't addressing me. She's speaking to Hervé, with whom she is a little bit thrilled. I think he reminds her of her late husband, the Frenchman she fell in love with and left England for. Even more fabulous, and I bet the main reason she goes all fluttery when he's around, is that Hervé is a baron. Or would be if France still officially had barons, which since the French Revolution it does not. His full name is Hervé de Villiers, the "de" in this case denoting former nobility.

"Just so," he repeats, no doubt making note of this expression for later use. Hervé is always up for adding to his

English phrase book.

I'm trying to think of a way to change the subject when Margaret does it for me.

"Oh, Amy, dear, by the way," she says, her brilliant smile revealing a piece of peppercorn lodged in her teeth. "I have a surprise for you and *Mademoiselle*." She means Catherine. "After dessert," she adds.

A surprise. Margaret adores surprises, the bigger and more extravagant the better. She even adored—and unabashedly welcomed—the big and extravagant surprise of Catherine.

Unlike me, to be honest. Even when the signs were becoming unmistakable, I was unable to accept that what Margaret had been claiming since almost the day we met was true—that there was, as she insisted with absolutely no evidence, an "itty bitty baby in this teeny tiny tummy" of mine. When I did finally go to a doctor and was given the big news, I thought I would never stop crying. I was terrified. I grew up without a mother. How could I be one?

"Smashing," says Hervé, reaching to take my hand and lift it to his lips. I can't help laughing. Hand-kissing is the kind of eighteenth-century, courtly gesture this man is totally able to pull off. I guess when you're a baron it comes naturally to you.

Margaret beams so hard I think she's going to burst a blood vessel. "Right. Shall we remove to the sitting room?"

"But of course." Hervé leaps to his feet to pull out first Margaret's chair and then mine. Manu again snorts. "This man, he exaggerates," he said to me not long ago. I had to agree. Everything Hervé does feels larger than life, theatrical. I've never met anyone like him.

We settle into the chairs Margaret arranged in a half-circle in front of the fireplace, where a log flickers even though it's still early September. I claim my favorite spot, a nut-brown leather armchair closest to the flames, the muted phone tucked out of sight beneath my thigh. Manu and Hervé sit opposite me and as far away as possible from each other. A silver tray awaits on the hammered copper side table, laden with Margaret's best demitasse cups, the ones so thin they're translucent. Even Hervé would have to concede the impeccability of Margaret's service, the vintage silver and Baccarat crystal and Limoges china and starched damask *serviettes*. "Presentation is everything," Margaret likes to declare. That's true. Beauty counts. It makes your life calmer. Sweeter.

Humming, she cuts and serves the three-layer chocolate cake that's been standing like a jewel box on the dining table this whole time. Up to now I've been happy to just admire it because—and this is a true miracle—I no longer obsess about my weight. Not the insane way I used to. I can accept the plate she offers without so much as a flinch.

Like Catherine, it's another recent big change in my life. Before Paris, before Margaret, my relationship with food was, to put it mildly, complicated. We were best friends and mortal foes at the same time. I even had a whole long list of food commandments that I not-laughingly called my "rules for the perpetual diet." Some were sensible ("Never eat processed food"). Some were screwy ("Go to bed hungry"). All of them made me crazy.

I never told William, or anyone, about the rules because I didn't want people to know how psycho I can get sometimes. I tell myself I need to start being more forthright, more trusting. But such openness feels risky. Dad passed away when I was still in high school; my mother died ten years before that. Loss makes you cautious. Wary. At least that's how it's worked for me.

Besides, obviously, I'm a textbook introvert.

Margaret leads the singing of "Happy Birthday," puts her plate down without taking even one bite, hops up from her chair, and disappears into her bedroom. Seconds later she reappears holding a cardboard box the size of a small footstool. It isn't wrapped in balloon-printed paper or festooned with a pink bow, so at first I don't realize this is the birthday surprise she was talking about.

"Happy birthday, my dearest child," she says, puffing as she plops the battered box at my feet.

I lean forward as much as Catherine will allow. "What can it be?" I exclaim, though I've just recognized this box. I've seen it numerous times, actually. Manu and I exchange glances.

"Come, come. Open it!" Margaret is perched on the arm of the chair beside me, her finely lined cheeks bubble-gum pink.

No one speaks, not even Hervé, as I fold back the worn

cardboard flaps. I do it carefully because by this time I've remembered what the box contains.

"Oh wow, Margaret!"

I lift out a tissue-swathed parcel and unwrap it to reveal a pair of tiny white knitted angora booties. I blink back tears because these aren't just any baby booties. These are the footwear Margaret's lost daughter wore, twenty-five-ish years ago, when Margaret, after years of trying, finally succeeded in giving birth to a late-life child.

I look over at Manu, who is smiling his first real smile of the evening. He has very white teeth, which make his blue eyes appear bluer and his dark curly hair appear darker. And his look is much more put together than when I first met him. In any case, Manu is very unlike William, who is monochromatic, with brown eyes and dark blond hair and a year-round Arizona tan.

At Margaret's behest, I unwrap and display every teeny-tiny undershirt, gown, sleeper, frock, cardigan, bonnet, and blanket. Some are designer. Some are handmade. None are pink, or blue, or even yellow or green. All are purest white and sacred to Margaret or to anyone who cares about Margaret.

Over the summer I've watched her sort through these items from time to time, so I should have recognized the box right away. But who could ever dream she would allow such treasures to emerge from their tissue paper shrouds and enter into the chaotic day-to-dayness of my messy life?

Which, today—if that really was William I saw, and let's face it, I know it was—just got a whole lot messier?

"Margaret." I swallow hard. "I can't believe this!"

"My darling girl." Her eyes, too, are brimming with tears.

Hervé fidgets in his chair and consults his watch, holding out his arm and pushing up the sleeve of his blazer so everyone is sure to notice the vintage Rolex. He's bored because nothing that is happening right now is about him. Well, too bad.

Manu, ignoring Hervé with exquisite deliberation, leans forward to gather Margaret's thin veiny hands into his own. "It is a magnificent gift, *chère madame*," he says in his gravelly voice. She giggles like a girl, and he grins at her the same way he grins at me when I remember to employ the subjunctive after "*il faut que*." Manu wants me to learn good French, and I do too.

"Oh, tosh," she murmurs as she leaps up and heads to the kitchen. "It's a trifling thing."

Manu looks at me and shakes his head. It's definitely not a trifling thing. One morning Margaret's daughter left the apartment to attend class at the Sorbonne and never returned. The extensive police inquiry that followed came up empty. Margaret, already a widow, became that saddest of all things, a mother who lost her child. She had a serious breakdown, and still remains physically and emotionally fragile. Manu told me this so I could understand and forgive her occasionally erratic behavior.

This is why, while she's in the little kitchen fiddling with the espresso pot, I wrap up all the baby clothes and return them to their carton. She should have a chance to renege on her generous impulse. Margaret already does so much for me. Taking more advantage of her than I already am would just be wrong.

I'm folding up the last diminutive cashmere onesie when my phone vibrates.

It's what I've been expecting to happen all evening. On one level I've even been longing for it to happen. Yet when it does, I leap out of my chair as if zapped by a cattle prod, and the phone tumbles onto the carpet.

Manu tilts his head to try to read what's on the touchscreen. Hervé, who's rattling on about a vintage wine cellar a friend of his just inherited, doesn't even glance at the fallen object. He's in agreement with Margaret, or she with him, that electronic devices have no place at social occasions. "It is an insult to the host," he said the first time he saw me take out my phone at a restaurant and place it on the white tablecloth next to my plate. You'd have thought it was a dirty gym sock.

I scoop up the phone and palm it against my thigh. It landed face up, and even by candlelight I was able to read the name over the text message: William Brodie. Not that I needed to. In my new French world, the only person who texts me is Manu. So who else could it be?

For a moment I stand perfectly still, savoring my surroundings. The butter-pat yellow walls, the chocolate and robin's egg blue Aubusson carpet, the clove-dark beams crisscrossing the creamy plaster ceiling—how I love this place. In these last few months it has come to feel like my place. The job I have with Manu feels like my job. The life I have here, in Paris, feels like my life.

William is known for not liking surprises. But, boy, he sure likes having the element of surprise.

"Excuse me," I mumble as I hurry out of the room.

three

AS I'M LOCKING the bathroom door behind me, my phone vibrates a second time. Then a third. In fact, I don't think it's stopped vibrating since it started.

I sit on the lip of the footed porcelain tub and watch in amazement as a long string of text messages downloads one after another.

Ames. Hey. I just landed in Paris.

In taxi now.

Btw, happy 30th.

Staying at same hotel you stayed in before. Room v small. Noisy buses going past every 3 mins.

You getting these?

Going out to eat now. Pizza joint around corner.

Just back from dinner. Amy, where are you?

Amy. Cut your crap.

I know you're getting these.

WTF?

Answer me NOW. I don't have all night.

Amy I'm warning you.

Listen. Really tired. Going to bed now. Expect to hear from you tomorrow.

I put down the phone. Whoa.

From the timestamps, and the contents, I can tell these

messages were composed and sent over the course of the last six or seven hours. But for whatever reason they all arrived just now, together. William's phone must have had trouble connecting to the French service provider.

I read through the thread two more times. It's comical in a way. Taken as a group, these messages could form a kind of highlight reel of our brief courtship and marriage. When I met William, at an office holiday party given by the company where we both worked, he was even-tempered and friendly. Factual. Genial. Charming even.

But as time passed, he grew impatient with me. Suspicious of my activities, dismissive of my troubles. Finally, at the end, he grew angry. Cold. Withholding.

Oh William. Was it my fault? Did I drive you to this behavior?

I scroll up and down the thread. Well, at least he remembers today is my thirtieth birthday. But that's not so terribly surprising, when you think about it. William is super good at keeping track of dates. He's never once forgotten to present me with a heart-shaped box of See's chocolates on February 14th or a dozen long-stemmed roses on September 4th, my birthday. The reason is simple: Dates are numbers, and numbers are his thing.

There's one more text, I now see. It consists of a single emoji—a big fat red question mark.

Weird. William learning to use emojis is not a development I would have predicted. Emojis are frivolous and open to misinterpretation. Texting itself is not fun for William, who hates typing on his phone. "The user interface is suboptimal for my thumbs," he once complained to me. I laughed at the time—he's such a geek—and can't help smiling a little now.

If only I had Kat to tell all this to. After all, if husband William can rematerialize in my life out of thin air, why not best friend Kat?

I get up and walk to the window, a lump forming at the back of my throat. Kat always knew the right thing to do. Even when she was wrong she was right, because Kat had a way of making me feel better about myself, my life, my everything. And then cancer came and took her away, stealing her life from her and her friendship from me.

The windowpane feels flat and cold against my forehead as I try to peer through the thick, almost opaque, glass. All summer I've been amazed at how late the sun stays up in Paris, which is much farther north of the equator than Phoenix. Now I'm amazed at how sunset seems to arrive five minutes earlier every day. But even if it were light outside, which it isn't, and I could see the street from this window, which I can't, I would never have the chance of spotting Kat as I still so often imagine her: striding along the sidewalk, a snarky grin on her face, her honey-colored hair long and thick and wavy, the way it used to be before the chemo.

Kat. Her death last spring is the real reason I snapped and came to Paris for my original "break." All through her long illness, we talked about and planned the trip to Paris we'd take when she got better. But she never got better. So after she died, I went on the trip alone, as a solace. An escape. A time in between my life as it was and my life as it was going to be. It didn't seem like too much to ask. William's opinion on this would differ, of course.

But even now I often picture her magically appearing at my side, alive and vital and well, bursting to tell the story of what a crazy misunderstanding it all was, the cancer and the three long years of futilely fighting it. "No way," she would say, smacking me wetly on the cheek. "That couldn't happen. We're too young. Let's go out for ice cream or drinks."

It's only a daydream. Kat never will magically appear. These days I don't drink, and when I eat ice cream, it's with Margaret, whose laughter I can now hear in the next room.

"Manu!" she is saying. "You wicked boy." He's always teasing her. It's sweet. Even when she sinks into bouts of sadness, as she often does, he never fails to find a way to make her laugh. Margaret and Manu's relationship is jokey, tender, and respectful, like a loving mother and son.

She even frets about him as if he were her own. "Manu is a young man capable of succeeding brilliantly at whatever he lays his hand to," she'll say. "If only he would finish school or settle down to a real job." It drives her to distraction that Manu, who himself turned thirty this year, is not on a corporate or professional track. Instead he chases after his twin passions, food and technology, and tends to get lost in them, sometimes to the point of forgetfulness. I try to tell Margaret not to worry. There are worse qualities to have.

I lift my head from the windowpane to listen. Manu is saying something I can't quite make out. Hervé is oddly, for him, silent. Wait. There he is. "*Madame!*" he exclaims, loud and clear. "Allow me to make a suggestion."

Funny. Not that long ago these people were complete strangers to me. Today they're at the center of the beautiful new life that I, with ridiculous luck and some work, have managed to create for myself.

Yes, I know it's a precarious life. According to God and the State of Arizona, I am still bound to William. Our business remains unfinished. Catherine is waiting for me, expecting me to do the right thing, which does not involve spending the whole night hiding out in the bathroom.

I turn my back to the window and tap out a brief text:

Hey. Just now got all your messages. They were delayed. It happens sometimes.

But before I press "Send," I pause. His last message was, "Expect to hear from you tomorrow." By now he may have managed to fall into a jetlagged sleep. If so, I sure don't want to be the one to wake him up with a text chime. A sleep-deprived William is never a cheery William. I delete my text, not wanting to send it off by accident.

Caution is wise, because he's going to go ballistic when he finds out I'm having a baby. He'll be enraged he wasn't immediately informed even though it was his fault for ignoring my many attempts to reach him. He won't believe me that it was July before I myself found out. He will bring up his "rights," just as Margaret has been doing recently.

"He at least needs to be told he's going to be a father," she reminds me on a semi-weekly basis. It's weird because, at first, she wasn't in favor of me leaving her and returning to William. Ha. No way. From the moment we met, by chance in a café, she seemed to crave my presence, my company. Manu says this is because I remind her of the daughter she lost. Yet as my pregnancy has progressed, more traditional notions have started to take hold in Margaret's mind. "Your baby is something you and your husband made together," she'll insist.

I don't disagree. Even before I knew for absolute sure about Catherine, my life in Paris has been shadowed by guilt, by a sense that I owe William something—a degree of allegiance, a measure of loyalty. At the same time, I'd like to just say, "Thanks a million, babe, for those lovely, lively sperm. Couldn't have done it without you."

Snark.

Out in the next room, Margaret laughs again. I'd love to possess an elegant silvery laugh like hers. She's nothing at all like my own mother, or at least how I remember my mother, who rarely laughed, but when she did, produced a squeak that sounded more like a sob. And who is, like Kat, dead and gone. Also like Kat, I wish I could have had more time with her, especially now that I'm about to be a mother myself. My situation gets a little scarier every day, to be honest. I adore Catherine, and want to meet her more than anything. But yikes.

I stand up, step to the sink, splash some water over my face, and use my wet hands to slick my hair behind my ears. No more hesitating. Must get going. Everyone is probably wondering what I've been doing in the bathroom so long.

Just before opening the door I check my phone one more time. No new messages have appeared. William, engorged with pizza and numbed with jetlag, must be sound asleep.

Good. Today is still my birthday, after all. I'd like to enjoy what's left of it. So I power down the phone and stash it under a stack of bath towels. If William does wake up and decide to text again, or call, I don't want to know. Not tonight.

Because, damn it, he has nerve, showing up here and threatening to put an end to my happy-ever-after.

four

AS I EMERGE from the bathroom into the sitting room, I feel as if I've stepped into the last act of an amateur stage production. Hervé is standing at the front door, buttoning his coat. Margaret is hovering nearby, clutching a white linen tea towel. Manu is seated beside the fireplace, elbows on knees, expression unreadable.

"Your invitation for a *digestif* is most flattering, *monsieur*," Margaret is saying. "Alas, I have a frightful amount of matters to attend to here."

"What's going on?" I ask. I was counting on a second slice of cake with my coffee. A *digestif* is supposed to come afterwards. If at all.

Hervé transfers his beady eyes from Margaret's face to mine. "Amy, I desire to invite you and *madame* to accompany me to a club."

"A club?" I cross the room to stand beside Margaret. It's nearly midnight. The last thing Catherine and I should do right now is go out clubbing.

"Yes. It is members only. Very exclusive." He rubs his palms together like a praying mantis.

"It sounds charming," says Margaret. "You, Amy, my darling, absolutely should go. And you, too, Manu, my dear boy," she adds, flapping the tea towel in his direction.

I hesitate. What I should do is stay home, help with the dishes, and go to bed. But the problem is that no matter how many dishes I wash, or how early or late I get to bed, I know I'm going to lie awake for hours obsessing over William. The man is staying only a few blocks from where I am standing right now. I can almost smell his signature vanilla-scented cologne. What's more, seeing him today, fleeting as it was, reminds me that my old desire for him is not dead. It's crazy, I have to admit. Always has been.

Yet I worry about leaving Margaret. "Are you sure? I don't want you to do those dishes by yourself," I say. She looks so tired. Her hands are trembling.

She chuckles. "Don't worry, my child. I'll save them all for you!"

"Good. You better. Seriously, I mean it."

She loops her arm through mine and leans against me. Usually I handle the cooking—I even buy the lion's share of the groceries, which is the least I can do seeing as I live here rent-free. But tonight, Margaret insisted on preparing the whole birthday dinner by herself, from *apéritif* to *entrée* to *plat* to dessert. Well, the dessert we bought at a bakery that specializes in American-style layer cakes. Our oven isn't big enough for something like that.

"I promise. No dish doing for me." She slings the tea towel over her shoulder. "Meanwhile, you young people should enjoy life! Have a *digestif* for me!" She laughs her silvery laugh as she reaches for the coat rack, where my black fingertip-length trench hangs from a curved brass hook. It was brand new when I first came to Paris last April. Now it's rumpled beyond redemption, partly because it was a cheapie coat in the first place and partly because it got completely soaked on a crazy trip I took down into the catacombs with Manu and some of his friends.

The memory makes me want to giggle. Exploring the forbidden Paris catacombs was the first true adventure of my life. Never in a million years would I go down there again, yet I love that such a place exists. When I walk the streets of Paris it's cool knowing a second Paris exists only a couple dozen yards beneath my feet, a city of shadows under the City of Light. I adore every single new thing I've learned about Paris and France. It's been awesome.

"Here." Margaret is holding up not my ratty black trench but her crisp tan Burberry. "Take my coat. The weather report predicts rain." She inserts my arms into the sleeves the way you would do for a child. "Off you go! I'll be asleep by the time you get home."

Before I can say another word, I've been gently shoved out the front door, followed by Hervé and—a half minute later—Manu.

The three of us clomp down the stairs in silence. My guess is that Hervé is annoyed Manu is along, and Manu is annoyed Margaret is not along. I, by contrast, am happy to be along. It's still my birthday, for one thing. For another, once Catherine is born I won't be able to just pop out for a late-night glass of whatever with friends. My life will be very different. I'm a little scared, as any sane person would be. But, also, I can't wait. Kat is no longer here to be loved, but Catherine will be, soon.

We step out onto the street, still in silence. I half expect to see Manu pivot on his heel and stride off down the sidewalk. Or return upstairs to spend the rest of the evening with Margaret. I wouldn't put it past him to do all those dishes by himself.

But Manu doesn't leave my side. When a cab pulls up, all three of us pile into the backseat, me in the middle, and we squeal off, heading west toward the rue de Rivoli.

As we speed along, I lean forward to peer out the side windows. This cozy enclosed spot, though it smells like cigarette smoke, feels like a good place to be right now. Tomorrow will be soon enough to find out why William has come to France. Tonight, I'm brimming with a mad joy.

After all, I'm in Paris.

I'm home.

Of course, this is ridiculous. I was born and raised in Phoenix, Arizona, and had never even traveled back East (much less overseas). But the first time I stepped onto a Paris sidewalk I felt wholly at ease. The sky was the color of pewter. The streets were shiny jet black from a night of rain. I walked for miles, sloshing straight through puddles, invincible in my boots and then-pristine black fingertip-length trench coat. It was, to date, the nicest walk of my entire life.

We are rocketing past the long, sober façade of the Louvre

when Hervé murmurs a few words to the driver, who a block later turns right off the rue de Rivoli and onto the broad avenue de l'Opéra. I scrunch down in my seat to gaze up at the Opéra Garnier, an ornate square building presiding at the end of the avenue like an enormous billion-calorie birthday cake.

It's funny. You'd think in a crowded metropolis like Paris there wouldn't be enough space for you to be able to admire things from a distance. But there is, and you can. Notre-Dame Cathedral is set on an island in the Seine, the Arc de Triomphe stands in splendid isolation at the top of the Champs-Elysées, and the Eiffel Tower can be spotted from all over town. You can turn down some anonymous little street and be treated to a perfectly framed snapshot view of an iconic monument, like the Sacré-Coeur or the Panthéon. It pays to keep your eye out. Be ready to be dazzled, Kat would say.

I'm wondering if our destination tonight is near the Café de la Paix—the café someone said the whole world eventually walks by—when our cab veers into the black maw of a poorly lit side street. All three of us pitch to the right, briefly pinning me between Hervé's bony shoulder and Manu's much more muscular one. My heart thumps. Without warning, we've plunged into one of the dark narrow lanes that Napoleon III told Baron Haussmann to replace with airy broad boulevards, all the better to march soldiers down to keep the rabble in line. Haussmann obviously missed this one. Perhaps barons are just not that reliable.

A hundred yards later the cab brakes, screeching, and Hervé opens his door before we've even come to a complete stop. "Come," he says, reaching for me. I don't need help exiting a car, just as I don't need help rising from a chair, but I allow him to assist me anyway. It's his thing. "No doubt he was brought up by Swiss governesses," Margaret once mused. "He has such lovely Old World manners."

Whether or not this is true, Hervé always seems to know the right way to conduct himself. He exudes a noble sense of self-assurance that I envy. Some people are just naturally confident, I guess. Not me. I often feel awkward or uncertain. I often do the wrong thing, or say the wrong thing, or make decisions hastily and fall into situations that most people would avoid. I react, instead of act.

That's got to change with Catherine on the way. Whatever happens or doesn't happen with William.

Manu leaps out of the cab a nanosecond before it lurches away, and I catch sight of Hervé's grimace in the red glare of the taillights. He was probably hoping the car would take off before Manu could get out. Honestly, the antipathy between these two is so thick you could cut it with a cheese knife.

"Where are we going?" I ask Hervé, but he doesn't reply. He only bares his whitened teeth in a glittering smile, happy to be the one with the upper hand. I mean, seriously. What is it with men and their need to control everything?

I reach out to brush Manu's elbow, to reassure myself he's still there. It's creepy here. We can't be far from the place de l'Opéra, where no fewer than seven major boulevards converge, but this forgotten *quartier* is hushed, deserted. The few street-level stores have long since closed up shop for the night, and the shutters on the upper-floor windows look as if they haven't been cracked open for decades. That's another surprising factoid about Paris. A mere half block from a bustling thoroughfare you can find yourself entirely, gloriously alone. All you have to do is round a couple corners, and poof, it's as if you've traveled miles instead of yards. It's uncanny. William would say there are wormholes.

We walk a few yards to the mouth of a street even darker and narrower than the one we're on, where Hervé pauses to pull two small flashlights from his pocket and passes one to me. Who knew Hervé was such a Boy Scout? I aim it so both Manu and I can navigate by its thin beam and am again reminded of our adventure in the catacombs. That was way scarier—black as ink, filled with icy pools and bottomless pits, studded with caverns hip-deep in human bones. "Weren't you terrified?" Margaret asked, her eyes wide. "Yes," I said. "But Manu was there. I never actually felt unsafe."

Margaret is easily disturbed so I didn't go on to explain that, in any case, safety is an illusion. It's a lovely story we tell ourselves, a fairytale that gets us through the night. Besides, she surely knows this, deep down. The loss of her daughter must have taught her that. The deaths of my mother when I was eight and my father when I was eighteen were how I learned.

Also, Kat's death.

I still miss her so much. Every day.

"*Voilà.*" Hervé touches my elbow.

We've stopped in front of a windowless unmarked door. It looks more residential than commercial, and for a second I wonder if this is where Hervé lives. Margaret and I often speculate about what Hervé's apartment is like. That it's baronial goes without saying, and both of us look forward to being allowed to see it someday. However, I'm ninety-nine-point-nine percent certain that while he might take me there, he would never take Manu.

Which is why I'm not surprised when he doesn't get out a key—the enormous antique brass key with a filigreed handle of Margaret's and my imaginings—but simply gives the door a push. It swings open noiselessly to reveal a smoky hallway, beyond which I can hear music and see tables and chairs.

As we step inside my first act is to scan for William.

I know. It's ridiculous. The odds against him being here are astronomical. Spotting him today has sent my brain into a whirlwind of speculation and paranoia and desire and panic. My worlds are colliding and most likely not in a good way.

"All right?" Manu touches the back of my hand, his blue eyes bright with concern, but all I can do is gaze around the room and think how William would hate the low ceiling, painted black, and the rough plank walls, also painted black, and (especially) the multitudinous votive candles littering the marble table tops. A firetrap, he would call it. The sole feature here that he might approve of would be the zinc bar. "Zinc is a living metal," he once told me. "It changes its color over time in reaction to its surroundings."

William is always divulging obscure pieces of information like this. Some are tedious. Some are intriguing. In the early years of our marriage he used to spend hours explaining how things worked. Engineering-type things like Tesla coils. Kat said I was nuts when I confessed to her that I thought this was adorable. But it was. Maybe it could be again. I shift away from Manu and let Hervé help me off with my coat, the hair on my arms standing up.

Not because the room is cold, or Hervé's touch is electric, or I've changed my mind about running straight to William's side, but because of the Bach cantata being played by an acoustic guitarist seated on a round raised platform in the center of the room. I recognize the piece right away because my mother was addicted to Bach. Whenever Dad, not a classical music fan, wasn't around she would put on her stack of battered records—we were among the last vinyl holdouts—and play her cantatas and chorales and preludes and hymns at full blast with all the windows open. We were the outcasts of the neighborhood. To this day, Bach gives me a stomachache and makes me homesick at the same time.

"Hervé, let's go somewhere else."

But Hervé doesn't hear me or doesn't choose to. He's acknowledging the aggressively thin woman gliding over to us. She smells of patchouli and is wearing a sequined black chemise that hangs from her shoulders to her ankles in a perfectly straight line.

By contrast, I have on a billowing white knee-length tent dress with shoulder pads, a vintage item of Margaret's lent to me for the evening. As a matter of fact, I now see I am the only person in the entire place not dressed all in black. And I'm definitely the only one here who is pregnant.

But the woman takes no notice of me or of the modest belly flaring out my white dress. She leads us toward a round table the size of a large pizza. "*Voilà*," she says.

The Bach piece has ended so I decide to give the place a chance. Besides, the guitarist is hot—tall, lanky, dark hair, blue eyes, one slender loafer-clad foot hooked behind a rung of his stool. He embraces that guitar like it's a woman, like I wish someone would embrace me.

Whoa. Down girl.

"You are *très belle*." Hervé reaches across the table to squeeze my fingers, and I let him—because all of a sudden I am yearning for the warmth of a human touch, of skin on skin. But when I catch the scowl on Manu's face I pull my hand away.

"Very gallant," I say to Hervé while smirking at Manu, who should know that Hervé's not only too young for Margaret but too old for me. In any case, I have no interest in prehistoric

Hervé, and he surely has no interest in pregnant *moi*. I would know, as my sexual antennae are finely tuned these days, thanks to hormones, and I guess, deprivation.

Anyhow, I don't feel beautiful. I feel as enormous and conspicuous as a harvest moon. Though I realize I'm not supposed to care about my size anymore, a lifetime of fat phobia isn't that easy to drop, not totally, not even during pregnancy. I guess I'll always be fighting those encroaching pounds one way or another. If not physically, then mentally.

Manu is shifting his chair closer to mine when his phone rings.

"Is it Margaret?" I ask as he unpockets his phone, glances at it, hops to his feet, and hurries away.

Of course Margaret would be my first thought. She's special to me, despite the fact that last April she purposely attempted to prevent me from leaving Paris—and her—by lacing my evening cup of herbal tea with what I found out later was a bit of her insomnia medicine.

Yes. That happened. The sequence is complicated. When William figured out (from credit-card charges) that I came to Paris for my "break," he followed me. We had a nasty fight. He returned to Phoenix. I wanted to follow him but was temporarily thwarted by Margaret and the aforementioned sleepy tea. When I did get back to Phoenix, William and I promptly had a second fight, the big one, the one where he told me he never wanted to see my face ever again. Literally minutes later, I boarded a plane and returned to France, where I've been ever since.

All of which is to say, I guess, that Margaret's sleepy tea plot was ultimately successful. I forgave her long ago. She is easy to forgive. She is a darling.

Just as Manu slips out of the room, phone pressed to the side of his face, he turns back toward me and shakes his head. Ah. So it isn't Margaret. It's probably one of his computer clients. They need help at all hours. Manu may not be ambitious in the way Margaret thinks he should be, but when he works, he works hard. His single-minded ability to focus is amazing.

"At last," Hervé murmurs, and for yet another moment of sheer ridiculousness I wonder if he engineered this phone-call interruption to get rid of Manu.

Yup, the day's events are definitely turning me paranoid.

"*Un Cognac, s'il vous plaît.*" He's addressing a waiter who, like the hostess, seems to materialize out of the ether. "And for you, Amy? What shall you take?"

"Um—"

"*Et pour madame, une tisane,*" Hervé instructs the waiter, and for once I'm grateful for his overbearing ways.

In some aspects, Hervé reminds me of William, who also likes to be in charge. When it comes to our marriage, William has always seen himself as the CEO and commander in chief. Not to mention the holder of the majority stock options, the signer-off on the budget, and the wielder of the absolute veto. I'm a little embarrassed to admit that at first I liked this nineteen-fifties-sitcom approach to domesticity. It made me feel safe. Normal. Not like the orphan I was. And am.

Our drinks arrive as the guitarist launches into a soft slow flamenco. Hervé takes a sip, leans back in his chair, and looks down his nose at me. "Amy," he says, "I ask myself, why does not Margaret leave the washing up to her servant?"

"What?" I have been busy feasting my eyes on the guitar player. "Her 'servant'?"

Hervé rubs his palms together, again reminding me of a praying mantis. "Just so. She should not have to concern herself with washing crockery. To prepare a meal is an art worthy of any lady. But to scrub and clean—"

It feels good to laugh out loud. "You think we should have employees to wash up after us?" I say this like it's a crazy idea, even though it's likely Hervé has servants. Maybe he can't imagine life without them. Maybe they are *incontournable*, as the French say. Something you cannot do without.

"Why not?" he asks.

I shrug and squint toward the door. Manu's taking a long time with his client.

But Hervé is not to be put off. "Tell me, Amy. Is Margaret quite well?"

"Of course she is," I reply, hoping this is true. "She just gets tired a lot."

"I am aware she lost a daughter." He lets his voice trail off suggestively. "But does she not have other family? In England, perhaps?"

I wonder how much he knows about the daughter, whose name no one has ever told me, and shrug again. "Not that I'm aware."

"Or friends?" he persists. "Surely she has connections in Paris?"

I sip my drink.

Hervé is undaunted. "I inquire, because I know how very important Margaret is to you. She is a most dear lady."

"She is," I agree. He's right about that at least. "You know that after her daughter disappeared she had a sort of breakdown, right?"

I pause, not wanting to go into too many details, though Hervé makes a good point. It's weird that Margaret is so isolated in Paris. So alone. She's lived here most of her life. Why doesn't she have a string of devoted friends or at least relatives on her husband's side? Why is it only Manu and me?

Of course, I'm not one to talk. In Phoenix, aside from William, I only had Kat. The rest of my acquaintances, from school and work, were just that—acquaintances. They started to slip away when I got married, William being even more solitary than me, and during the years that Kat battled cancer, they disappeared entirely. I haven't tried to get in touch with any of them since. In a way I'm angry with these people. Not because they disappeared in my time of need but because they're still alive when Kat is not. How dare they? It's so unfair.

Hervé smiles his feline smile. "Ah well. You and I must therefore be her family, n'est-ce pas?"

"You and me?" I say this way too loudly for a French public place.

Hervé scowls. "I mean simply that we ought to care for her." He has lowered his voice to a whisper, as if to compensate for my American-style volume. "For example, we can help her manage her apartment. It is magnifique."

He's right about that too. Margaret's apartment is indeed magnificent. Even though I've been inside only one other apartment in Paris—Manu's tiny studio—I've come to realize that a place with two full bathrooms, a washer and a dryer, hand-blown eighteenth-century glass in the windows, a working fireplace, and an entire wall of exposed stone that is who knows how old is very likely extraordinary.

Hervé perseveres. "Perhaps she has other properties as well? Investments? Holdings?"

I glare at him. "Holdings?"

This isn't the first time Hervé has pumped me for information about Margaret. Sometimes it even seems he asks questions to which he—as a friend of her husband—should already know the answers. I really wish Manu would finish his phone call. He could help me deal with Hervé.

"But of course. I assume she keeps a country home. Perhaps more than one." He picks up his snifter, swirls it, and puts it down again. "Amy, my dear child, it is not uncommon for people of Margaret's class to possess considerable fortunes. I am just proposing that we could perhaps assist with her affairs."

I peer down into my tisane. The waiter brought not *verveine*, which is my favorite, but *citronnelle*, which is just OK. Hervé's questions are ridiculous. If Margaret has a "considerable fortune," she's never mentioned it. Nor would it occur to me to ask. I'm about to tell Hervé that Margaret's so-called affairs are none of his, or my, damn business when Catherine baps me in the bladder.

As usual, her timing is excellent. I leap to my feet and catch the eye of the elegant hostess, who nods toward a hand-lettered sign at the far end of the room: *Toilettes*.

I hurry away without excusing myself to Hervé. I don't like him much right now. I'm not sure I ever did.

five

I SQUINT TO READ the tiny Roman numerals on the egg-sized Waterford crystal clock Margaret recently gave me to keep on my bedside table.

Eight o'clock. William has been in Paris for fifteen hours. More or less.

It's more than past time to make my move.

First, I power up my phone. When I got back last night, I retrieved the phone from its hiding place under the bath towels but did not turn it on. It was past two a.m. I was exhausted. Disgusted. The final portion of my "special day" had been spent parrying Hervé's questions about Margaret's private affairs and waiting for Manu to return from his phone call, which took ages. When he did appear, he announced he was leaving and suggested I do the same. In short, the "members-only nightclub" was kind of a bust. I ended up going home in a cab, alone.

I should've fallen asleep right away. Instead, I tossed and turned and considered the idea that William chose to arrive on September 4th on purpose, as a kind of birthday surprise. Which would mean that now, in addition to being mad about not getting an immediate response to his text messages, he's mad his surprise flopped. I worried for hours, yet I was still unwilling to risk phoning and waking him.

So this morning I'm glad to see no fresh texts from William.

Also no voicemails or emails. I guess he's waiting for me to respond. Maybe he's evolving. Just as I am. Or maybe, and perhaps more likely, he's zonked out. A long flight east makes waking up in the morning a real bear.

I set the phone next to the clock, hop out of bed, and head for the bathroom. The apartment is hushed and still. Margaret, who normally brings a morning cup of milky English Breakfast tea to me in bed, is not yet up.

This also makes me glad. With the excitement of my birthday dinner passed, she might now have the bandwidth to notice something going on with me. Margaret may be capricious, but she's also observant. She was the one who insisted I take a pregnancy test, only days after we met. However, the wand she provided was out of date, weirdly showing up as both positive and negative. I didn't even know pregnancy wands could go bad. But, apparently, they can and do. Either way, I was convinced I couldn't possibly be pregnant, which is why it took me so long to go to a doctor.

In a funny way, I'm in Paris because of a defective pregnancy test. Because if it'd been accurate I never would have gotten on an airplane after that final fight with William. I would have come clean about my situation, and we would have reconciled. Probably.

At the very least I would've stayed put in Arizona, where I've got health insurance and citizenship. No sane woman would flit off to a foreign country, alone and pregnant. Fortunately, the cost of health care in France is remarkably reasonable, and so far, I've been able to pay for my doctor's visits out of pocket. But as for a long-term plan, well, guess what. I don't have one. The confirmation of my pregnancy still feels so new. I'm still in the reeling stage.

And who knows? Maybe the whole issue is about to be resolved for me. Maybe it's the right thing.

I pull on yoga pants and my favorite long sweater, and let myself out of the apartment. Catherine flutters like a hummingbird as I thump down the three flights of stairs and burst out into the brisk morning air. Most babies fall asleep when their moms are in motion, but Catherine does the opposite. She perks up. She'll be an athlete. Or a dancer. Something physical.

Minutes later, I'm hurrying up to the door of the Hôtel du Cheval Blanc, quivering with apprehension, fatigue, excitement, and hope. Also hunger. I neglected to eat breakfast, or even to grab a slice of leftover birthday cake on my way out the door. But this morning my plan—my sane, adult plan—is to meet up with William and invite him out for a proper French breakfast. Buttery *croissants*. A steaming hot *café crème*. A good way to start the day and maybe the rest of my life.

I'm reaching out to open the smudged glass hotel lobby door when I spot William. Like yesterday, I shiver all over. Like yesterday, he's standing at the reception desk, though this time with his back to me. He seems to be waiting to speak with the deskman, who's on the phone.

This wasn't the plan. I never dreamed William would be up and out of his room so early. I assumed I'd have time to get here, station myself in the lobby, and be waiting for him to come down, a smile on my face and a baby in my belly—the element of surprise, for once, belonging to me.

I pull back my arm. I'll just wait for him to come out. It's better this way—after all, it would be weird to have a deskman witness my first meeting with William after so long. Awkward. A public sidewalk is, paradoxically, much more private.

Meanwhile, I get out my apricot lip gloss and apply it while studying William from behind. Odd. His hair is unwashed, his shirt is wrinkled, and his shoulders are slumped forward. Slovenliness is not like him. Slumping is especially not like William, who as a former military man is known for fabulous posture.

He must be even more exhausted than I am. The bargain Hôtel du Cheval Blanc is located right next to a busy bus stop— even now a pair of turquoise and white city buses is huffing and puffing in the street behind me—and from my own brief stay here I remember how the rumbling of engines kept waking me up every ten minutes. Poor William. Buses combined with jetlag may have made his night at least as restless as mine, if not more.

I tuck my hair behind my ears and straighten my own posture. Any second now he'll turn. He'll stop short when he spots me. His eyebrows will shoot up. Then he'll smile (a little), cross the small lobby, and step out onto the sidewalk. Where I'll be ready and waiting. "Hello, Will," I'll say. "Long time no see."

As for what comes next, well, I don't know. My future, including my relationship with William, is a big fat question mark.

The deskman finishes his phone call. William steps forward. His back is still to me, so I clearly see him pluck a rectangle of white printer paper from his hip pocket. But I can't tell what it says on the paper because when he unfolds it and holds it up his shoulder blocks my view. All I can see is the deskman shrugging. William, who obviously doesn't know that a shrug is French for "I don't know, and I don't care," flattens out the paper on the desk and begins to gesticulate with both arms.

This is another oddness. William isn't the kind of person who gestures while he speaks. All his movements are controlled and intentional. It's one of the qualities that attracted me to him. William is a brainiac, but he's also very physical, graceful, and I've often thought how Catherine must get her athleticism from her father.

When William's gesticulating elicits nothing but a second shrug, he refolds the paper, jams it back into his jeans pocket, and turns around to face the glass lobby door.

He's not smiling. His forehead is creased. His jaw is clenched. As he moves toward the door I shrink to the side—I can't help myself—so that when he steps out I'm standing off to his left, about six feet away, yet close enough to smell the vanilla of his aftershave and see the individual hairs of his new stubble beard.

This is it. William should be spotting me. Right. About. Now.

But, incredibly, he doesn't.

Instead, his eyes sweeping right over me, he turns and stalks away, shoulders hunched, hands plunged into the pockets of his jeans.

I'm about to open my mouth to shout his name when I recall that not only has William failed to get whatever information he was seeking from the deskman (strike one), he is operating on little sleep (strike two). Worse, he hasn't yet had his coffee because the Hôtel du Cheval Blanc doesn't serve breakfast (strike three).

He's clearly in a black mood, a black-enough mood that he doesn't even notice me—his own wife—standing in plain view.

I follow. He moves at a rapid clip, as if he knows where he's going. Two blocks later I realize his destination is the Café de la Poste. It's the café nearest the hotel and therefore the logical breakfast destination. Still, this is yet another thing that feels odd. The Café de la Poste is where I ate my first meal in Paris. It's where Margaret and I first met, last April, when she came to my rescue after my purse was stolen, another one of my little misadventures. We often still come here to grab a cup of coffee or eat lunch. It's a little annoying. William is retracing my steps, sleeping in my hotel, breakfasting at my café. All of this is probably accidental, but still.

At least he doesn't sit at my table. That would be too weird. He chooses a spot near the bar, his back to the door.

While he waits to order, I conceal myself behind a card rack outside the bookstore across the street. Yes, I do feel silly. "What does it mean," Kat would certainly ask, if she were around to ask anything, "that you find yourself tailing your husband down the street like a cartoon detective? What does it mean that you don't just walk up and talk to him?"

It's a pretty good question. It most likely doesn't mean anything good. But I have Catherine's welfare to think of. William always needs a jolt of caffeine before he's fit for human companionship. Besides, my plan is totally to "walk up and talk to him." I just want to do it in my own time and in my own way. Not haphazardly, how I used to do things.

William is speaking to the waiter—in English, I'm sure. Unlike me, he isn't burdened by years of French lessons and therefore feels no compunction to try to speak it. He addresses everyone in English and assumes he'll be understood. And, apparently, he is, because a minute later the waiter appears with a basket of *croissants* just as delicious-looking as the *croissants* I order in French.

It's torture. Normally at this time, I'm sitting across the cherry wood dining table from Margaret, sipping a second cup of English Breakfast tea and nibbling on a *brioche*. Or a *tartine*. Or a *pain au chocolat*. Or a *croissant*. I dig around in my tote bag, locate a packet of trail mix (now that I'm pregnant I always carry food with me, for emergencies), and toss back a handful of cashews.

Two minutes later, however, I chortle out loud. The waiter

has returned to William's table bearing a teeny tiny cup of coffee. I know exactly what happened. William ordered a *café*, using one of the only French words he knows, and received not a good old cuppa joe but a thimble-sized shot of inky black espresso. And William hates espresso. Despises it. He doesn't even much care for lattes. In this respect he's like his granddad, patriotically insisting on drinking only thin watery American-style plain black coffee. Perhaps he learned this in the army. But it's surprising, because otherwise he's such a foodie. He's the one who made me a foodie. "Cooking is an art at which I predict you can excel," he said, back in the early, fun days. He opened up the world of fine cuisine to me. I'll always be grateful to him for that.

If I were sitting at that café table with William, I could make sure he receives his cup of American-style coffee—it's called a *café allongé*. I could even try talking him into ordering a *café crème*, which is the proper beverage to accompany your breakfast *croissant*. If I were at William's side, as many people might say I ought to be, I could explain all this and more. I could help him discover a Paris most tourists never see. He might be impressed, even grateful.

Or not. William usually prefers to be the one possessing the superior facts and data. It's his thing. He needs it, craves it, which is why I've always been happy to grant it to him.

Anyway, right now he's getting along just fine without my help. When he points to the espresso and shakes his head, the waiter instantly removes it and returns less than a minute later with a large steaming *café allongé*. Done and done. William has no need to speak French. Perhaps he has no need of me.

I take out my phone to check the time. Nine-thirty. Margaret must be awake by now, wondering where I am. In addition to forgetting to eat breakfast, I forgot to leave her a note. I also still haven't done the dishes from last night. My best move right now may simply be to text William—briefly, pleasantly, maturely—and suggest we meet later today. Like for lunch. That would give me time to go home, check on Margaret, have breakfast, shower, do up those dishes, and put on more of a power outfit than yoga pants and a sweater.

It's a plan.

I'm about to start tapping my message into my phone when

William takes out the same folded sheet of paper he showed the deskman at the hotel, unfurls it, and uses it to flag down the waiter, who steps forward, frowning, to look.

This waiter is the same dark-haired lugubrious guy who last April served me my first wonderful breakfast in Paris. (It was an omelet with French fries. Yes, French fries for breakfast. I felt so naughty.) He's almost always the waiter who serves Margaret and me when we come here. Every time we enter, he and she kiss each other on the cheek like old pals, though I don't think they even know each other's names.

The waiter now has the mysterious paper in his hands. He holds it out at arm's length, squinting at it, while William sips his coffee and lounges back in his chair, his posture relaxed, expansive, as if he wants the waiter to be absolutely sure who is the alpha male here. Not for the first time I wonder if I know everything there is to know about this man whom I married so hastily and so thoughtlessly. "Your mystery man," Kat used to call him. Once she even suggested he might be an axe murderer. It was a dumb joke. William isn't an axe murderer, or a Russian sleeper agent, or a CIA operative in deep cover, or a participant in the Witness Protection Program, or anything else special or out of the ordinary.

He's a regular guy. An engineer from Minnesota. Nice. Normal. Loves math, science, baseball, and babies. Changes the oil in my car for me. Taught me how to make pasta from scratch. Those are just a few of his many fine qualities. I tried to explain all this to Kat, but for a long time she wouldn't hear it. She was jealous of William, resentful of our love, never thought he and I were a good fit, and even once tried to break us up. Which makes it all the more touching that at the end she came around to him. Some of the last words she said to me were, "Take a closer look at Will. I don't want you to be alone."

Kat loved me more than she loved herself. Nothing is more rare.

Meanwhile, I'm itching to see what the heck is on that sheet of paper. A bus has halted traffic between my lookout post and the café, so I dart across the street and sidle up to the window. Again, I'm barely six feet away from William. Again, he's oblivious.

I'm shifting to a better vantage point when the waiter flips the paper over to check the opposite side, and I at last get a look at what he's been studying for so long.

It's a photograph.

Of me. Pre-pregnancy, pre-Paris me.

Now that's bizarre.

William comes to France looking, I assume, for me. He gives no advance warning. When he arrives he doesn't call me directly. He texts instead. But he also comes equipped with a photo of me, as if foreseeing the need to do a little amateur detective work. Perhaps he's feeling guilty for ignoring my many attempts to get in touch and is worried I'll refuse to see him. My failure to immediately answer his texts would confirm that—he has no idea the messages didn't arrive until hours later.

I'm not sure whether to feel flattered, creeped out, or amused.

The waiter is refolding the sheet of paper when, somewhere nearby, a car alarm starts to shriek. He looks around, sees me standing out on the sidewalk, and his eyebrows shoot up.

Only last week this same waiter served Margaret and me warm goat cheese salads and apricot tart. Now I'm the subject of some American guy's sleuthing. What must he think?

We stare at each other for approximately an eternity and a half. Finally, the waiter returns his gaze to William, the faintest flicker of a smile floating across his face.

Then he shrugs.

Even William must have figured out what a French shrug means by now.

The spell broken, I turn and scurry back across the street, clutching my belly with one hand and my tote bag with the other. This time traffic is being held in place by a taxi, so Catherine and I again make it across without being run over. I head straight into the bookstore and stop only when I reach the back wall, where I feign interest in a display of rainbow-colored notepads while trying to steady the pounding of my heart.

It's a while before I'm calm enough to steal up to the front of the bookstore and peek through the open doorway. The car alarm has stopped. The taxi is gone. Traffic is flowing freely again. William is still sitting in the café, his back still to the window, munching on a *croissant.*

The waiter is nowhere to be seen. Wait, there he is. He's standing outside on the sidewalk, puffing on a cigarette, and looking straight at me. I lift a hand and wave. He inclines his head.

"*Merci,*" I mouth.

He winks, tosses the cigarette into the gutter, and reenters the café.

"You can count on the French to be discreet," Margaret once told me when I asked her why none of her neighbors seemed to care, or notice, that a pregnant American woman had taken up residence in their building. "The concept of privacy is important here," she explained. "You are left to live your life as you please. All people ask is that you do the same for them."

What a nice custom.

I'm still standing inside the bookstore and considering my next move when William takes another *croissant* from his basket. It's his third. I assume he'll inhale it as rapidly as he did the first two, but instead he puts it down and gets out a selfie stick.

This is the last thing in a million years I would expect him to do. William has never owned a selfie stick. He disapproves of them. He thinks they're stupid.

He fumbles a bit attaching the phone to the clamp, an indication that this is William's first-ever selfie. But only he and I are aware of this. Only he and I hold our breaths as he frames a photo of himself with the *croissant.* He doesn't pretend to take a big bite out of it or act goofy in any way. He just gazes gravely into the phone, cradling the *croissant* next to his cheek, almost close enough to touch his new hipster facial hair.

Wrinkled shirt, private eye sleuthing, a selfie stick. None of this jibes with what I know of my controlled, conservative husband.

The one thing I do know is that if William were in my place, he wouldn't act in haste. He would take the time he needs to gather facts and data, form a working hypothesis, and determine a reasonable, prudent course of action. "People do things backward," he used to complain to me. "They make up a theory and then look for ways to support it."

True. That's how people are. And that's why I'm sure he

would absolutely approve of the fact that—after he's devoured the third *croissant*, paid his bill, and exited the café—I again choose to follow him from a distance.

Facts and data. You can't have too much of the stuff.

He wanders down the wide boulevard, taking his time, pausing every few yards to snap a selfie. At the bakery with the red-and-white-striped awning, he positions his face so he shares the frame with a window display of tarts and cakes. At the wine seller's, he gestures with his thumb toward the open door and winks. Two blocks on, he poses beside a wooden cart filled with oysters and mussels on chipped ice. He walks right past the tiny flower shop that sells only roses. He takes no notice of the store that sells only white dishes.

I trail him as if tethered by a cord. At any second, I'm poised to dash into a boutique, dart down a side street, or duck behind a lamppost, should he unexpectedly turn and look back. But he never does. William has seemed to forget all about why he has come to Paris. He's seemed to forget all about me.

Six blocks later he veers left. By this time, he's collapsed the selfie stick and stowed it back in his pocket. His stride grows longer, more fluid, and it becomes difficult to keep up with him. After all, I'm sleep-deprived and hungry, and have the still small but precious weight of Catherine to slow me down. If William knew I was a mere dozen yards behind him, carrying his unborn child, he would not be walking so quickly.

He would freak out.

William's parents died in a car crash when he was three. He was raised by his granddad, just the two of them on a hobby farm in Minnesota. One of the first things I learned about him was his strong desire to have a family. It was how our story started, actually. We met in December, nearly five years ago. In late January I got pregnant (that first time was unintentional too). By early March we'd married, bought a house, and started to furnish a nursery.

The miscarriage came not long after. To William it was an enormous disappointment. To me it was more complicated. I wanted time to process my grief, to process all the changes in my life—it had all happened so fast. Waiting a year didn't seem unreasonable. Then Kat got sick, and she remained my sole focus for three years.

I know William wants to be a father almost as much as Catherine needs to have a father. He will be thrilled when I tell him the news. Hell, if he hadn't been ignoring me all this time, he'd have known for weeks already. I feel sorry for him.

Moving even faster now, he reaches the quai des Célestins, where he turns right.

The sole interesting feature of the quai des Célestins is that it runs parallel to the Seine. If you stay on the side farthest from the river, however, it's a pretty boring walk. I shun it because it's devoid of food. Not a single bistro, café, restaurant, cheese shop, *crêpe* stand, falafel joint, sushi vendor, bakery, *pâtisserie*, *épicerie*, *supermarché*, or deli. Not even a mini-market.

In Phoenix I hoarded junk food. In Paris I focus on the good stuff—*croissants* made with real butter and sorbet made with real fruit and *crêpes* made with real buckwheat flour. When I'm out walking, I choose routes that take me past the ready-to-eat food shops called *traiteurs*, where I can admire platters of creamed spinach and buttery mashed potatoes and béchamel-enrobed *endives au jambon*. I find excuses to wander by *boucheries* so I can inhale the mouth-watering aroma of the roasting chickens set out on Ferris-wheel-style rotisseries every morning. I will go blocks out of my way to loiter in the open-air aisles of greengrocers and ogle the bins of feathery escarole and jewel-like raspberries, and—when the vendor is not looking—cup my hands around fuzzy peaches and dream about the downy heads of newborns.

Not that I can't just buy some peaches. I can. I have a job, savings, and a place to live. I have friends and a life and maybe even a future here. Just last week, Margaret's lawyer sent us a pile of forms so I can apply for a French residency card.

William is now coming abreast of the Hôtel de Ville. We've been wandering for more than two hours, and when I catch sight of his face in the reflection of a window, I see he is almost smiling. The caffeine and carbs have kicked in. The exercise has lifted his mood. I apply another layer of apricot lip gloss, finger-comb my hair, and button up my ratty trench coat. Now is beyond time to catch up to him and say, "Hey, Will. I got your texts. Wanna have lunch?"

We rebooted our relationship that way once. We'd had a

disagreement, and after not speaking to me for a couple days, he showed up at my place with a packed picnic basket and a plan to drive up to Sedona for the afternoon. "Don't go," Kat counseled when I hastily texted her for advice. But I ignored her and went. And had a good time. Maybe too good, as it resulted in that first, short-lived pregnancy.

A lot of people would be jealous that I seem to get pregnant so easily.

An enormous tour coach passes me, swerves to the curb, and proceeds to disgorge tourists—Scandinavians, judging by their height and blondness. I lose sight of William. He is tall but not as tall as your average Norwegian.

I take the opportunity to phone Margaret, who should be up by now. When she doesn't answer, I find a stout cement bollard to sit on and eat some more trail mix. Observing William all morning has reminded me of the many things we have in common. We both like *croissants*. And long walks. And wine, shellfish, and bakery displays. We're both orphans. In fact, this shared experience of vast loss is what first drew us together. It made me sympathize with him and feel I understood him.

Now we have something else in common. Something new and wonderful—Catherine. Maybe she'll be what brings us together for good. Maybe that would be the right thing.

The Viking throngs disperse, but William is still nowhere to be seen. I finish the trail mix and dial Margaret again. No answer. I wander for a couple blocks and am screwing up my courage to finally text him—because this game of cat and mouse is getting ridiculous—when I round a corner, and there he is. He's seated at a café across the street, not inside but outside on the sidewalk terrace, facing the street.

I'm halfway across the street, heading straight for him, when I notice he's talking on his phone.

Damn.

This isn't how I want things to go. For my big reveal, I want and need to have William's undivided attention. Catherine deserves no less. Hell, even I deserve it. So I find another bollard and sit down. Not hiding this time. Not behind a car or a sign or a kiosk. Out in plain sight. But he's immersed in his call and doesn't notice me. I'm starting to wonder if I'm invisible. Or so changed that I'm unrecognizable.

Or perhaps it's just that whoever is on the other end of the line is enthralling.

But it's most likely Robert from work. William would naturally want to check in with the office, and Robert is entertaining—if you enjoy bathroom humor. Also, his job or anything related to his job always completely absorbs William. Work is his passion, maybe his chief passion. So I sit and study the swell of his biceps and the indent of his waist. He hasn't gained weight, as I initially thought. He's been going to the gym. He's ripped.

William listens with enviable focus, his shoulders shaking with laughter. A blonde woman takes a seat at a table near him, and unlike me, catches William's eye. He's always said he prefers brunettes, like me, but the way he looks at this blonde indicates he notices them too. Another surprise, in this day of surprises.

The phone call drags on. William leans back in his café chair and props his right ankle on his left knee, revealing a pair of shoes I haven't seen before. Black suede ankle boots, very hip. Not the kind of stylish footwear I would expect William to select or even know about.

New shoes, a new beard. If I didn't know better, I'd think he's met someone. But I do know better. William is painfully shy around women. Aside from me, he's had only one other serious romantic relationship in his life, with a girl in Minnesota who left him to sing in a bluegrass band. No, most likely his new look is related to his recent promotion. The company owner wears a stubble beard and ankle boots. Now William does too.

I take out my phone and notice it's past noon. At first this means nothing to me, except to remind me how hungry I am, but as William carries on his endless call I realize that noon in Paris is four a.m. in Phoenix. Way too early for a work-related call.

William smiles—he has a killer smile—and throws his head back in unrestrained laughter. I have not seen him laugh this long, or this hard, for ages. It gives me hope. It also confuses me.

six

I SIT ON THE UNCOMFORTABLE cement bollard watching
William talk and laugh for what seems like thirty years, but which,
according to my phone, is only thirty minutes. This morning his
behavior started out odd, and it's becoming odder. For example,
he's unaware, or doesn't care, that he's using up a ton of data on a
single call. That's not like William. Unless the company is paying
for the roaming charges. That would explain it.

My stomach is growling. My feet are tired. I'm starting to get
a headache. Just last night I heatedly told Hervé that I never nap,
but I would love one now, just for twenty minutes—what
Margaret calls a "nice lie-down."

So without further ado, I turn my attention back to my
phone.

Hey Will. Welcome to Paris.

I push "Send" and wait.

And wait.

It's maddening. His phone must have pinged. Even if he has
the sound off he would have felt the thing vibrate in his hand.

I try again.

*Hey. I got your texts. They were delayed and didn't arrive till late last
night. That's why I didn't answer.*

This time he removes the phone from his ear and glances at
it. Ah. Finally. I stand up. Surely he'll end his call with Robert or

whomever and text me right back. Or call me. Or—here's an idea—switch his focus to across the street and recognize me, his wife. His pregnant wife.

But no. He returns his phone to his ear and resumes his conversation.

Unbelievable.

This is too much. I head for the nearest Métro station. I glance back a few times, but William remains deep in conversation, nodding attentively, the smile faded from his face. I suppose it's important. It better be. Whatever, I'm not up to playing second fiddle to a phone call. He saw my text and ignored it. The ball's in his court now.

The distance that took two-plus hours to meander takes mere minutes by Métro, and I even get to sit down—a fifty-something woman offers me her seat, nodding at my midsection, and I gratefully accept. I don't try calling Margaret again. She's obviously done something to her phone, which she often knocks off the hook or manages in some other way to render inoperative. Anyway, I never get good service down in the Métro, even though they say they offer free Wi-Fi.

Just as I'm pushing open the heavy street door of Margaret's building, my phone rings.

Great. He waits until I get all the way home before calling. William, your timing is awful.

Tempted to let it go to voicemail (which would serve him right), I get out my phone anyway, only to see that the smiling face on the touchscreen is not William's. It's Manu's.

Oh no.

The lunchtime deliveries. I was supposed to meet Manu at ten-thirty.

I clap the phone to my ear. "Manu! I am so sorry! I forgot all about the deliveries!"

"*Aimée?*"

Manu uses the French version of my name, pronouncing it "*Em-ay.*" I've never corrected him because it sounds so much more beautiful than plain old "Amy." Plus, every time I hear it, I think how "*aimée*" means "beloved."

"You forgot?" he asks. I can tell he's upset because he's speaking to me in English, which he does when he wants to be absolutely sure I understand.

I let the massive door latch behind me and move a few steps deeper into the entryway. "Manu, listen. I am so, so sorry."

I really am. Today is Thursday, our biggest day. Normally we meet up at his apartment and take his van to a restaurant to pick up the pre-made lunches—on Thursdays we swing by three restaurants. But this morning I was so wrapped up in thinking about William that I never once thought about Manu, much less about all those hungry office workers waiting for their sandwiches and salads.

"*J'ai tout à fait oublié*," I add, as if repeating the apology in French will somehow make my thoughtlessness less terrible.

"*T'as oublié?*" he repeats, his tone incredulous. You forgot?

"Yes, I—it—"

I stop and try to order my scattered thoughts. I want to tell Manu what I've been up to all morning, but I also want to reveal the news in the right way. William's arrival is so momentous. Manu may be hurt that I didn't confide in him immediately, which would have been the natural thing for me to do. He knows the whole story of my shotgun marriage and of Kat's death and of my numerous unsuccessful attempts to get in touch with William. In fact, he knows my entire life story, chapter and verse, as we have tons of time to chat while stuck in traffic on our daily deliveries. I've surprised myself by confiding in him so completely. He's too easy to talk to, that's the problem.

I lean my shoulder against a cool wall of metal mailboxes. The entryway is drafty and coldish, even on hot days, but it's a good place for private conversations because it's almost always empty. "Manu, I have some pretty interesting news," I begin, part of me thinking I should first ask if the deliveries went OK but the rest of me too overwhelmed by my own problems to focus on Manu's. "Yesterday, on my way back from the bakery, I saw—"

"Amy! Amy!"

Someone is shouting my name. I take the phone from my ear and step forward into the interior courtyard, a serene indoor/outdoor space created by walls of cream-colored stone, a floor of square light gray cobbles, and a ceiling of pale blue sky.

"Amy!"

For a mad, sad second I imagine it's Kat. I often think I hear her, or see her—even in Paris, a place she'd never visited. She still exists in my head and my heart, though, where I guess she'll live forever. In that way you never really lose the people who die. At least this is what I tell myself.

"Amy dear, where are you?"

Of course, the voice floating down from above doesn't belong to Kat. It's Margaret. Which makes a lot more sense.

What doesn't make sense is how hoarse and raspy she sounds. Not her usual pure clear tones.

"Listen, Manu, Margaret is calling me," I say into my phone as I hurry across the courtyard toward the foot of *Escalier B*, the staircase that leads up to Margaret's (and my) apartment. "She sounds weird. I have to go. I'm sorry. I'll call you back as soon as I can."

He'll understand. Manu knows all about Margaret's fragility. Anyway, I don't wait for him to answer because Margaret is shouting my name again, her voice even louder and shriller than before.

"Ammeeee—? Are you coming? I saw you out the window. Hurry, darling, hurry!"

The last syllable is cut short, causing me to pause and grasp the worn wooden handrail for support. What if William has discovered where I'm living? What if he's up there with Margaret right now, freaking her out with a million questions? I consider turning back. Running.

But no. That's ridiculous. William is either chattering on his phone or chowing down on a big French lunch. Also, the very idea of turning back is out of the question—in four short months I'm going to be a mother. A parent. My turning and running days are over. Time to grow up. Way past time, I guess.

"Amy? Hurry, child, hurry!"

She's shrieking now. I take the stairs two at a time, and when I round the last landing, she's standing in the open doorway of the apartment, her mouth agape and her long thin arms stretched out toward me. She's barefoot and wearing her bathrobe even though it's nearly one p.m.

"There you are! At last!"

"Margaret! What—what is it? What's wrong?"

She bares her teeth in a too-wide, too-bright smile and darts forward to grab my hands as I mount the last few steps. "Come, child, come! You will never believe what has occurred!"

Her breathing is labored and her face flushed. I worry she's having a heart attack or a stroke. My mother died of a stroke. One minute she was her normal self, yelling at me for being the bratty little kid that I no doubt was. The next, she was gone. Completely, permanently gone. That's how it happens sometimes. We think things will last forever, that people will stay with us forever. Until they don't.

"Margaret, please tell me what's going on." As she tugs me into the apartment I check the coatrack for signs of William's jacket. I know. It's insane.

"Oh Amy. Oh Amy. I cannot find the words!" Margaret lets go of my hands and takes me by the shoulders, her icy fingers digging into my flesh.

"Margaret, what is it? Are you all right?" I try to squirm away, but she has a surprisingly powerful grip.

"All right? Oh yes. It is all happening, it is indeed."

She again flashes the too-big smile, revealing the chip on one incisor, and pushes me into the sitting room.

As I stumble forward the first thing I notice is a pair of blood-red leather slippers. They are lying in a T in the center of the chocolate and robin's egg blue Aubusson carpet as if someone has just kicked them off. The slippers don't belong to me, or to Margaret, though they're similar to a Moroccan-style pair she sometimes wears. These are far more exotic, however, with long pointy toes and extravagantly embroidered uppers.

The presence of the slippers bothers me. Our apartment is never in disarray. The Limoges figurines are always dusted, the creamy lace curtains are always starched, and the Baccarat vase is always filled with fresh cut peonies or roses and placed just so on the marble mantelpiece. Margaret and I do not leave items of clothing lying about.

Nor do we let dirty dishes sit out after meals. But now the cherry wood dining table is strewn with the remains of lunch— the uneaten half of a leek quiche, some green salad, a nearly empty bottle of white wine, and what's left of my birthday cake.

It takes a second hard push from Margaret for me to notice the woman sprawled in the nut-brown leather armchair next to the fireplace. My armchair. She's about my age, or maybe a few years younger, and is wearing a flowing black caftan. Her feet are bare—the exotic slippers must belong to her—and are very dirty. So is her shoulder-length ash blonde hair. She has unusually huge round eyes that she fixes on my face and doesn't move, even to blink, as Margaret ushers me across the room to stand before her, like a peasant being presented to a princess.

"Amy!" Margaret says, her voice shooting up another octave. "Amy, allow me to present my daughter, Sophie."

My polite smile freezes in place. Margaret has a daughter named Sophie?

To the best of my knowledge, Margaret had only one daughter—the one whose name no one has ever told me. The one who vanished without a trace, whom I supposedly resemble, whose clothes I often wear, and in whose bedroom I now reside. The girl who long ago wore the gorgeous baby clothes Margaret gave me for my thirtieth birthday just last night.

This lamented lost child is how Margaret and I met. After Margaret recovered from her breakdown, she started taking up with young women who reminded her of her daughter, often picking them up at random, as she did me at the Café de la Poste. "They weren't all as *sympa* as you," Manu said to me when he explained all this. *Sympa* means nice. It made me feel he approved of me, which made me happy.

"Sophie, darling," Margaret is saying. "Amy is the young friend I've been telling you about. The American? The one expecting a child?"

Sophie barely glances at my baby bump. She's too busy chewing on her thumbnail and jiggling her knee. She possesses none of Margaret's elegance and warmth, and doesn't even seem to physically resemble her, except for the fact that her enormous round eyes are green. For a split second I wonder if she's a home invader. After all, any amount of weaponry could be concealed under the voluminous folds of that caftan. She could be holding Margaret, and now me, hostage. I hang back, half expecting her to whip out an AK-47 and start demanding our cash and jewels, but after a few seconds she apparently remembers her French manners and holds out a small, none-too-clean hand.

We shake. We do not kiss on both cheeks, which would be

the normal greeting in France between two similarly aged young women (even on first introduction) and which means I may have been purposely snubbed.

"Why don't you two girls chat," Margaret says, clasping her palms together like a mother superior. "I'll put the kettle on."

Sophie remains seated, so I sit opposite her, in the chair Margaret usually occupies. "Um, hi," I say. I try not to stare at the elaborately beaded caftan, which like her feet and hair is filthy. As a matter of fact, I have never seen such world-class dirt on anyone. Not even on a homeless person on the street. It seems impossible that any daughter of Margaret's could let herself get into such a state.

"It's Sophie, right?" I ask. "Nice to meet you. Have you been at school? Traveling?"

Sophie has leaned forward and is eyeing the diamond bangle bracelet Margaret gave me last May. It was a gift "for no reason," she said. I told her it was too extravagant, but she insisted, and I decided to wear it, but only on a sort of loan.

I pull my sleeve down over the bracelet and refrain from asking Sophie any of the other many questions running through my tired, malnourished brain—Why doesn't anyone talk about you? Where have you been all this time?—because I'm pretty sure she would not reply. We sit together in stiff silence, listening to Margaret rattling dishes and tunelessly humming in the kitchen. At one point, Catherine gives my lower ribs a soft nudge, reminding me how worn out I am, how much I'd like to have a bath and a nap, and how good that leftover quiche smells. My eyes wander to the dining table.

Lunch remainders mean Sophie must have arrived around late morning. Maybe earlier because not only is Margaret not dressed, her usually perfect silver hair is sticking out in all directions. I recall the multitude of mood-regulating pills Margaret still takes and wonder if we're heading toward trouble.

"How long do you stay?"

I jump. These are the first words out of Sophie's mouth.

"How long do I stay?" I repeat. I can't tell if she wants to know how long I've been here or how long I intend to be here.

"You. Here." She waves a grimy hand around the apartment. "When?" If she recognizes how rude this sounds, she doesn't care.

"You're asking when I'm leaving?"

"*Oui.*"

My breath catches. I've never heard anyone say "*oui*" quite in the way Sophie says it. She squeezes the life out of the word. She exterminates it, expelling it through her lips in a brief violent blast of air. They say French is a beautiful language, and it is, but I've come to realize it depends on who is speaking it, and how. And why.

"Well," I begin. "I'm going to have a baby."

Sophie sits back and lifts her left eyebrow in an expression that in Arizona would mean, "No shit."

"And I am, sort of, living here," I continue. "With Margaret, with your mother." I run my thumb over the bracelet. "She's wonderful, your mother. An amazing woman. So kind. So good."

At this point I stop. I'm not saying anything Sophie doesn't, or shouldn't, already know.

We've lapsed into another uncomfortable silence when Margaret enters the room carrying a large silver tray laden with her English bone china tea set. Not the Cornishware mugs with the wide blue stripes we use for everyday, but her best vintage Spode with the tiny pink roses.

"Right. Here we are."

Margaret is breathing heavily, but before I can jump up to help her—Sophie keeps her butt firmly planted in my chair—she places the tray on the hammered copper side table. "*Ouf.* Good job I laid by these lovely bon-bons. You never know when you'll be in need of a proper celebratory sweet, I always say!"

Smiling so widely I worry her face will split in two, she produces a small golden box of a dozen Godiva chocolates from underneath the table, pulls a brocaded footstool forward, and plops down on it. "I'll be mother," she says. That's what English people like to say when they pour out the tea. It's a thing. She knows I find it funny, and she giggles at me as she tips a splash of milk into each of the three dainty cups.

Other than that, we are silent as our tea is sugared and milked and passed around. I open the box of chocolates with the Swiss Army knife Manu gave me for my birthday, which is still difficult to believe was only yesterday, and Margaret proffers them first to

Sophie, who grabs the box and gobbles up two pieces rapidly one after another, as if she fears someone will take them away from her. I salivate at the sight of the chocolates and continue to puzzle over the possibility of Margaret's having two daughters. But the truth is I'm having a hard time making my brain work. Last night I got less than four hours of sleep, and it wasn't sound sleep. This morning I walked for miles. And I'm famished. I sip my tea, wishing I had the nerve to help myself to some chocolates. But the box is on Sophie's lap. Miles out of my reach. Like William.

"Amy." Margaret is speaking to me but does not take her eyes off her daughter's waxy face. "Is it not the most marvelous thing you could ever imagine? I still cannot believe it. The most marvelous thing." She shakes her head as if to clear it of cobwebs and stretches forward to caress Sophie's fingers. She doesn't seem to notice how dirty and broken the fingernails are. Sophie does though, pulling her hands away and tucking them under the folds of the caftan.

"Oh, are you tired, darling?" Margaret's voice swoops up yet another octave. "But of course you are! Come. You can take a rest on my bed. Or would you like to have a bath first?" she adds brightly. "Perhaps that would be better."

Aha. So she does notice the dirt.

I can't help smirking as Margaret hops up and hastens toward the bathroom. She's halfway there when Sophie surges to her feet, jostling the tea tray and almost knocking over the footstool. She's shorter than I thought she would be, one of those people who oddly look taller when sitting down.

"*Your* bed?" She places the box of chocolates on the mantelpiece, a good six feet away. "*Mais pourquoi?* But why? I have my own bed, do I not?"

The fact that Sophie speaks English with a French accent surprises me. By all rights she should sound endearingly British, like Margaret. But Margaret's French is also impeccable. Maybe that's what she spoke with her husband and children (and I'm still trying to work out if Margaret did indeed have more than one child), making English Sophie's second language.

Margaret spins around, needing to reach out to place the tips of her fingers on a bookcase for support. "Yes, you do, my darling girl. But, at the moment, dear Amy is using your room."

Sophie's green glassy eyes flicker toward the door of my room. As well as an entryway, sitting room, dining area, kitchen, and the two baths, Margaret's apartment possesses a pair of good-sized bedrooms, plus a third, smaller, chamber currently furnished as an office that lately we've talked about converting to a nursery.

By Parisian standards it's a very large apartment. But it has just started to feel very small.

Margaret squints at me, as if trying to remember who I am, and then rushes to Sophie's side, her smile radiating like a Phoenix noonday sun. "But soon we'll have everything sorted! Soon. For now, *ma fille*, I reckon you are greatly in need of a lie-down. We'll leave the bath for later. Come now."

I feel a twinge of unjustifiable envy. Lately Margaret has taken to referring to me as *ma fille*. My child. I have to confess to loving it. But Sophie is a real *fille*, and Margaret doesn't so much as glance in my direction as she loops her arm around Sophie's waist and starts to usher her toward her, Margaret's, room.

"*Mais non*! I will take my own bed!"

Sophie jerks free of Margaret. Her motions are violent, and I worry Margaret will be thrown off balance. But she grabs her mother's elbow, as if to steady her, and glares at me as if daring me to intercede. I continue to sit there wordlessly, because really I am just stunned, as well as tired and hungry and filled with sudden foreboding. Then Sophie whirls away from her mother, stomps into the second bedroom (mere seconds ago my room), and slams the door shut behind her.

For a minute we both stare in silence at the defiantly closed door. But when Margaret turns to me, the radiant smile has reappeared.

"Ah, Amy dear, I do apologize." She is whispering, as if Sophie could possibly have already fallen sleep. "You understand. She is spent. And the dear girl always becomes a bit huffy when she's tired. Rest, that's what she needs. And a bath." She laughs, retrieves the box of chocolates from the mantelpiece, pops one into her mouth, and sinks into the chair Sophie just vacated.

My tea has cooled, but I gulp it down anyway. I am much in need of tea.

"I still can't fathom it," Margaret murmurs. She presses her hands to her cheeks, which have gone bright pink again. Her lips are quivering. Her eyes are glittering. Despite the fact that she continues to smile, I have the strong sense she is millimeters away from bursting into tears.

Margaret often reminisces about the daughter who disappeared, going on about "my daughter this" and "my daughter that." But at the same time, she's never provided details about exactly what happened. I've refrained from broaching the subject or even asking the daughter's name, because I don't want to pry. And I understand the pain. I know too well how, each time you think of the loved one you lost, you lose that person all over again. It never seems to hurt any less. Every time is like the first time.

As Margaret sucks on a chocolate I wrestle with the idea that the person in the next room—my room—is the missing daughter. The lost and now found, feared dead yet now somehow miraculously brought back to life, precious, perfect child. It's the sole rational explanation. If I weren't so brain-dead, I would have figured it out immediately.

"Margaret, you've never really told me about Sophie." I pronounce the name as gently as I can.

Margaret inserts another chocolate into her mouth. "I fancied Manu filled you in on all that."

"All he said was—"

"Manu!" Margaret leaps to her feet. "I've not told him the grand news! I must phone him." She takes a shaky step in the direction of her office, where the apartment's telephone resides, and sinks back down in her chair again.

"Goodness. I fear the events of the morning have rendered me a bit wobbly. Lend me your mobile, will you, Amy?"

I pull my phone out of my pocket, find Manu's number, and hand it over.

She holds the phone a few inches from her ear, as if it's a ferret that might bite. I notice she isn't wearing earrings. Margaret always wears earrings. It's another oddness, in this day of oddnesses.

After a pause in which it becomes apparent Manu is not picking up, she leaves a voicemail, in that stiff way many older people have. I listen as hard as I can, but though my French has improved greatly over the past months, the only words I'm able to understand are "Sophie," "*une surprise*," and at the very end, "*Rappelle-moi aussitôt que possible.*" Call me as soon as possible.

Manu tends to procrastinate when it comes to voicemail or email. He usually responds only to texts. But I'm positive he'll return Margaret's call as soon as he gets the message. No one could fail to register the note of near-hysteria in her voice.

"Margaret," I say to her as she passes the phone back to me, "will you please explain a little more about what's going on?"

But instead of answering she again manages to rise to her feet. "I must check the contents of my larder. Would you like to accompany me to the *supermarché*, Amy?" She heads toward the kitchen, steadying herself along the way by grabbing onto tables and chair backs. "Let's see. Sophie always takes hot chocolate in the mornings. And she is partial to Marmite on her *baguette*. That's the English half of her!" She turns and winks. "Will you help me make a list? And come along to tow the caddy for me?"

What I would really like to do is eat and have another cup of tea, but I don't even reach for a chocolate before following Margaret into the kitchen and retrieving the two-wheeled shopping caddy from where it hangs on a hook behind the door. The caddy is used only for major expeditions, when we need to stock up on heavy items like laundry detergent or olive oil. Normally we food shop every day, buying just what we need for our next couple of meals.

Margaret is on her knees on the red tile floor, rummaging through the tiny refrigerator, peeking into plastic containers. "What shall we have for dinner? We've loads of leftovers from last night. But should I make something special? Will you help? She is so tired. Did you see how tired she looked? I wager she won't want to eat much. And I for one don't think I could manage a bite. Aha! We do have some!" She sits back on her heels and smiles up at me, waving a small brown jar of Marmite in the air.

"Margaret." I rescue the Marmite just as it is slipping from her grasp. "Margaret, please, listen. Why don't you come sit down? You're shaking. Look."

She holds out her hands and stares at them as if they belong to someone else.

I close the refrigerator door, help her to her feet, and lead her back to her chair in the sitting room. "Would you like fresh tea? Or maybe a small glass of sherry?" Sometimes Margaret has a little sherry to, as she says, settle her nerves. Even in the middle of the day, like now. If I weren't pregnant, I'd have a shot myself. My nerves are jangling like live wires.

She shakes her head and again pulls the Godiva box onto her lap. I assume she'll finally offer me one, but instead she lobs a candy into her own mouth, then another, and then another. It's not the way Margaret consumes anything, much less chocolate. Margaret always eats mindfully and never too much at one time. She likes to tell me that once you pass sixty you need only half the food you needed before. Maybe that's why she still has a pretty trim figure for someone her age.

"Hey, save some for the rest of us."

I am teasing her, hoping to make her smile, but Margaret continues to eat, munching and swallowing joylessly, like a child who's been ordered to finish her Brussels sprouts or else. Only when the box is empty does she let it slide to the floor. Her eyes are dull. Her jaw is slack.

"Margaret, tell me what's going on with you," I again implore, though by this time I'm rapidly coming to my own conclusions. "Talk to me. Please."

seven

MARGARET DOESN'T TALK TO ME. She claps her hands over her cheeks and starts to sob, rocking back and forth in her chair. Before I know it, tears are running down my face too. Crying is contagious.

I'm trying to convince her she needs to lie down when Manu arrives. Thank God.

After I relate to him all I know he kneels in front of her chair. He is pale and serious. "Please, *madame*. You should take a rest, *juste pour un petit moment*." Just for a little while.

But Margaret, who is normally delighted to see Manu, barely seems to register his presence. She continues to weep, hiccupping and holding a crumpled tissue to her reddened nose. It's unsettling to see an older adult sob openly, like a child. My mother never cried, at least as far as I knew. Dad did once, toward the end, but it was only because he didn't want to die and leave me all alone in the world. William has never shed a tear in my presence. Not when I lost that first baby, mere weeks after our hastily planned wedding. Not even at Kat's funeral. He did hold my hand, however, and I remember hoping he felt a little of what I felt, or at least sympathized.

Manu grasps Margaret by the shoulders and shakes her a little. "*Chère madame*. Soon Sophie will awaken. Do you not want to be rested and ready to greet her?"

At the sound of the word "Sophie," Margaret drops her tissue and cocks her head like a spaniel. Manu seizes his opening.

"*Viens.*" He gets to his feet. "Come."

Each of us taking an arm, we guide her between us to her room, where she willingly enough lies down on the bed. I cover her with a cashmere throw, and she closes her eyes. Five minutes later she's snoring.

"*Eh bien,*" Manu says when we return to the sitting room. He takes the spot where Margaret usually sits, and I settle into the chair opposite—"my" chair—which now smells a little funky from Sophie's dirty feet and clothes. Or maybe that's just my imagination.

"*Aimée. Ça va?*"

"*Ça va.*"

I smile a tiny bit, because I like how "*ça va*" can be both a question ("how's it going?") and an answer ("everything is fine"). It's the world's most versatile phrase. You can go a long way in French on the strength of "*ça va*" alone.

Manu picks up the golden Godiva box, glances inside, replaces the lid, and returns it to its spot underneath the hammered copper side table. Even though the box is empty, the entire room is redolent with the aroma of chocolate. I can practically taste it.

"*C'est incroyable,*" he says.

Ha. "Incredible" doesn't begin to cover the events of the past twenty-four hours. William has come to Paris. Sophie has returned to Paris. Margaret, though physically in the next room, is emotionally and mentally far away. How I yearn to wind back the clock to when our biggest problem was deciding what kind of cake to have for my birthday.

"Yeah," I mutter, as I pluck a sugar cube out of the Spode sugar bowl and pop it into my mouth. At this point, any calorie source sounds good to me.

"The police." Manu pauses, his normally deep blue eyes faded to an almost gray. "The police told us, told me—" He rubs his face, and I feel a fresh stab of remorse for forgetting about the lunchtime deliveries. He's exhausted. Maybe even more than I am, if that's possible.

But before I can launch into further apologies, he continues.

"We believed that she was gone for always."

I nod. Sophie is indeed the missing-presumed-dead daughter. I can't believe I didn't figure it out right away. Worse, I'm still confused. "Manu. I'm wondering. How could she have been gone all this time without ever getting in touch?"

What I don't ask is: How could a person be so horribly cruel? To anyone? After all, it's one thing to lose people you love because they die. It's quite another to be robbed of a cherished someone because he, or she, just can't be bothered to keep you in the loop. Even a person as self-absorbed as Sophie appears to be must realize how much Margaret adores her. Yet apparently, she was capable of just taking off without saying a word.

I leap from the chair and pace around the room. To be honest, I did more or less the same thing to William. While he was away on business I implemented what Kat and I called "The Plan" and took off for Paris without saying a word. Surely knowing I wouldn't want to execute The Plan without her, Kat left me both explicit instructions ("Go. To. Paris.") and an airline gift certificate. At first, I resisted, hesitated, but when William started demanding that I just "get over it" (meaning Kat's death) I booked a flight for the very next day. It was easy. Easier than maybe it should have been. Even if for only a "break."

"*C'est incroyable*," Manu says again.

"Yes. Yes, it absolutely is."

I want to elaborate, to tell him how rude Sophie was, then decide not to. I need to be careful about what I say and how I say it, because Manu and Sophie used to be a couple. Maybe he even loves her still. Maybe beneath that grave but calm exterior he's overjoyed, overwhelmed. I return to my chair and curl up as much as the presence of Catherine will allow. "Tell me again what happened. When was the last time you saw Sophie?"

"It was two and a half years ago. Indeed, I saw her the night before she disappeared." He reaches for Margaret's abandoned cup of tea, now surely stone cold, and drinks it down in one go. Wow. Manu is not a tea person, especially tea with milk in it. Normally I'd comment, make a joke, but I don't think Manu is in the mood to be teased right now.

"Did she seem weird?" I say instead.

"*Pardon?*"

"Nervous? Like maybe she was planning to run off?"

"No. I do not think so. *Elle paraissait contente.*"

I try to imagine Sophie "seeming content."

"And—afterwards—was anything missing?" I ask. "Like, did she take clothes? Or—"

Here again I stop myself. The police would have already asked all these same questions. It is no doubt unhelpful, and possibly painful, to be asked them again.

Besides, I've spotted another item that doesn't normally belong in Margaret's sitting room—a backpack. Or, rather, daypack, propped in a corner behind a potted philodendron. When new, it must have been a light khaki. Now it's dark with dirt and can only be the property of Sophie.

"*Quoi?*" What? Manu turns to look. When he spots the daypack, he shoots up from his chair, strides to the corner, grabs the pack, and tips out its contents. I cringe because whatever is inside is likely to be as filthy as the outside, and I just cleaned this whole room yesterday. But when he kneels down on the carpet, I go to kneel beside him. His cologne is woodsy, like a crisp fall day.

"Is this everything she brings?" he asks when the only objects to fall from the pack are a voluminous black robe and an embroidered black leather wallet. Nothing else. No bras, no underwear, no toiletries, no shoes.

Speaking of shoes. "Well, those must be hers." I nod toward the blood-red leather slippers still forming a T in the center of the room.

Manu stretches out his arm to grab one. "Tell me," he says, turning it round and round in his hands. "How does she look?"

"Sophie? OK, I guess. She seemed stressed. And dirty."

I don't tell him how dirty. Nor do I elaborate on how jumpy she acted. Because who knows? Maybe she's always jumpy. Anyway, there's no way I can describe Sophie's appearance or behavior without sounding as if I hated her on first sight. And I don't hate her. I hardly know her. If she's Margaret's daughter, she must have some redeeming qualities.

Manu holds up the slipper. "I ask this to you because—these *babouches?* They are not her style."

"These what? 'Bah-boosh'?"

"It is the name of this shoe. *Babouches*. They are *typique* of *Le Maroc*."

I reach for the other slipper and run my thumb over the intricate embroidery. *Le Maroc*. A lot of life in France is influenced by relatively nearby Morocco. Food especially. You can find a couscous restaurant on practically every corner. Once Margaret took me to a cozy Moroccan-style *salon de thé* not far from here, where they served the most comforting mint tea I've ever tasted. She was also the one who told me that the little mini-markets you see all over Paris are traditionally owned and operated by Moroccans. Many tourists don't realize that France has long been home to many people of Arab descent, and that this number increases every year, a fact snobby Hervé never ceases to deplore.

I put down the slipper and pick up the hem of the long black robe. "This is probably from Morocco, too, isn't it?"

"Yes. It is called a *djellaba*."

I start to ask him to spell the word for me—it sounds like "jell-ah-bah"—but he's searching through the leather wallet and frowning. I shift closer to him to get a better look at the sheaf of violet, burgundy, and chartreuse bills he has pulled out of the wallet. "What now? Is that Moroccan currency?" I ask, though it has to be. Given the *babouches* and *djellaba*.

Manu doesn't reply. Perhaps he's not familiar with the English word "currency." I lean my shoulder against his for a moment, just for the feel of his warmth, his solidity, and then get to my feet. Manu's mind and probably heart are a million miles away. Besides, Catherine doesn't like me to sit in one position for too long, much less on my heels on the floor.

I circle the room a couple of times to uncramp my legs. The Godiva chocolate aroma has begun to fade, succumbing to the stronger perfume of the half-eaten leek quiche still standing out on the dining table, and on my next pass, I break off a piece of the buttery crust and pop it into my mouth. Scrumptious. "Well, I guess it's safe to conclude that Sophie has recently been in Morocco. How much money is there?"

"*Beaucoup*." He rifles through the wallet a second time.

I help myself to another shard of quiche crust and try to picture Sophie sticking up a remote Moroccan bank, or swindling a wealthy Moroccan businessman, and then fleeing to Paris to hole up in her mother's apartment until the excitement dies down. But no. I don't think so. For Sophie, this seems way too purposeful and energetic.

"*Aimée*." Manu has spread the money across his knee and turned the wallet inside out. "Look. She does not carry papers."

"Papers?" I cross the room to stand over him. It's wrong to go through someone else's stuff. It's also wrong to be enjoying it as much as I am.

But playing detective with Manu is so much fun. Since William arrived in Paris the question of what will happen next in my life—what should happen next—has been hanging over my head like a sharpened sword. But right now, in this moment, Manu and I are on the same side, working together. It's a lovely, comfortable feeling that I would like to have last as long as possible.

He looks up at me. "*Carte d'identité. Passeport.* They are not here."

I shrug. French people keep their identity papers on them at all times—I think it's a law or something—but still I see no reason for him to be scandalized. "Maybe she has them with her. In there." I jerk my head in the direction of the room that so recently I was thrilled and honored to call mine. Sophie could have been wearing a money belt under that huge caftan. Hell, she could have been wearing half a dozen money belts.

He shakes his head. "*Peut-être.*" Perhaps.

I return to my chair and perch on one arm. "Morocco. Couldn't she have called home? If she wanted to?"

After all, as Margaret often marvels, nowadays anyone can call from anywhere. Over the past months I've phoned William in Arizona dozens of times and left him a voicemail every single one of those times. He ignored me completely until yesterday. Come to think of it, he's still ignoring me.

Manu lifts his eyebrows. "Exactly. It is *un mystère*." Earlier he was speaking in a low voice, but now he's no longer bothering, and I wonder whether he wants Sophie to overhear, come running out, and leap into his arms.

"Sophie is *égoïste*," he adds. "But she would not allow her mother to anguish, to believe that she is—" He sighs and stuffs the Moroccan money back into the wallet.

If Manu is still in love with Sophie, would he call her egotistical? Maybe. Or maybe it's all he can do to keep from racing into the next room and covering her grimy face with adoring kisses. I reach for another sugar cube, pop it into my mouth, and let it dissolve on my tongue. Margaret has told me more than once how Manu and her daughter used to be, as she put it, "an item," and how the daughter was the one to break it off and how Margaret was so sorry. Manu himself has never addressed this topic with me, and I've never asked him about it. I've been assuming he would tell me on his own, when he was ready.

Now, though, I'm not sure I want to know. I ignore the pang of what feels like jealousy and blame my raging hormones. I realize I should be supportive of Manu's happiness. After all, I would go nuts with wonder and joy if, say, Kat were to magically reappear in my life. But if Sophie comes bursting out of the bedroom, I'm heading to the kitchen. I don't want to have to sit here and watch their reunion. I would much rather wash the dishes from last night. I gaze at the quiche still on the dining table. "We'll just have to ask her when she wakes up. What time is it?"

Manu pulls his phone out of his pocket and glances at it. "*Dix-sept heures.*"

Dix-sept means seventeen, which means it's five p.m. Even in normal everyday conversation, people in France use a twenty-four-hour clock to keep track of time, like in the military. Yes, it's awkward. You often have to stop and do a little mental arithmetic when someone tells you the time.

"Did you have lunch?" I ask. "I can heat up that quiche. And there's still asparagus from last night."

Catherine and I seriously need food. But I'd be offering to whip up a snack even if I weren't hungry because I don't want Manu to leave. I don't want to sit here by myself listening to Margaret and Sophie snore on the opposite sides of their respective doors. And when they do emerge from their slumbers I don't want to have to deal with them on my own.

I'm afraid he's going to say he's too stressed out to eat, but he nods and follows me to the kitchen. Together we rummage through the refrigerator, locate the leftover asparagus, cheese, and pâté from the night before, and decide the quiche will taste fine at room temperature.

In less than five minutes we've assembled a tasty, healthy meal and arranged it on the small table for two that stands beside the window in the kitchen.

Now's my chance to tell him about William.

"Manu. I have something important to talk to you about."

He's glancing up at me when my phone pings.

A text. From William. Finally.

Manu, who knows he's the only person I ever text with, puts down his fork and gives me his full attention. I wave my phone, grateful to it for providing me the perfect opening for what I want to say. "You'll never guess who this is."

Manu smiles. "Tell me."

I'm opening my mouth to answer when Sophie barrels into the room. She's changed out of the black caftan and into a blue-and-white striped silk dressing gown, another item Margaret gave me to wear as my own and that was probably Sophie's originally. Her big round eyes are, if possible, even bigger and rounder than before, and she's dragging a carry-on behind her. My carry-on.

"Sophie!" Manu leaps to his feet.

But she barely glances at him because all her focus is on me. "You leave. Now."

I stand up, remember that I have Catherine to think of, and sit down again, glad the table is creating a barrier between us.

"Your things." She advances on me, fists clenched, chin jutted forward. "They are here. Go. Now."

"My things? You went through my stuff?" I ask, even though I just went through her stuff. Or at least helped to.

Before she can answer, Manu grabs her hand and kisses her on the cheek.

"Sophie! *Te voilà!*" Here you are! He starts to kiss her on the other side—the rule is two though many French people do three or even four cheek kisses—but she pushes him away and gives the carry-on such a hard shove that it skitters across the tile floor, smashes into a table leg, and tips over.

"Sophie!" Manu hastily closes the kitchen door. "*Ta mère, elle dort.*"

But Sophie doesn't appear to care that her *mère* is sleeping, just as she doesn't care that she should be greeting Manu with more recognition of the gravity of the situation—*Sophie! Back from the dead! It's a miracle!* All her energy is on vanquishing me, the intruder, the interloper.

I fold my hands in my lap. This isn't the first time someone's told me to just "go." William said it last April, during that final fight. "Don't bother showing up back here again," he growled over the phone. Like my first, Kat-facilitated, departure from Phoenix, it was easy to make sure that indeed I was not there. Actually easier, as at the time I was already at Sky Harbor Airport, return ticket to Paris in hand. I'd already guessed how angry William would be, and what he would think and say and do. I was prepared.

This time, however, I'm being ejected from my living situation with no place to go. No Plan B. What's more, the stakes are infinitely higher than they were last April, because it's no longer just me. It's me and Catherine. Catherine who needs me to do the right thing. I'm about to tell Sophie that she needs to seriously chill when Manu reaches out a forefinger to stroke her cheek. "Sophie!" he whispers. "*Calme-toi.*"

Amazingly, this works. She shoots me a final nostril-flaring scowl before transferring her gigantic eyes to him. "Manu!" A Margaret-like smile spreads across her face, she flings her arms wide, and they embrace in a very un-Parisian full-body hug.

I remain seated at the table, not wanting to watch yet not able to look away either. Many long excruciating moments later, when they finally step apart, Manu wraps his arm around Sophie's shoulders and escorts her to the sitting room, speaking to her in the rapid-fire French I will never understand no matter how long I stay in Paris.

Which I'm accepting cannot be much longer.

eight

IT'S TIME TO GET STARTED on that Plan B.

But first I eat the rest of my quiche, finish the asparagus, and gobble down a half-dozen thick slices of cheese. Catherine and I need nourishment. Then I wash and put away the dishes from last night. No way am I going to leave this mess for Margaret to deal with. Or Sophie, who if she did lift a finger to do dishes, which she probably wouldn't, would likely break half of them anyway. I noticed her hands really shake.

Only when the kitchen is clean do I read the message from William.

Hey. Got your texts. Thx. But a big problem just came up at work. Am about to start teleconference. Probably will be long. Will get back to you tomorrow morning.

What the what?

William flies to Paris. On his first day here, he sends a flurry of texts asking-slash-demanding me to call him. On his second day, he ignores me completely until early evening (now), then texts to say he "will get back" to me.

I sink down into a chair and cover my face, ready to give up on ever understanding him.

But then I remember this is William, who lives for his job. A work emergency is not unusual. Neither is scheduling a business teleconference while on a personal trip. Last spring, he got a big promotion from staff engineer to chief engineer—the position he'd been gunning for since starting with the company. I'm sure he's been working twenty-four-seven ever since. When it comes to his job, William never puts off for tomorrow what he should do today.

Unlike me. I'm excellent at putting things off. Especially difficult, scary things.

But this time it's not me that's the problem. It's him. So I wheel my carry-on past Sophie and Manu in the sitting room, where Sophie is saying, "*Mais je ne pourrais pas!*" and Manu is shaking his head.

Since I have no idea what it was she "could not do," nor do I care, I let myself out of the apartment, closing the door softly so as not to wake Margaret.

Out on the landing I shrug into my old black trench and sit down on the top step. Frankly, I'm surprised Manu let Sophie evict me in such an abrupt and rude way. But Manu isn't a big multi-tasker. He prefers to focus on one problem at a time, which in this case is Sophie. And who wouldn't be a little overwhelmed? His old love has returned from the dead. Many questions remain to be answered. Though he's not showing it, he's probably just as freaked out as poor Margaret is.

Also, I have the feeling that people are used to giving Sophie her way and that she is used to getting it.

Whatever. Sophie isn't my issue right now. My issue right now is finding a place to sleep for the night. For approximately two and three-fourths seconds I consider going over to the Hôtel du Cheval Blanc and to William. After all, we are still husband and wife. But I don't want our first meeting in months to start with me crawling back to him, homeless and helpless. When we reunite—if we reunite—I want it, need it, to be as equals.

Besides, William's exact words were "get back to you tomorrow morning."

I have my phone out and am starting an Internet search for hotels when I think of Hervé. Maybe I could ask him to let me stay at his place. Why not? He kind of owes me one after being such a jerk last night. Plus he's bragged about his fabulous *maison* to Margaret and me at least a million times. He even insists that "house" is indeed the correct term when we suggest the word he probably means to use is "apartment." Or as Margaret would say, "flat."

Whatever you call it, I'd bet a hundred euros it has enough room for Catherine and me. What's more, Hervé truly enjoys being the dispenser of favors and largess. He might even volunteer to come fetch me in his red Fiat, another possession he's gone on and on about. In return I could offer to cook him a nice dinner. It's been a super crazy, super confusing, super tiring day. Yes, he'll want to hear all about the events that led to me needing a place to sleep, but right now I'd give a lot to be picked up in a warm comfortable car and delivered to a place of refuge. Temporary as it may be.

I'm clicking over to "Favorites" when the door to Margaret's apartment opens and Manu slips out.

"*Aimée?* I am glad I have caught you."

"Manu!" I scramble to my feet. "Is everything OK? Did Margaret wake up?"

"No. No. She still sleeps." He yawns and rubs his eyes, looking like he could use a catnap himself.

"And Sophie?" I dutifully ask.

He shrugs. "*Elle est—ça va.*"

As a response, in addition to "everything is fine," *ça va* can also mean "things are so-so." It depends on the tone.

"She is very tired," he adds. "So she takes a pill. I think she will sleep until tomorrow."

"Oh."

I drop the phone into my tote. Strictly speaking, I don't need to conceal the fact that I was calling Hervé, but at the same time I know Manu would not approve. "Why do you spend time with this little man?" he asked me once. "He can be fun," I said. I was too embarrassed to admit that, like Margaret, I'm a little dazzled by the whole baron thing. You don't run across many titled nobles in Phoenix, Arizona. Now that I've met one, I want to enjoy the experience. While I still can.

Manu picks up my carry-on. "I have come to escort you *chez moi.*"

"Your place?"

"Yes. You and *Mademoiselle* will require a bed for tonight." He glances at my stomach.

"You're kidding. Really?" I picture Manu's tiny studio. It's always clean, but there's only one place to sleep—a French-style futon known as a clic-clac. There are no armchairs, only bar stools. A cluttered metal desk takes up one corner. An oversized filing cabinet occupies the spot where an armoire might be. It's snug and strictly a one-human living space. "But what about you? Where would you sleep?"

He starts down the stairs. "Do not worry. I will stay with a friend."

I follow, suddenly feeling happier and more optimistic than I have all day. As curious as I am about Hervé's "house," Manu's offer comes with no exhausting interrogation or other attached strings. "You can always trust him," Margaret assured me once. "Even though it was he who took you on that dreadful catacombs escapade."

I knew this before she told me. Manu is never the person you have to worry about, never the one who will turn out to be something other than what you thought.

We step out onto the sidewalk. This morning when I was shadowing William all over the fourth *arrondissement,* the sun was shining from a cloudless blue sky, but now a sharp rain is coming down heavily enough to require an umbrella. We share mine, elbows bumping, shoulders brushing.

"*Aimée,* I regret that Sophie asks you to leave, so unkindly. She is not—herself."

"No problem. Don't worry." I choose my words with care. It's possible Sophie is normally a sweetheart of a person and that her behavior today was an aberration. Not probable, just possible. "Most people would be upset to come home and find a stranger sleeping in their bed," I say. "Like Goldilocks."

I glance at Manu and wonder if French parents read this same fairytale to their children. But I don't press the point, because isn't Goldilocks a greedy annoying brat who in the end gets eaten by bears? If Manu is still in love with Sophie, and she with him, and they reunite in a blaze of rapturous glory, I'll need to be diplomatic and supportive. Manu's my friend. His happiness should make me happy.

We skirt a puddle. "To speak of Sophie," he says. "She explains to me what happened to her. She tells me she was—I do not know the word in English—*kidnappée?*"

We are crossing a street, but I stop right in the middle. "Kidnapped? Seriously? You've got to be kidding me."

He shakes his head.

"No way! She's telling you that all this time she's been, like, held hostage somewhere? And this is why she never got in touch with her mother? Or you?" We're standing only inches apart—it's a small umbrella—but I have to raise my voice to be heard over the clatter of rain, which has started to come down "in ropes," as the French say.

"*Oui. Exactement.*"

"And you believe her?" Kidnapped. Held hostage. It feels ridiculous to even use words like these.

"I do not know what to believe," he says, his face grave. He's taken my elbow and is leading me the rest of the way across the street when a gust of wind puffs our umbrella inside out. Raindrops pelt our faces. Wind whips our hair. I shiver, wrap my coat over the roundness and innocence of my belly, and glance up and down the street to check for William, whose hotel isn't that far from here. My paranoia is becoming a mania. To be honest, I'm not sorry that our first face-to-face encounter in months has been postponed until tomorrow. William has a volatile side. He can surprise you. I wonder if he'd say the same thing about me.

Manu struggles to close and reopen the umbrella, and when we're again sheltered from the elements, he loops his arm through mine. "*Ça va?*" The rain tap-taps over our heads. A passing Renault slows to avoid spraying us with gutter water.

I smile. Manu can be as gallant, as baronial, as Hervé. I've been incredibly lucky all these months to live with Margaret and work with Manu. I was even starting to believe in the possibility of things working out for me to stay in France, as if it was meant to be. Kat was a big believer in the concept of "meant to be." I never have been. I've never thought it was smart to assume that things happen for the best. Because they often don't. Life owes us nothing, Dad always used to tell me. It's what we make of it.

"So I guess she really was in Morocco all this time," I remark a half block later.

"*Oui.* But that is all I know. She does not say more. She

needs rest."

I suppose she does. Sophie's fantastical story has made this strange day even stranger. After all, I could have predicted William's eventual arrival in Paris. We're married. He would never leave such a huge loose end to dangle free. All summer long, I've known that sooner or later I would have to settle with him or for him.

Sophie's reappearance, on the other hand, is staggering.

"So after she told you that she was, um, kidnapped, what did she do?"

"She began to—*pleurer*."

"Cry."

I provide the English word without thinking. Manu and I have an agreement to translate unfamiliar words for each other so that I might improve my French and he his English. It's working.

"*Merci*," he says. "She began to cry and to be angry, because she saw we had looked into her *sac à dos*."

"Backpack."

"*Ah bon*. And then I ask to myself, 'What about *Aimée*?'" He squeezes my arm. "I recall that when Sophie is unhappy, she stays unhappy for many hours. So I give her the pill, *et me voilà*." And here I am.

I can't help but feel a flush of victory. Sophie is back at the apartment, dead to the world. William is shut up in his hotel room on his conference call, happy to be in a situation where he's clearly the one holding the reins. Manu is here with me.

"Thank you," I say.

"For what?"

"For letting me stay at your place."

"It is nothing. It is my pleasure."

"Well, I really, really appreciate it."

We arrive at his building, where I relax the instant we step into the courtyard. Here no one can find me. Here Catherine and I will be safe. Sheltered.

"*Aimée*, tell me now." We are trudging up the stairs—Manu lives on the sixth floor, no elevator. "Tell me why you are so *troublée*."

I wait until we reach his door before answering. Then, gasping to catch my breath, I announce my momentous news.

"William. He's here. In Paris."

Manu peers into my eyes before turning away and inserting his key into the lock.

"He wants me back," I add.

I don't know this for sure. But seeing Sophie wrapped in Manu's arms today has made me want to have someone's arms wrapped around me.

Yes, this sounds desperate. But I've had a long dry spell, hug-wise and romance-wise. Paris is supposed to be the city of love—but for me, not at all. I've been on a different track.

When I enter the apartment, I kick off my wet shoes, shrug out of my ratty coat, and pad across the room to stare out one of the two tall windows overlooking the courtyard. Margaret would be pleased to see that the African violet she gave Manu earlier this summer now has five blossoms. I want to ask him how he can get a plant to flower in such low-light conditions. I want to offer to make us a pot of coffee. I want to suggest that he try coiling up his millions of computer cables and stowing them out of sight.

Stupid, casual, unimportant things—that's what I want to be talking about.

Instead I return to the fateful topic at hand. "William? You know, my husband?"

Manu takes off his jacket and hangs it up. "*Oui*. I know." His voice is barely audible.

"Well, I saw him on the street when I was on my way home from the bakery, completely by chance. He was actually checking in to my old hotel!" I plop down on the clic-clac and pick up an orange-and-white-patterned pillow to cradle in my lap. "He's texted a few times since then. He wants to talk to me."

Manu perches on a barstool, his face smooth and expressionless. "When did he arrive?"

"Late yesterday afternoon." Just about twenty-four hours ago. Seems longer. I hug the orange and white pillow, wishing it could hug me back.

"Did he call first to say he comes?"

"No. He showed up with no warning whatsoever." I chuck the pillow to the side, peeved by Manu's composure. How annoying that he doesn't seem the least bit surprised by my announcement. I suppose he guessed something important was happening during the birthday dinner last night, when I kept checking my phone. It would explain why this morning, when I failed to appear for the lunch deliveries, he didn't contact me right away. He went ahead and did all the work himself, then checked in with me later. It would be like him.

"Do you answer his texts?"

"*Have* I answered them, you mean?" I am oddly enraged by Manu's subdued reaction. Or maybe I just feel guilty about flaking out on the lunchtime deliveries. "Yes. I have. He put me off. Says he's busy."

Manu tugs at the corner of his eye with the tip of his right index finger. In the rich vocabulary of French hand gestures, which is a language unto itself, this means he doubts my veracity.

Or perhaps he's doubting William's veracity. Either way, I shake my head. "Seriously! First, he seemed impatient to see me. That was yesterday. Today he's had some work emergencies, so he says he can't meet up until tomorrow." William has not yet specifically stated he wants to meet up. I'm just assuming it.

Manu nods. "*Alors.* What can I do to aid you?"

I lean down to retrieve the pillow from the floor and to hide the fact that my lower lip is quivering. Manu is not criticizing me for failing to handle this better, as I suspect many people would. He simply asks what he can do to help.

"Thanks for offering, Manu. I mean it. But, really, there isn't anything you can do. It's my issue. I have to deal with it."

For a moment neither of us says anything. We both know this development likely means I'll be returning to Phoenix soon. Manu has been my biggest supporter when it comes to staying in Paris—he and Margaret will discuss for hours how I could manage to apply for a residency visa without getting in trouble for staying past the legal ninety days tourists are allowed in France. But all along I've been skeptical. People from Phoenix, Arizona, don't generally end up living in Paris, France. At least no one I've ever known has. It's too offbeat.

I'm thinking how great it would feel right now to curl up on the clic-clac and close my eyes, just for ten minutes, when Manu stands up. "And you will. Deal with it. *N'est-ce pas?*"

"Yes. Absolutely." I'll not only deal with it, I'll do the right thing. Catherine deserves no less.

He grins at me. "And now, *Aimée*, I am sorry, but I must depart, to check on Margaret."

I leap to my feet, which is not so easy anymore as the clic-clac is low and Catherine keeps me earthbound, if not grounded. "Will you call me? Later?"

He moves around the room, locating things. "Here are clean towels for the bath. Here is a key. Here is a pillow and blanket. Do not worry. Sleep well. *Je t'appellerai demain.*" I will call you tomorrow.

Before I can think of anything to say that will delay his departure, even for five seconds, Manu is gone.

The silence he leaves in his place drops around me like a cloak. You might think of Paris as a big noisy metropolitan city, and it is. But what you may not know is that within Paris there exist places as hushed and tranquil as the remotest countryside. Manu's studio is one of these. It's even more serene than Margaret's far-grander three-bedroom apartment, which faces the street and gets traffic noise.

I yawn, stretch, and eye my carry-on still standing by the door where Manu left it. It's been days since I've updated *Fun French Food.* That's my blog. I don't have many followers yet, but it's been huge fun adapting French recipes into dishes I think Americans would like—dishes that are both easy and authentically French. Someday I'd love to do a whole cookbook. I should check to see if Sophie put in my laptop, though I don't particularly feel like blogging. My belly is finally full, and I feel like sleeping.

But then I remember the money belt. When I arrived in Paris last April, I carried nearly three thousand dollars in cash with me. It's my stash. It's what keeps me from being completely vulnerable to William. It means I'm not a penniless waif he needs to rescue. Or rule.

Which is why I've spent very little of it, keeping it in my money belt buried in my underwear in the bottom drawer of the armoire in my room. The room that Sophie is now occupying.

My stomach flipping and flopping like a trout, I lunge for the carry-on, unzip it, and dig through the contents.

The computer is here. Some clothes and shoes. But no toiletries. No underwear or socks. And no money belt.

The missing underwear, however, could mean that Sophie never opened the bottom drawer of the armoire and therefore never saw the money belt. To be on the safe side, I fire off a quick text to Manu:

Manu, remember I keep my money belt in the armoire in my room! Bottom drawer. I don't want Sophie to find it!

His answer is prompt:

Do not worry. Sophie sleeps. I guard all.

I thank him, then power down my phone to save on battery (naturally, Sophie did not pack my charger) and head for the bathroom. Before I do anything else tomorrow morning, before texting or calling William or even eating, I need to go over to Margaret's and rescue my money. At the same time, I can retrieve the rest of my clothes because, oddly, the only clothes Sophie packed are the ones I brought with me when I first came to Paris—pre-pregnancy jeans that don't button anymore and form-fitting tops no longer roomy enough to accommodate my expanding girth. My small precious collection of maternity items, found on sale or at flea markets, is entirely absent. Meanwhile, I stand for a while under a hot shower, reminding myself for the zillionth time that I don't need to worry about money.

At least not in the short term. I'm in better financial shape than most thirty-year-olds. In addition to the three grand in my money belt, I have savings in the bank back in Phoenix, plus a car, plus half the equity in our house. I have no college debt because Dad's life insurance policy paid for my degree. "You're such a miser," Kat said once. "Will-boy probably married you for your money."

That's not true. And I'm not rich—I was the first one in my family to go to college. But I know William was impressed when he got a look at my trim finances. It's the sort of thing that's important to him. And, I guess, to me.

Showered and wearing one of Manu's clean T-shirts, I spend a good ten minutes struggling to transform the futon into a bed. Apparently, you need to be French to operate a clic-clac. Or at least in a less exhausted state. Finally, I give up, settle myself into the crook between the seat and back, and arrange the cotton blanket so my feet are tucked in.

I close my eyes and inhale the clean soapy fragrance of

Manu's shirt. It's soothing and makes me think of him and our time together. No. I shouldn't be going there, shouldn't set myself up for more confusion in my life. I roll uncomfortably onto my other side and thoughts of Sophie fill my mind. Manu must have wondered what was behind Sophie's less-than-factory-fresh condition. Actually, it kind of backs up her kidnapping claim. From what I know of hostages, they typically do not have access to bathing facilities.

Boy, I can't wait to hear the rest of that story.

nine

I SLEEP FOR TWELVE HOURS, waking from time to time to listen to the sound of raindrops tapping the windowpanes. It's the best lullaby in the world. If you'd been born and raised in Phoenix, Arizona, you'd love the sound of rain too. You'd appreciate it for the gift it is.

In the morning I hop up from the futon, pull on the same clothes from yesterday, power up my phone, and wait. William has been in Paris for nearly forty hours. You'd think he'd want to do what he came here for. Whatever that is.

But—once again—I get nada. No texts, no voicemails. No emails either. From anybody.

Well, at least nothing crazy happened during the night. I can rescue my money belt, talk to Margaret for a bit to be sure she's all right, and—without fail—be back here at eleven sharp to join Manu for the lunch deliveries. Yesterday was so over-dramatic and out of control. It stands to reason that today things will be more normal.

First, however, I type out a pleasant, neutral-sounding text:

Will. Hey. Good morning. I'm assuming you're still asleep. Jetlag! I get it. Take your time. I have stuff to do this morning but can meet this afternoon. Coffee? Around three? Let me know.

There. Friendly, prompt, and informative. Just the sort of communication style William prefers.

I'm rounding up my shoes and socks when my phone rings, slicing through the silence of the room like a cleaver through a melon.

Damn. William may be up after all. He's a seasoned traveler and could've already beat jetlag. Nevertheless, as I reach for my phone I pray that it's Manu, calling to say *bonjour*, or Margaret, calling to say oh-my-darling-girl-please-come-home.

It's none of the above. It's Hervé.

"*Bonjour, ma chère.*"

"*Bonjour.*" Hervé is the last person I feel like talking to, but I don't want to be rude.

He says nothing, probably remembering the last time we spoke, the night of my birthday, when he quizzed me about Margaret's assets and I got so mad.

"What's up?" I finally ask.

He fake-coughs. "I call you with a surprise. Do not go to work today. Tell your associate you must have the time free. I insist, dear Amy!"

I sigh. "Hervé. You know that can't happen. I have to go to work today."

But he carries on as if I haven't even spoken. "I will come to look for you *chez* Margaret in thirty minutes. Wear the red Christian Dior." Hervé's a little like a kindergarten teacher in that his suggestions manage to sound super fun and non-optional at the same time. "*Ciao, ma belle.*"

"What? No, wait! I'm not at Margaret's. Hervé!"

Too late. He ends the call and doesn't pick up when I dial him right back. Of course not. He knows what I'm going to say, and he doesn't want to hear it. The thing to remember about Hervé is that it's always about Hervé.

I pad over to one of the windows and consider my options. It might be good to briefly meet up with him. After all, it would be wise to arrange a roof over my head for tonight *before* meeting up with William because I don't see myself, no matter what is said between us this afternoon, spending the night with him tonight at his hotel. It would be too soon. And I feel guilty taking over Manu's studio two nights in a row. Hervé's place might be the perfect solution.

It sounds like a plan, but still I linger at the window. Outside, the sun is peeking through the clouds. Inside, Manu's African violet has produced a new periwinkle blossom overnight. My mother used to grow African violets, a whole row of them lined up on a glass shelf in the kitchen. She was particular about keeping them only in an east-facing window and never getting water on the leaves. But they all died after she died because neither Dad nor I could ever get the hang of caring for them. Yet to this day I love African violets. They remind me of what it was like to have parents.

Catherine stirs. *Oui, mademoiselle.* I know. Time for us to get going.

Needless to say, I can't wear the Christian Dior tunic. Sophie didn't pack it. Hervé will be annoyed because he gave it to me just last week. Well, not "gave," exactly. He was lending this item to me, he said, because I should have something nice to wear when we go out. When I asked how he happened to possess a piece of women's clothing he smiled his feline smile and purred, "Ah, but that is my secret."

He cracks me up. Margaret and I have a ton of fun puzzling over his many mysteries.

Had a ton of fun. Damn Sophie. Everything's changing now. Plus, I haven't had the chance to wear that tunic even once.

I'm pulling on my socks from yesterday when I notice they both have huge holes in the heels. Great. Well, I'll have to wear them anyway. The rain has stopped, but the day remains cloudy. It looks too cold to go out with bare ankles.

Unless. They'll still be there.

Conscious of the need to hurry, I lay the carry-on across my knees, work my hand under the lining, and grope around until I locate what I'm looking for, a worn plastic baggie. Inside is a pair of thin white nylon ankle socks. I press them to my cheek. My mother has been dead for twenty-two years, so it has to be my imagination that I think they still smell like her—lavender mixed with Ivory soap. When I pull them on, I feel a little silly wearing white socks with black shoes, black yoga pants, and a black coat. But my ankles will be warm. And the socks make me happy.

Like most things, they're connected to Kat. "Hey," she said. We were clearing out my parents' personal effects. "You complained about being cold. Put these on."

I reached out to catch the pair of balled-up white socks she pitched across the room to me. "No way."

"Well, then, don't moan to me about your icy feet." It was December and chilly, which in Phoenix means the low sixties. She headed for the windowsill. "What about these ceramic pigs? You wanna to keep one as a souvenir?"

"Gack, no." I chucked the socks into a bag marked Goodwill.

I was eighteen, and it had taken me until midway through my first year of college to tackle this job. Dad had passed away nine months earlier, and I'd been living alone in a house completely unchanged since my mother's death ten years before. Her clothes were still hanging in the closet she'd shared with my father, and her collection of ceramic piglets still lined every windowsill in the house. Dad insisted on keeping everything exactly the way it had been on the day my mother died with no warning from a massive stroke.

"Yow!" I'd stepped on a box cutter. Bright red blood welled up between my toes, and I was hopping up and down on one foot.

"Medic!" Kat yelled.

Kat was one of those unflappable people you like to have around in a crisis. She helped me to the bathroom, where she washed the cut, doused it with hydrogen peroxide, and bandaged it with tape and gauze. "Here, put these on." She had retrieved the discarded pair of my mother's socks. "Shoes too."

I obeyed.

"Look," I said a minute later.

"What? You bleeding again?"

"No, I've just realized something. My feet look exactly like my mother's. Same size. Same shape. I didn't think I physically resembled her at all." I held up my non-injured foot and wriggled my white-nylon-clad toes. "Is it possible to inherit feet?"

"Why not?" Kat asked. "Besides, they are very cute feet. You never told me your mother was cute."

Maybe because I didn't think of her as cute. I never got to really know my mother. Sometimes she seemed like the distant aunt you see only on holidays but are expected to kiss even though she makes you feel unworthy. Sometimes she called me *mija*, and baked my favorite cookies, and sewed tiny elegant clothes for all my dolls, and did my math homework for me after I went to bed.

The point is I kept the socks. They are the only things I still own that belonged to my mother. I tell myself she would like it that I brought them with me all the way to Paris. She might have even found it funny.

In any case, my plan is to change into different, better clothes the minute I get to Margaret's. I'm rounding the corner onto her street, wondering if I should've phoned first, when I see Hervé has beat me here. He's standing out on the sidewalk.

With Sophie.

They're engaged in what appears to be a cordial chat and don't notice me. Hervé is impeccably turned out in a navy blue blazer, gray wool trousers, and polished leather loafers. Sophie is wearing white jeans and strappy high-heeled sandals. And my red Christian Dior tunic.

Unbelievable.

I hurry to join them, towing my carry-on and wearing yesterday's outfit and feeling like a poor relation.

Hervé and Sophie continue their conversation—in French—leaving me, as I so often am, on the outside looking in. In Phoenix, I understand everything. In Paris, I am out of the loop a good ninety percent of the time. In many ways life will be a lot easier if I go back to Arizona, to English, to the familiar, to William. No matter how long I stayed in France I'd always be a foreigner. An outsider.

When I can stand being ignored no longer, I poke Hervé in the arm. "Hey. You're early. Didn't you say a half hour?"

The flow of French stops short, like a faucet being shut off, and he turns to me. "Ah. Amy. *Te voilà.*" There you are.

His impeccably groomed eyebrows arch as he takes in my rumpled trench coat and baggy-at-the-knees yoga pants. When his gaze reaches my mother's white ankle socks he visibly recoils. I almost giggle. Yes, the socks are tacky. But this is who I am. Or at least part of who I am. Or was.

Sophie murmurs something I can't understand. Her eyes are bloodshot but she looks ten million times better than yesterday, with now-clean hair and wearing my Christian Dior tunic, which,

I hate to say, she carries off far more successfully than I ever could have. Nor was I ever able to walk in those high-heeled Manolo Blahnik sandals, even though Margaret was always urging me to wear them, along with the rest of her missing daughter's couture wardrobe. Manu says it's because I physically resemble her. But I don't see it at all.

I nudge Hervé again as I fish my keys out of my tote bag. "Why don't you come on up? Margaret would love to see you. Have you had coffee?"

I extend the invitation without thinking, not remembering that the apartment upstairs is no longer mine to invite guests to.

Sophie, however, does remember.

"That is *impossible!*" She uses the French pronunciation. *Ahm-poh-see-bluh*. "As I just tell to *monsieur*, my mother, she is ill. She cannot receive visitors today." Her round eyes narrow to half-moons, making it crystal clear that if there were a list of visitors who cannot be received my name would be at the top of it.

"Margaret is sick? What's wrong? Is Manu here?" I reach past her to punch the building code into the keypad. If Sophie were less wrapped up in herself, she would realize how fragile her mother is.

She grabs for my hand. "*Mais je dis non!*" But I say no. Her voice is different today. Less sharp. More throaty. And she's pale, even paler than yesterday.

I'm at least three inches taller than she is, so I just bat her away. That's the way to treat Sophie—like a pesky insect. The last thing I would expect is for her to physically retaliate.

I would be wrong. A sharp blow to my shoulder as I'm leaning into the door to push it open catches me off balance. I teeter sideways, dropping my keys and windmilling my arms through the air. My only thought is Catherine. I must protect Catherine.

"*Attention!*"

Hervé steps forward just in time to save me from landing on my ass in the street. I feel a flash of surprise and gratitude.

When I regain my equilibrium, I turn on Sophie. "Are you insane? What is wrong with you? Can't you see I'm pregnant?"

Sophie neither responds nor apologizes. She scoops up my keys, which landed on the sidewalk at her feet, and stations herself in front of the doorway, legs wide, arms folded, chin set.

OK, so she's stronger than she looks. Still, it's ridiculous. Sophie can't lock me out. My stuff is here. Margaret is here.

"Listen." I disengage myself from Hervé's grip. "I *need* to go up to the apartment. I'd like to check on Margaret, for one thing. And I'd like to quickly shower and get the rest of my clothes. For example, that top is mine. Give it back, please."

"Top?" She says the word as if she's never heard it before.

"Yes, you know what I mean—"

Hervé interrupts, his eyes glittering. "*Du calme! Du calme!*" He's definitely enjoying this.

"Your *chemise, mademoiselle.* It is, I believe, the property of Amy."

Sophie puffs her lips in what a lot of people would think is an adorable moue and straightens the silky hem of the Dior tunic. I suppose she assumed anything in the armoire that was couture must automatically be hers. Or maybe she put it on because none of her old stuff looks good on her. She is extremely thin. Skeletal. Wherever Sophie was for the past two or three years, she was not eating or living right. If she weren't being such a total bitch, I'd feel sorry for her.

She is being a total bitch, however, so I dart forward to grab my keys.

But once again she's too quick for me. "*Non!*" she cries, concealing the keys behind her back and fending me off with her free hand.

This is madness. We're standing out in the open street. The Hôtel du Cheval Blanc is only four blocks away. What if William were to happen along and catch the three of us facing off on the sidewalk like gang members?

Hervé retakes my arm. "Do not worry, *chère* Amy. You can refresh yourself *chez moi.* I have another ensemble for you to wear. We will call Margaret—may we telephone her, *mademoiselle?*" He's now addressing Sophie, who nods, never taking her mongoose-like gaze off me.

"*Bon.* My car is just here, Amy. Come," he says as he leads me to a red Fiat illegally parked across the street.

Sophie wins another round.

As I get into the car, I glance back to see her punch in the code to the building and slip inside. She must have come down to the street when Hervé rang to tell him that Margaret was unwell.

A small part of me is pissed off that she again got the upper hand. A larger part of me is freaking out about Margaret, William, the safety of my money belt, and the exact location of where Manu slept last night. Somewhere other than Sophie's bed, I hope. Not that it's any of my business.

On the bright side, without even having to ask, I've been invited to Hervé's. So there's that.

ten

WE ZIP ALONG the quai du Louvre. You might assume Paris traffic to be perpetually awful, but sometimes the streets are near empty, and motorists tootle along like in an old Audrey Hepburn movie.

Also like in an old Audrey Hepburn movie, a large wicker basket filled with bread, fruit, chocolate, water, and wine is occupying most of the Fiat's tiny back seat. Evidently Hervé's original plan was to whisk me off on a lovely picnic somewhere outside of Paris. Judging by the size of the hamper, the quantity of white-paper-wrapped packages that I assume are cheese and pâté, and the presence of champagne, he intended to invite Margaret too.

"I can't do this, Hervé." I dig around in my tote bag for my phone. Manu hasn't texted me yet this morning, but he deserves reassurance that I'll be on time to help him with today's deliveries.

"Do?" He scowls.

"Sorry." I smirk. Hervé's least-favorite English word is "do." It has "too many employments," he often complains.

"I can't cancel out on Manu and go with you today," I add. "It's impossible. Sorry. I did appreciate your help though. Back there with Sophie. Thanks."

He slides into the left lane without even glancing into a rearview mirror. "*Mais, ma petite.* You forget you come to me for a change of wardrobe. And to refresh yourself."

I nod. "Yes, that's true. You're a lifesaver, Hervé. But please understand that I do need to work today. It's my job." As if to bring home my point, I push "Send" on the text I typed to Manu, telling him I will absolutely, for sure, without fail, be at his place to go pick up the lunches.

The horizontal lines on Hervé's forehead deepen into a frown. He's irked. Which is not good. I was just about to broach the subject of me staying at his place for the night.

"Your colleague can do his own work," he sniffs. Hervé never refers to Manu by his actual name. It's always "your colleague" (which he pronounces like "koh-leg") or "that one" or just "he."

"His business is not your responsibility," he continues. "Your responsibility is to care for yourself and for your *bébé*."

"I know that. Don't you think I know that?"

I'm annoyed with myself for being annoyed. And I'm aggravated that Hervé has the nerve to lecture me about responsibility when, in general, he puts precious little energy into caring about, or even thinking about, anyone other than himself. Even that picnic in the backseat has more to do, I'm sure, with Hervé's priorities than my pleasure.

"Listen. I *am* fulfilling my responsibilities. By having a job. Isn't that what people do? What women do? At least in the twenty-first century they do. We're not living in the nineteen-fifties." I lean heavy on the "do's," not by accident.

Hervé clamps his mouth shut and concentrates on his driving. I turn my head and gaze out the side window. This day, which started out so positively, is already falling apart. Why is it that every little plan I try to make dissolves into chaos?

A few minutes later he swerves the Fiat into an underground parking garage and guides it into a space marked *"Privé."* We got here in seemingly no time, and it occurs to me that unless you count Manu's van, I haven't been in a private vehicle since leaving Phoenix, where driving is practically a state religion. I haven't missed it one bit. Cars don't feel special the way cabs and buses and trains feel. I suppose Parisians think of car travel as special, and cabs and buses and trains as boringly ordinary. I suppose I'm just a silly romantic.

We continue our journey on foot, still not talking. I'm busy looking around. It's surprising. All these months, when Margaret and I wondered about Hervé's *"maison,"* we assumed it would be an elegant eighteenth-century apartment in a stunning building in the sixteenth *arrondissement*, which is the fancy area. But a street sign tells me this is the less-than-fancy fifteenth, and the narrow, unmarked door Hervé stops in front of is spattered with graffiti and squeezed between a Chinese deli and an orthopedic shoe store.

He punches a series of numbers and letters into a keypad. If you lived in an apartment in Paris, you would access the street door of your building like this—with a code, not a key. Everyone does.

"Entre, chère madame." He pushes the door open and holds it for me.

I hesitate before stepping over the threshold. "So this is where you live? Seriously?"

He smiles the way he does, mouth tightly shut, lips curling up at the corners like a cat's. "You will see."

Because I do want to see, I allow him to take my elbow and escort me not into the swank foyer of Margaret's and my imaginings but a long, narrow, low-ceilinged corridor. The white plaster walls are blotched with water stains, and the red hexagonal floor tiles are cracked and in some places missing. The odor of urine prickles my nostrils. My stomach lurches, and I glance back over my shoulder as the door clicks shut. To return to the street, to the light and traffic and noise and safety of other people—of Paris—all I have to do is retrace my steps and push that button labeled *"Porte."* That releases the lock. "Always have a fallback," Kat used to say.

Which is smart advice that in my life so far I don't think I have taken even once.

The corridor is short, less than ten feet long, and ends in a second door just as graffiti-spattered and unimpressive as the first. Hervé enters a second series of numbers and letters into a second keypad, but instead of opening up the door when it unlatches, he leans over to give me a kiss. It's the kind of dry, chaste, peck-on-the-cheek a brother would give a sister, and it makes me chuckle. Fussy, prudish Hervé, shorter than me, older than me, with less upper body strength than me, is not someone I ever need to feel suspicious of or uneasy about.

"Now, *ma chère enfant*. Close your eyes."

I laugh. "You're killing me here." He shoots me a quizzical look, and I'm glad to have the upper hand for a moment, if only linguistically. But he still doesn't open the door. He waits. Finally, I cover my eyes with my hands.

What I expect is a creak of hinges. What I get is a gust of air so aromatic and fresh it completely obliterates the urine smell. For a fantastical instant I imagine we've somehow been teleported out of the urban hallway and set down in the rural countryside. After all, you never know about Paris. In Paris, magic is always ready to happen.

Without waiting for permission from Hervé, I drop my hands and open my eyes. "Oh my God."

He smiles again. "*Et voilà. Bienvenue au paradis.*" Welcome to paradise.

On the day I met Margaret she said to me, "You'll find that Paris has many *jardins secrets*." And she was right. Yet never in a million years could I have imagined a secret garden as amazing as this. For one thing, it's unusually big, about the size and shape of a tennis court. For another, it's bursting with flowers of all sorts—roses, hydrangeas, mums, asters, calla lilies, and others I don't know the names of. I even see, at the back of the garden, a trio of plum trees with actual plums hanging from the branches.

Breaking away from Hervé, I head directly for a stone sundial presiding in the center of the garden and sit down on one of the two stone half-circle benches flanking it. The seat is surprisingly warm. In fact, it feels much warmer here in the garden than out on the street. If William were here with me, he might explain that the high walls formed by the surrounding buildings trap and reflect the sunlight, magnifying the heat and perhaps accounting for the profusion of flowers so late in the season. I might think this is cute. I always have.

I lift my face to the sun, now fully emerged from the clouds of last night's rain, and draw in a long, deep breath. Funny. The floral component of my day started out with a single African violet in Manu's apartment. Now I am surrounded by dozens and dozens of waist-high rose bushes.

Hervé catches up to me, but I wave him off. I don't need to know the life story of the sundial's sculptor or the scientific name for a plum tree or whatever other arcane subject he's no doubt about to expound upon.

I need a few minutes to myself.

When Kat was dying she actually found time to worry about me. "I don't want you to be alone," she said more than once. Well, she's getting her wish, in a way she never dreamed of. Ever since Margaret dragged me to the *maternité* to confirm what by that time even skeptical me was starting to suspect was true, I've been by definition no longer alone. Catherine is with me, always. It's a good thing. But also a scary thing.

I need to do right by her. That is paramount.

Hervé taps my shoulder. "*Viens*, Amy. Come."

"Wait just a minute. Please." I am reaching into my pocket for my phone. I want to take a photo. A hundred photos.

But then I spot the tunnel.

When Margaret told me Paris is full of secret gardens, she should have mentioned it is also full of tunnels. Around ninety percent of the Métro is underground. The catacombs consist of a crisscrossing network of subterranean arteries and chambers, miles of them, comprising a virtual city beneath the city. Aboveground, sort-of tunnels occasionally appear in the form of narrow shop-lined streets roofed with glass. They're called *passages* and were, Manu told me, a precursor to the modern shopping mall. This made me burst out laughing.

And now, on this slippery, off-balance day, a day when I have so much to deal with and decide upon, I'm confronted by a new kind of tunnel—a living tunnel, its walls and ceiling formed by a luxuriant wisteria vine.

I pocket my phone and leap to my feet.

Hervé chuckles as he leads me into the tunnel's leafy mouth. He knows he's captured my fancy.

At least he doesn't chitchat, for which I'm glad. Privileged, spoiled Hervé could never experience this fragrant path the way I do, as something magical, like Dorothy's yellow brick road or the winding grassy lane that tempted hobbits to wander away from the shire. And not only magical, but historical. I know without being told that the closely fitted cobbles under our feet were set in place centuries before Phoenix was so much as a flyspeck on the map.

The wisteria tunnel isn't long. About thirty feet. At the end I expect to come to another locked door or a foyer or a set of stairs. Anyone would. Like every other Parisian I've met or heard of or read about, Hervé has to live in an apartment, likely one larger and more opulent than Margaret's, but still an apartment of some kind.

Which is why I do not expect to find myself standing in a small square cobblestoned courtyard, staring up at a castle.

OK, it's not truly a castle. There are no crenellated battlements. No moat, no drawbridge. But there's a turret—a tall round stone tower with narrow slit windows and a steep conical slate roof that makes me think of a witch's hat. And there are balconies, roomy enough for Juliet to pace back and forth on, calling out for Romeo.

Margaret would go bonkers over this place. Even Manu would be reluctantly impressed. As for William, he'd no doubt just remark how expensive such a large place would be to heat and cool. He'd point out the mullioned windows on the ground floor and mention how all those little panes would be a bitch to keep clean. William is pragmatic, which is a fine quality. Within reason.

Hervé trots up to the shining mahogany front door like a tomcat returning home after a night on the town.

He knows I will follow, and I do. The entryway is flanked with topiary shrubs snipped into perfect cones and topped by a stone pediment incised with foot-high numbers. I step back to make out a one, a seven, an eight, and a six. "Is that when the house was built? In seventeen eighty-six?"

Hervé has removed a disappointingly modern-looking key from the inside pocket of his blazer and is inserting it into the door. "But of course."

To Hervé none of this is special. It's just home-sweet-home. Me, I would not be surprised to spot Rapunzel peering down at us from one of the narrow slits in the turret.

As we step into a cool foyer, I look around for the morning-coated butler that by all rights should be the next extraordinary thing to appear. However, the house is silent and still, and no one greets us as Hervé escorts me across a shining floor of black and white diagonal tiles and up a helix-shaped stone staircase. Its grandeur does not surprise me. At this point, nothing would.

We rapidly climb three flights to the top floor. I think I hear music coming from somewhere, but I can't be certain. Maybe it's just the sound of the house breathing.

At the end of a long-carpeted corridor he flings open a door. "*Voilà.*"

OK, I was wrong when I said nothing more could surprise me. The suite of rooms—first a sitting room, then a bedroom—that Hervé shows me into is five times the size of Manu's studio apartment. The walls are paneled in white with painted gold trim, like the palace at Versailles. The ceilings are frescoed with Renaissance-style murals of cupids and flowers. "Yikes," I whisper to myself.

Hervé has been towing my carry-on all this time, and now he parks it next to a massive armoire in the bedroom. The armoire is gilded and inlaid and carved and sculpted and marbled to within an inch of its life, and is probably older than the Declaration of Independence. I'm running my hand over the silky smooth wood of the door panel when he taps my shoulder. "Inside you will find clothes to fit you, I think," he says. "But first I must show you one more thing."

He leads me into a third room, a bathroom. In contrast to the rest of the suite, it is stunningly modern, and Hervé beams with pride as he points out a Japanese toilet with an electric seat warmer and accompanying bidet, a marble-topped vanity with professional-quality make-up lights, and an enormous freestanding slipper tub. When he draws my attention to the walk-in shower, I almost moan.

It's been months since I've taken a comfortable shower. At Margaret's, lovely as her place is, there's only a tub where, to wash my hair, I have to kneel on the hard, cold porcelain and fold over. Last night at Manu's I took a stand-up shower, but the stall is so narrow it's impossible to turn around without knocking my elbows against the glass sides. I've been wondering how I'll manage as I get less bendy and more bulky.

"What do you think? Better than America?" We are re-descending the spiral staircase.

I nod. I am, as Margaret would put it, gobsmacked.

On the ground floor he ushers me into a sitting room spacious enough to deserve two carved marble fireplaces.

"Please be seated." He indicates a pair of brocade settees facing each other in front of the nearest fireplace. I sit. A small wood fire flickers in the hearth, and a massive silver tray laid with a coffee service and a plate of *madeleines* is positioned on the low table between the settees. The coffee smells hot and strong and fresh. Maybe there is a butler around here somewhere after all. A butler who magically knows when to put out refreshments.

"This place is amazing, Hervé."

He smiles, sits across from me, and picks up the coffee pot. "I think, Amy, you are no longer staying at Margaret's. Is this not correct? You are welcome to be my guest here. For as long as you need."

I swallow. "Really?" Most likely Hervé is just trying to curry favor with Margaret, but still, I can hardly believe my good fortune.

Then again, Paris has been a lucky place for me. From day one, I've stumbled into great situations. If it weren't happening to me personally, I wouldn't believe it possible. But good things still do happen in this bad old world.

"Wow, Hervé. Thank you. That would really help. I don't need to stay long. Maybe for just one night."

I silence myself. I don't want to get into details that would lead to a discussion of William and whatever my plans are. For one thing, I don't know myself what my plans are.

He picks up the plate of *madeleines* and offers it to me. "As you wish. There is plenty of room here. As you can see."

I take a *madeleine*. "Yes. It's dazzling. But this morning I do still need to go to work, you know." I check the time on the ormolu clock shining down from the mantelpiece. Nine forty-five. "In fact, I need to leave pretty soon."

He winks. "Even so, you will have time for a small refreshment. And shall we not telephone Margaret?"

As I very much want to check on Margaret, I nod enthusiastically while reaching for my phone with one hand and taking a bite of a *madeleine* with the other. *Fun French Food* is definitely going to include a recipe for *madeleines*—a snap to make if you know the secret, which is to prepare the batter a day in advance. That's the way to achieve the cake's signature hump.

I finish one *madeleine* and start on a second while listening to the phone ring. No one answers. There's no option to leave a message either, as Margaret has never mastered voicemail. It reminds me that yesterday I forgot to check if her phone is plugged in. I glance through my texts. No answer from Manu. Or from William. Most likely he's still asleep, but it's almost as if by entering the secret garden I have been taken out of the world of real life, where William exists, and into a Brigadoon-like enchantment, where I'm free to let my imagination go nuts. Not that my imagination needs help to go nuts.

Hervé pours coffee into the elegant gold and white cups. "No matter. We shall try again. Tell me about Sophie."

"Sophie?" I put down my *madeleine* and check to see if Manu has responded to my text. He has not. "Sophie is Margaret's daughter."

Hervé glares at my phone until I drop it into my tote bag, then shrugs one bony shoulder. "Ah. Does not Margaret have other children?"

"No. I don't think so."

I yawn and rub the small of my back. Sophie has been in my life less than twenty-four hours, and you know what? I'm already tired of thinking and talking about her.

Hervé, who never notices people's moods, places his cup on the table between us with a sharp click. "I would like to request your kind assistance, Amy." He locks his eyes onto mine. "You have heard me speak of the wonderful discovery of the vintage wine cellar. Well, I have interesting news. We can bring these bottles to market in a short time if we only have the, how do you say, seed money. It would not be a large amount. I am sure Margaret would find it all very amusing."

"Hey. Wait." I wave my hands in the air to stop him. "You want *me* to talk to Margaret about investing money in your wine business?"

He clasps his hands around his knees and smiles his feline smile. "But of course."

I knew there had to be strings attached. Here they are. I stand up. "Listen, Hervé. Thanks for rescuing me from Sophie, and for the snack. And for a bed to sleep in. But I don't want to talk about Margaret or Margaret's money. I mean, seriously. It's just not appropriate." I glance at the clock. If I hurry, I'll have enough time to shower and change.

"Amy, I insist—"

But I never learn what Hervé is about to insist upon because his small eyes shift to focus on something behind me.

I turn to see a woman in the doorway. She is fifty-ish and thin, with the intricately lined face of a lifetime smoker. Her straw-straight blonde hair is cut in a bob, a popular French style. One of my first rebellious acts in Paris was transitioning from elbow-length to chin-length hair. Since then I've discovered that even people it doesn't flatter choose this cut. Like this lady.

"*Oui?*" Hervé's voice, usually so mellifluous, has turned brusque.

She stands with her fists on her hips and glares at him. She has on an apron, which would indicate she's the provider of the coffee and *madeleines*. But I can't be sure. She seems surly for a servant.

Hervé sighs and rises to his feet. "*Un instant,*" he says to me. His face is unreadable as he moves quickly into the foyer to join the woman, who narrows her eyes at me as he closes the door. Whoever she is, she's less than thrilled to see me.

I need to get going, but I decide to take another minute to drink some coffee and have a third *madeleine*. With my initial hunger sated, I can tell it's a *madeleine* from the grocery store, not from a superior or even a regular bakery. It tastes "industrial," Margaret would say. Powdery, dry, and with a chemical sweetness. Frankly I'm surprised that snobby Hervé would put up with substandard baked goods. But then my visit here wasn't planned. Maybe that's why the servant woman is so angry. Or maybe she's wondering what happened to the richly laden picnic hamper, which I just now realize Hervé left in the car.

I wash down the last of my *madeleine* with a final swig of coffee, pick up my tote bag, and approach the closed door, where I try to make out what's being said on the other side. But the door is solid mahogany, the tones are low, and the French is machine-gun-like. At one point I hear a sharp "*Mais non!*" but can't tell if it's Hervé or the angry servant woman. They both have pretty deep voices. After that, the talk grows fainter, then fades away entirely.

I'm about to place my hand on the doorknob when my phone rings.

Manu. Finally.

"*Aimée? Où es-tu?*" Where are you?

Poor Manu. I've been such a terrible co-worker of late. He's probably worried I'll flake out on him again.

"Listen to me," he says before I have a chance to reassure him. "There is a problem. With Margaret. Can you come? Now?"

"A problem?"

"Yes. Please come. Right away. *Maintenant.* I meet you in the street in front of her building."

He ends the call before I can tell him where I am or ask him where he is.

No time to shower and change clothes. Or even socks.

I'm getting a bad feeling, but I grab a fourth *madeleine* before leaving the warm salon. Out in the chilly foyer, Hervé and the woman have moved their argument to the bottom step of the spiral staircase. I can't imagine why Hervé would allow his cook, or maid, or whatever she is, to talk to him this way.

I pause, wishing to say goodbye, but when neither of them acknowledges me I turn, cross the shining black and white tiles, and let myself out the front door.

If Manu says to come right away, he means come right away.

eleven

I CAN'T RESIST pausing midway through the wisteria tunnel, just for a few seconds, to soak in its beauty. My time in France has taught me how nourishing beauty is, how you can come to crave it, and how it can become essential to your happiness.

Leaving Paris, if I do, is going to be difficult. Phoenix is not that attractive of a city. And William himself doesn't put much emphasis on beauty, the surface look of things. He'd tell you it's the inner workings that count, the functionality, and I suppose he'd be right.

Twenty-five minutes of Métro-ing later I'm hurrying up to the door of Margaret's building for the second time today. Manu is standing out front.

"*Enfin,*" he says. Finally.

He steps forward to do the double-cheek kiss thing. It's called *la bise.* I've grown to love this custom, though at first I was shy about kissing Manu all the time. Giving *bises* to Margaret and Hervé is like smooching an older relative, but Manu is my age and a guy. Sometimes the press of his smooth cheek against mine is so warm and tingly that I forget to say "*Bonjour.*"

"I don't have my keys. Sophie took them."

"*Ne t'inquiètes pas,*" he says. Do not worry.

He steps aside to let me punch in the building code. At least Sophie couldn't change that.

"What's happening?" I ask as we mount the creaky wooden stairs side by side.

"I am not sure. Sophie called and asked me to come."

I turn my head to hide my smile. If Sophie had to call Manu it means Manu spent the night somewhere other than in her arms. I tell myself I simply think Manu deserves better than Sophie. As for why Manu didn't answer my texts this morning, I bet it was because he was involved in somebody's software issues. Manu gets forgetful when he's deep into computers. Like I do when I'm cooking. We're alike in that way.

At the door to Margaret's third-floor apartment, my throat goes dry. Only yesterday I possessed the keys to this place. I called it home. But I say nothing about my run-in with Sophie earlier, how she physically barred my entry. Manu may not want to believe she would act in such a way, and I don't want to be put in the position of having to convince him.

"*A l'attaque,*" he murmurs as he presses the doorbell.

Not that he plans on attacking anybody. It's just a thing French people say when they're about to start doing something. When no one comes to the door, he rings a second, then a third time. Nothing. The whole building is perfectly silent. It's mid-morning on a Friday, and our neighbors, whom I've never met, are likely at work.

I'm about to start pounding on the door with my fists when it finally cracks open to reveal a thin strip of Sophie's unsmiling face.

Manu steps forward. "Sophie, *bonjour. Laisse-nous entrer.*"

When she sees him, she swings the door open, though her eyes harden as she spots me. If I were alone she would probably push me down the stairs. But Manu is here so she stands aside and lets us file past. I study her. Earlier this morning she was arrogant, bulletproof even, but now her sallow cheeks and trembling hands seem as if they could possibly belong to someone who was kidnapped and held hostage for two or three years. If this outlandish story is true, I'll need to start feeling compassion for her. Sophie doesn't make it easy though.

With the exception of the red leather slippers still sprawled in the middle of the carpet, the sitting room looks as orderly and elegant as it always does. Yet the feel of the place is different.

Something's missing.

"Where's Margaret?" I demand.

Because that's what's missing—Margaret, rushing forward in a cloud of Shalimar, brimming with smiles and kisses and offers of tea. Without Margaret the apartment is merely a gorgeous interior. In a way William is right. True beauty needs a functioning core. It needs history and constancy. It needs a heart.

Sophie turns away from me. She's still wearing my red Christian Dior tunic. Her blonde hair is swept into an artful ponytail, and her feet, yesterday so dirty, are now smooth and clean. I can see how men would be attracted to her. She's like a doll, with her big round eyes and pale porcelain skin. But, today, a broken doll.

Manu sheds his jacket. "Sophie. Tell us what is wrong. Where is your mother?" He speaks in English, whether for my benefit or to force Sophie to remain on a more formal footing, I don't know. Either way, I'm grateful.

She flounces down into the brocade *fauteuil* but two seconds later leaps back up.

"I do not know what to do!" she wails, pacing back and forth, kicking one of the red leather slippers across the room. "She will not get up from the bed. She will not eat or drink. She will not let me call the *médecin*." She stops and turns to look at Manu, her green eyes glistening like marbles. "I do not think it is a physical malady. I think it is her spirit."

Manu nods. "*Exactement*. It is the shock."

Sophie's smooth forehead crinkles, as if she has no idea what he could possibly mean.

"Your sudden return," I explain, "has overwhelmed her."

Sophie's huge eyes grow huger, as if to say, "Huh?" Maybe she's not that smart. OK, I know it's mean of me to add stupidity to the list of her faults, but I can't help it.

"Let me talk to her." I head for Margaret's closed bedroom door.

"*Non.*" Sophie blocks my path.

I brush past her. This time she's not going to get the better of me. "Margaret?" I rattle the doorknob. "It's me. Amy."

"Am—Amy?"

I turn to look back over my shoulder. Sophie's hands are

clapped over her mouth. Manu, standing behind her, frowns. We're all sharing the same thought, I am sure—that the thin voice drifting from the room, while it can belong only to Margaret, sounds as if it's coming from a child. A small, lost, frightened child.

"Margaret, I'm coming in." I step forward and open the door, ignoring Sophie's loud whispered, "*Arrête!*" behind me. So often people tell you, "Stop!" when the thing you most want to do is "Go!" For too long, I listened to them.

Margaret's bedroom, normally bright and cheerful, is shuttered and gloomy. She lies flat on her back in bed, the pink quilted coverlet pulled up to her chin. Her lined cheeks, usually rosy, are dull gray. Her eyes, usually a light sea green, are mud brown. Her teeth are chattering.

"Margaret, are you cold?" I throw open the shutters to let the sunshine in. It's a perfect fall day. Crisp. Clear. "Let me cover you with another blanket."

I'm unfolding the cashmere throw she keeps at the foot of her bed when her head rears up off the pillow.

"Get away!" she hisses.

I shrink back. Once, long ago, my mother said those exact words to me. I'd tried to crawl up onto her lap; she wanted me off. Now I think she must have been tired that day or hot or headachy or depressed. But the sting of that rejection went deep into my child soul. I have vowed to never talk to Catherine like this, no matter how overwhelmed or cranky I feel. I must not.

But gracious, well-mannered Margaret, so different from my mercurial and difficult mother, is glaring not at me but at something behind me.

I look back and see only Sophie. She followed me into the room like a terrier and is now standing a few inches inside the door, her round face ghostly against the dark wood of the paneling.

"Make it go!" Margaret's voice, usually so clear-toned, is guttural. "Make it go awa-a-ay! Amy!" She stretches out her arms to me, her face contorted in anguish, and I realize the "it" Margaret is referring to is Sophie. Oh no. This is awful.

I drop the cashmere throw and rush toward Sophie, waving my hands to shoo her away. But she doesn't budge. She stands as rigidly as a department store mannequin, her red-painted mouth a lowercase "o" of astonishment.

Manu appears as I'm grabbing Sophie by the shoulders. Perfect timing. "Here," I say to him, spinning her around and pushing her into his arms. As he ushers her away I slam the door shut.

Sophie is out. I'm in. Yeah, karma's a bitch. Yet I pity the real pain I saw in her eyes. Margaret is Sophie's mother, the one person in the world from whom she has a right to expect unconditional love and acceptance. As we all do from our mothers.

But right now my priority has to be Margaret. I hurry back to the bed. "It's OK, she's gone."

I put an extra emphasis on the "she," again out of pity for Sophie, who—whatever she is—is not an "it."

The terror on Margaret's face has transmogrified to petulance. "Amy, my dear girl. You've been away ever so long. Where in the world have you been?"

I sit beside her on the bed and stroke her icy cheek. "I was— out for a bit. But I'm here now. Don't cry."

Too late. She's already crying, and like yesterday, I'm disturbed to see a woman in her sixties weep with such utter abandon. I've always believed that with age comes serenity. I've never thought of older people as having passionate, unbridled emotions. They usually look so sedate.

But Sophie's return from the dead, so to speak, has turned Margaret's world upside down and inside out. In her addled state of mind, she probably thinks she's seeing a ghost.

Margaret rolls away from me and buries her face in her pillow. "I've been calling and calling for you, Amy. For ever so long."

"What? You called for me?"

My pity for Sophie begins to dissipate. She knew her mother wanted me, but she declined to deliver the message. She even kept me away by force. Here I've been making excuses for her behavior—after all, who wouldn't be upset to return home after a prolonged absence (for any reason) and find another girl, a sort-of substitute daughter, living in her room, sleeping in her bed, wearing her clothes, and being mothered by her mother? If I had a parent as lovely as Margaret, I would want her all to myself. Forever.

But Sophie has been back in Paris for only a day, and her parent is already a blubbering, hysterical mess.

"Margaret." I cup my hand around her trembling shoulder. "You're shivering. Would you like me to make you a nice hot cup of tea? Or a *tisane*? Does that sound good?"

I had her at "tea." She pauses mid-sob and twists to look at me, the corners of her mouth lifting into the beginnings of a small smile.

"There. You see?" I grin at her. Our roles have reversed. I'm the mother now, the comforter, the provider of tea, the crooner of soft words. It's a lovely feeling. And, maybe, good practice for Catherine.

"Everything will be all right. I'll go put the kettle on." I arrange the cashmere throw over her legs and turn to leave the room.

But when I open the door Sophie is standing there, her arms wide open, just the way Margaret opened her arms to me yesterday, when she was standing in the doorway to the apartment and calling for me to come. Now it's more obvious how they could be mother and daughter.

I step to block Margaret's view. Manu again appears, grabs Sophie around the waist, and drags her away. I turn back to the bed and to Margaret.

It all happens very fast. But not fast enough. As if a switch has been flipped, Margaret has moved into full freak-out mode. She rolls her head back and forth across the pillow. Strands of white hair stick to her damp cheeks. A vein in her forehead throbs. Her normal aura of Shalimar has been blotted out by the salty stench of tears. "Don't leave me!" she moans. "Don't leave me with—that!"

This time I immediately understand what the "that" is.

"It's OK. It's OK. I won't leave you, Margaret. I'm staying right here with you." I sit beside her and stroke her thin arms through the blanket, trying to quell her trembling. Yesterday, I believed I'd lost Margaret, my new beautiful friend and potential mother substitute, and I was scared. Today it seems as though Margaret has lost herself, which is much scarier. None of this wild emoting goes with the Margaret I thought I knew, the crisp cheerful ever-so-British Margaret forever putting the kettle on or running a bath. Manu said she had a complete mental breakdown when Sophie went missing. It must have been like this.

When Margaret's sobs dwindle to intermittent choking sounds, it occurs to me to ask about her pills. I've never asked what they're for, that subject being none of my business. But whatever the pills' purpose, if she's been steadily taking them, then abruptly stops, she might have a reaction of some kind. Like chills, the shakes, and paranoia.

"Margaret, have you been taking your medication?" I strive for a conversational tone but cannot completely erase the tremor from my voice. I nursed my dad as he succumbed to multiple sclerosis. And Kat as she battled cancer. But neither of those experiences prepared me for this.

Her eyes flutter open, and she blinks up at me. I try to catch a glimpse of her pupils, because maybe instead of not taking anything, she's been taking too much of something. But I can't really tell.

"You know, your pills? There's a pink one, I think, and some blue ones." I squint at the clutter of bottles and vials on the dressing table across the room. "Could I look at them?"

When she doesn't object I slowly rise to my feet, patting her shoulder. "I'm just going over here, to your dressing table. See? I'm not leaving you."

She lies quietly, watching me through slitted eyes, and all seems well until I reach the dressing table and pick up the first bottle. That's when the shrieking commences. I rush back to her side, but before I get there, she's launched herself out from under the covers, leapt to her feet on the bed, and started to jump up and down. Her arms are outstretched, her spine is flexing, and her head is lolling back onto her shoulders, as if she's riding a bronco.

I don't know what is more disturbing—the high eerie pitch of her keening or the fact that she's naked.

twelve

OK, SHE'S NOT NAKED.

She's wearing a white cotton bra and underpants, and also socks—not thin synthetic ones from Walmart like my mother's (which I'm still wearing), but a thick woolen hand-knitted pair that I've seen her put on when she's especially cold. Even in the summer, Margaret gets chilly. She's maybe too thin.

I've grabbed her dressing gown from the armoire and am struggling to insert her flailing arms into the sleeves when the door opens and Manu strides in.

Thank God.

"Margaret! *Madame.*"

His voice is low, but it seems to penetrate her screams, and the crying begins to abate.

"Margaret." He grabs her hands. "Please. You must try to calm yourself."

Together we manage to get the robe on her, tie the belt in a lopsided bow, smooth back her hair, and wipe her cheeks dry.

"We're here," I say to her. "We're here. It's OK."

She stares up at me and shakes her head, as if to say that nothing is certain anymore, not even our physical presence.

Her sobs slowly die down, and all grows still. Calm. Manu and I are sitting side by side on the edge of the bed, our thighs touching. Margaret is curled into a loose ball across our laps. I am cradling her shoulders, and Manu is massaging her toes. Her eyes, sea green again, dart around the room, from time to time focusing on Manu's face as if he is the savior, the answer to everything that is wrong in her world.

She's just starting to relax, her arms and legs growing heavy, when the door flies open, and Sophie again bursts in.

Incredible.

Sophie is either very stubborn or a very slow learner. How can she not know that her presence is the last thing her mother needs right now? I try to signal to her with my eyebrows to leave before Margaret sees her. But the damage has already been done.

"No! No! No!" Margaret again starts to writhe in our arms. Her face has gone from white to red to purple. Her body in the silk dressing gown is hot and slippery.

Sophie just stands there in the open doorway, her lower lip quivering, her eyes dull. I want to shout, "Get out of here, now! What are you? Stupid?"

But that's the one thing I can't say. Margaret is Sophie's mother, and this is Sophie's home. Not my mother. Not my home. All I can do is try to hang on.

"*Mon Dieu.*" Manu slides out from under Margaret's long and now stiffly outstretched legs, grabs Sophie by the elbows, and starts to propel her toward the door. This third time, however, she puts up more of a fight.

"*Maman!*" she cries, wrenching herself from Manu's grasp, and against my better judgment, I'm again moved to pity Sophie. No daughter wants to see her mother screaming and thrashing like a lunatic. Daughters need their mothers to be heroes. We need them to be better than any human being can ever really be.

Mothers know this. Even I know this. Surely Margaret does. But now her screaming has risen to an ear-splitting crescendo. I struggle to prevent her from rolling off my lap onto the floor. Sophie evades Manu's attempts to pull her away and drops to her knees at my feet, her mouth gaping wide and revealing a missing molar. No wonder she keeps her lips pinched together most of the time.

I shout into Margaret's ear. "Margaret. Please. Look at me."

But instead she's looking at Sophie, who's also weeping loudly. Sophie is as prone to outsized emotion as Margaret is, I realize. That's another way they're alike.

Luckily for all of us, Manu is like Kat, in that he's the kind of person you want to have around in a crisis.

"Sophie, *viens*." He grabs her under the armpits and hauls her to her feet. She kicks and spits like an angry kitten, but he manages to eject her from the room—for the last time, I sincerely hope—and close the door behind her, wedging a chair under the knob.

The ghost monster once again vanquished, Margaret's screams stop, abruptly and completely this time, like snipping a ribbon in two. Manu and I look at each other in astonishment, and all of a sudden, it's as if there's no Sophie and it's back to just the three of us. Oh, I'm going to miss this.

I'm starting to relax when—faster than it takes to tell it—Margaret flips off my lap, lands on her knees, springs to her feet, and bounds across the room like a fawn. Manu reaches out to grab her, but she's too fast for him. It's astounding really. Before either of us can even call her name, she disappears into the adjoining study, the room that would make such a perfect nursery but that now, because of Sophie, will never be one. The door slams shut, and we race to try the knob, but it's locked. Margaret's periodic bouts of madness always seem to have an underlying thread of intelligence. Just when you think you've got her figured out, she hits you with another surprise.

"What now?"

Manu's opening his mouth to answer me when we hear the first crash. Then another, and another, and another, each one louder than the last. The din can probably be heard throughout the building. I'm certain Catherine can hear. I want to reassure her, to say, "No, my little one, this isn't what the world is like; this isn't how people act. Not usually."

I slap the solid panel of the door with the palms of my hands. "Margaret! It's Amy! Let me talk to you, let me see you. Please?" I want to remind her that she has friends, that good things are still out here, waiting for her, that the world is beautiful if not always just.

My response is a heavy thud followed by a tinkling of broken glass. It could be the television. Or maybe the computer. Or the window. Manu and I again turn to each other, and I know we're both thinking the same horrible thought. What if Margaret jumps out the window?

I pound on the door as hard as I can. Manu rattles the knob. We join our voices together and call to her in unison, and we're rewarded by a pause in the crashing. But then we hear the whoosh of something heavy sliding across the carpet, followed by a boom and a thud and more breaking sounds. I cover my face with my hands. This is not the kind of situation I've ever had to deal with before. My mother used to get angry—she had moods. She never smashed things though. The worst she did was yell, at me or at Dad, and grab the car keys to go for a drive.

I didn't recognize it as a child, but to escape, to flee—that was the overwhelming desire wafting from my mother like a powerful perfume. Perhaps that's why I ran away to Paris. It's a family trait.

Manu touches my shoulder. "Is there not a key?" He shouts to make himself heard. This is madness.

I shake my head. "No! I don't think so!"

The only interior key I know of in the whole apartment is the one that goes to the bathroom door. We keep losing it because it keeps falling out of the lock.

Manu kneels down and positions his lips at the keyhole. "Margaret! *Madame! S'il vous plaît. Je vous en prie!*"

Please. I beg of you.

It's odd he should use formal language like "*je vous en prie.*" Manu and Margaret always say the familiar *tu* to each other—they really are like mother and son. But the decorous *vous* seems to spark some reflex of politesse in her because the sound of breakage dies away.

I'm resting my forehead against the door when I realize that no noise is scarier than noise. Now we can only imagine what she's doing in there.

"What next?" I whisper to Manu.

Me, I'm out of ideas. This isn't my country. Margaret isn't my mother. Manu is at least French and her longtime friend. Possibly her future son-in-law. I shudder at the thought. When Manu called me earlier and asked me to come here fast, I was glad William had, temporarily at least, put himself on the back burner. But when I look around this room, all I can think is how out of place I am. A foreigner, a stranger in a strange land.

Manu squints at me—it's his thinking squint, the one he uses when deciding which catering client will need to go last—then pulls his phone from his hip pocket.

He stands. "Please remain."

I nod. I will remain.

When Manu opens the bedroom door, Sophie's round face looms like a white balloon. I was hoping she'd been scared off. Or given up and gone somewhere, anywhere. Sophie disappeared out of Margaret's life once before. Poof. Why not again?

"Sophie," he murmurs, taking her arm and closing the door behind him.

I sit on my heels on the carpet outside the locked study door, my hands folded in my lap and my head bowed. Catherine doesn't move. William and his presence in Paris seem very far away. Not the slightest squeak comes from the study, not even when I call, "Margaret? How about a cup of tea?" No sound comes from the sitting room either—if Manu and Sophie are talking, they're being quiet about it. I don't even hear traffic noise from the street.

The silence becomes worrisome. Margaret isn't a young woman. She may have passed out in there or had a seizure or a stroke. Or something. What if when we get to her, it's too late? What if Catherine is somehow being damaged by all this madness going on outside the sanctuary of my body?

I scramble to my feet and pace. I've often wondered why Margaret chose this room as her bedroom when it's so much smaller than the other one, the one I'm no longer entitled to think of as my own. Only the biggest and the best for Princess Sophie, I suppose. Margaret gave her everything she had to give, and Sophie repaid her by disappearing and then reappearing and in the process robbing her mother of her mental balance. Even if the disappearance wasn't her fault, even if she truly was kidnapped, the way she engineered her return was thoughtless and screwy.

Dad liked to crack, "Insanity is hereditary—you get it from your kids." An old and pretty dumb joke. But did I, too, drive him crazy with concern, with fear, with love? Catherine isn't even born yet, and I'm already obsessing over what's good for her, what's best for her, is she all right, will she be happy, will she be safe.

I make Margaret's bed, sit on it, and again notice I'm still wearing my mother's white socks. The nylon is so thin I can see my toenails through the fabric. I take them off. Once the socks have worn out, they'll be gone. Forever. Like Kat. Like my mother. I smooth them over my knee, fold them, and slip them into my pocket. Later I'll wash them out, by hand, and return them to their plastic baggie.

Since there's no clock in Margaret's bedroom, and my phone is in my tote bag out in the sitting room, I'm not sure how much time passes before I hear the familiar creak of the apartment's front door, followed by the lilting hum of French voices. I've just stood up when the bedroom door swings open, and Manu appears, followed by a half-dozen uniformed men.

They're dressed in loose-fitting navy blue jackets and matching trousers, striped around the arms and legs with wide yellow ribbon. The backs of the jackets are stenciled in all caps with the words, "*SAPEURS POMPIERS PARIS.*" They're wearing shining silver helmets that make them look, to me, like space-age knights. Margaret's charming ladylike bedchamber feels suddenly awash in testosterone.

"*Ici?*" one of the knights asks, tipping his gleaming headgear in the direction of the closed study door.

Manu nods. "*S'il vous plaît. Elle est très fragile.*"

The knight who spoke, the "head knight" in my overactive imagination, nods. He knows his patient is fragile. That's why he's here. He came to do a job, the nod says, and how he does it is up to him, the trained professional. Manu and I are at best just bystanders, at worst potential impediments. But at least he lets us remain in the room as he swiftly approaches the door and begins to run his fingertips over the panels, the handle, and the hinges.

The hinges. Manu and I could have tried to disassemble them and remove the door ourselves. Then we wouldn't have had to summon this intimidating platoon of military types, who are sure to terrify Margaret out of what's left of her wits. But the events of the day have clearly spun out of our control. That much is obvious.

I retreat to the far corner. Manu sits on the edge of the

dressing table. Sophie remains, thank God, elsewhere. The head knight rattles off a string of commands to one of his sub-knights, who hustles out and instantly returns with a large canvas bag of tools. Their competence is breathtaking.

As two of the sub-knights begin to ease the door from its hinges, I inch forward, poising myself to rush past them into the study. I can't allow Margaret to feel as if she's being taken into custody for breaking some unknown regulation. She is innocent and good and kind, to her core.

But when they lift the heavy door from its frame, the first sight we see is Margaret's wide smile. She is sitting cross-legged on the floor in the middle of the small office and is, fortunately, still wearing her robe. She's not bleeding anywhere that I can see. She seems to have completely forgotten about Sophie and the shock and anguish of her sudden reappearance.

Instead she's clapping her hands with delight. "*Les pompiers*! *Bravo!*"

I return to my corner. The sub-knights fall back as the head knight picks his way through the various shattered electronic devices and kneels at her side. He smiles, winks, and proceeds to take her pulse with a tenderness I wouldn't have given him credit for.

Margaret is captivated. She flutters her eyelashes at the head knight. Glances around coquettishly at the assembled sub-knights. And why not—they're all super good-looking, which finally leads my exhausted and malnourished brain to cough up the information that "*pompier*" means "fireman." Apparently in France firemen are just as hunky and adorable and beloved as they are back home in the States. It must be an international law.

Manu grins at me. Margaret squeezes the head knight's knee, which he accepts as his due, patting her shoulder and shifting to one side so that one of the sub-knights, maybe a medic, can move forward with a syringe and inject something into Margaret's arm. She doesn't flinch, so thrilled is she to be at the epicenter of a crowd of gorgeous men in uniform. A half hour ago the apartment echoed with screams of anguish, but now everyone is smiling and low-key and under perfect control. It's all so French.

The *pompiers* don't take Margaret away with them, though a stretcher was part of the paraphernalia they transported up the three flights of stairs. After the medic gives her the injection, two of the beefier sub-knights pluck her up from the study floor and carry her to her room, placing her on her bed as effortlessly as if she were a doll. She lies back, smiling up at them like a trustful child. I spread the cashmere throw over her, sit down at her side, and take her thin dry hand in mine.

My own trustful child stirs. How are you doing in there, little girl? You're probably ready for some peace and quiet. And a snack.

I sure am.

thirteen

SOPHIE THROWS a world-class hissy fit when Manu tells her she has to leave the apartment.

"*Mais non!*" Her volume is loud for a French person, many of whom are so soft spoken I sometimes have trouble hearing them.

Manu glances at the door to Margaret's room. "*Chut. Ta mère.*" But he doesn't need to worry. Margaret won't be waking up anytime soon. I'm pretty sure the medic dosed her with a sedative strong enough to bring down a musk ox.

"It is only for a short while," he adds, returning to English. "You must give your mother time to recover. Your return—the surprise has been too great. Seeing your face distresses her. She does not know what is real."

Sophie hid out in the kitchen the whole time the *pompiers* packed up their gear and Manu and I cleaned up the broken glass in the study. But now she's in full possession of the sitting room, pacing back and forth across the Aubusson carpet, picking up priceless knickknacks and tossing them from hand to hand before putting them down again, doing and undoing her ponytail, and in general behaving as if she could use a slug of whatever it was they gave Margaret. I would be glad to jab in the needle myself.

Yes, Catherine's impending arrival has made me resolve to be a kinder, better person. But still I don't see how I could ever come to like Sophie. Maybe she grows on you. Manu seems to be devoted to her.

"*Je ne comprends pas*," she says.

This is ridiculous. She certainly does understand. Or if she doesn't, she should. Kidnapping or no kidnapping, you don't just show up after years of unexplained absence and expect everything to be all hunky-dory. Not if the person you left behind is someone as emotionally fragile as Margaret. I keep my thoughts to myself, however, as some of those knickknacks are pointy and heavy, and Sophie is completely capable of hurling them in my direction.

Manu stands up. "*Ecoute*. Listen to me. For now, you must go. You can stay *chez moi*. Just for one night. Perhaps two."

His words are conciliatory, but his tone is the exact opposite. In fact, I didn't know Manu had that much steel in him. What is his history with Sophie, I wonder, that he can be so firm, even hard, with her? Wasn't she the one who broke up with him? Now I'm not so sure.

Sophie puts down the Lalique crystal vase she was waving about and glares at him. "*D'accord*," she mutters and stomps off to her room, formerly my room. She doesn't neglect to scowl at me as she passes.

"Will you stay here?" Manu asks me. "In case Margaret awakens?"

"Yes, absolutely. As long as you need." I keep an eye on Sophie through the open door as she stuffs a pair of jeans and a clean top into an oversized handbag. Both items of clothing belong to her. At one point she changed out of the red Christian Dior tunic, so at least she's back to wearing her own clothes. That's a step in the right direction.

As Manu ushers Sophie out the front door he flashes a smile at me over his shoulder, and my heart lifts. My failure to show up for the lunchtime deliveries yesterday is forgotten. We are a team again. I heave a sigh of relief.

It's awesome to be alone in the apartment.

My first action is to head to my room. Thank God. My money belt is still right where I left it, in the bottom drawer of the armoire hidden beneath a wad of bras and camisoles. I fan through the bills—looks like it's all there.

Not long after my shotgun wedding, I got into the habit of

asking for ten dollars cash back at the grocery store and five dollars cash back at the dry cleaners every week. It's evidence, I guess, that from the beginning I failed to fully trust in the permanency of my marriage. But I never dared to analyze this behavior. All I knew was that the slowly accruing bills made me feel safer. Stronger. I kept them in a Tupperware container behind my cookbooks, where William (who keeps his recipes "in the cloud") was certain not to look.

As Kat used to say, you never know.

I return the cash to the belt but not the belt to the drawer. It's no longer a safe hiding place. Instead, I roll the belt into a tight ball and wedge it deep into one of my shoes—ugly, clunky walking shoes that Sophie would never be tempted to try on. That'll do for now. I don't want to have to wear the thing. It's not comfortable around my stomach.

My second action is to check my phone. It's just past noon. But William still hasn't responded to the text I sent him earlier this morning. Hard to believe he could still be asleep, but he may have been up late last night dealing with his work emergency. And there's jetlag. It's only his second full day in Paris. Whatever, his uncommunicativeness is a good thing. I can't meet up with William now. I need to stay with Margaret until Manu gets back.

My third action is to scramble myself a couple of eggs, which I eat standing up, gazing out the kitchen window at the flower boxes across the courtyard and feeling steadier with each swallow. When the eggs are gone, I wipe my plate clean with a bit of stale *baguette* and pop it in my mouth. Except for Hervé's "industrial" *madeleines* from this morning, I haven't had anything to eat since late yesterday afternoon.

This is no way to run a pregnancy.

I'm still hungry so I eat a banana. When that's done, I pour myself a tall glass of orange juice and use it to wash down a prenatal vitamin. Finally, I put the kettle on, laughing quietly to myself because it's what Margaret would do in this situation. In any situation, tea is Margaret's go-to. Decades of living in Paris haven't erased her intrinsic Englishness. We are who we are, at our core. If I were by some miracle to stay in Paris, I would always remain basically American. The thought makes me feel sad and glad at the same time.

Don't ask me why. I wouldn't know the answer.

While waiting for the kettle to sing I find and eat three dates. It's my latest food craze—dates and tea. Manu is teaching me to pay attention to the way flavors interact. In this case, the sweetness of the dates lingers on the tongue and mellows the flavor of the milky tea, turning it almost into a dessert. Margaret, not a foodie in spite of her fidelity to "superior" bakeries and the like, finds this all a bit silly. "It's not what you eat," she says. "It's whom you share it with." Exactly. Life is about other people, how you treat them, how you love them, how they love you in return. When William and I got married, I believed I loved him and he loved me. Somewhere along the road, things got muddled.

I make the tea in my favorite blue-striped cup and wander around the apartment as I sip it. I check on Margaret, who is still sleeping soundly, her breathing regular, her mouth curved into a serene, Mona-Lisa-like smile. She looks almost like her normal self, except her face is thinner. Sunken. Like me, she hasn't had much to eat in the last twenty-four hours.

I know what I'll do. I'll make soup.

Soup is my specialty. Back in high school, when all free time was devoted to taking care of my dad (who by that time was in the final stages of MS) we lived on take-out food and frozen pizzas. Except for Saturday night. That was soup night. Even in the dead of summer, when normal Phoenix residents subsist on salad and iced tea, hot hearty soup was my go-to. Salad is colorful and cool, and good for you if you don't go overboard on the dressing, but soup feeds your soul.

Both eating it and making it. And, as if by design, the tiny refrigerator in the kitchen happens to contain all the right ingredients for my famous homemade chicken noodle soup— chicken legs and wings and backs for the broth, eggs for the noodles, onions and carrots and celery for the soup itself.

Perfect. I heap the chicken pieces into one of the round enameled cast-iron pots the French call a "*cocotte*," throw in a quartered onion, two celery sticks with their leaves, three small carrots, a bay leaf, and add enough cold water to cover. I peel the carrots first, as carrot peels can make a broth bitter. I don't put in garlic, as Margaret doesn't care for garlic, but I do include a tablespoon of peppercorns tied up in a square of cheesecloth.

While that bubbles I dump a few handfuls of flour into a deep narrow crockery bowl. I don't measure. The proportion of wet ingredients to dry depends on the freshness of the flour, the size of the eggs, the time of year, the level of humidity in the kitchen, and—for all I know—the stage of the moon. Cooking is part science and part sorcery, unless you are William, for whom it's all science.

Poor William. He's never approved of the way I cook, especially the way I make noodles. Not only do I not measure the ingredients, I use my bare hands to mix them. "Disgusting," he said the first time he observed me doing this. But he's not here, and it's fun to plop the sunny yellow egg yolks, one by one, into the snowy flour and plunge in both hands, squeezing and mixing and kneading until the shaggy mess transforms into smooth dough. I use only egg yolks as the liquid for my noodles (no whites, no milk or water). It makes them richer and yellower.

I push my hair back with an elbow. Cooking is the one thing in my life I've never had to work at. Cooking completes me. Too often I've lost track of this important truth about myself. In fact, for too long, food was my archenemy. I believed I had to battle it, tame it, the way you subdue a dangerous animal. I was afraid to love what I loved.

Until I came to Paris and met Margaret. She was the one who taught me how what you think you fear is often the thing you love the most. She showed me that passion doesn't need to slide into excess, and denial can be just as indulgent as indulgence. Despite her performance today, Margaret isn't crazy. Far from it.

I knead the noodle dough until it's as smooth as a baby's bare belly and cover it with a clean white tea towel. Time to remove the chicken and veggies from the pot and turn up the heat to reduce the liquid. It won't be a true bone broth—those are simmered for ten hours or more—but this will be good as is and will allow me to use the cooked meat for the soup itself. The onions, celery, and carrots are spent, however, so I chop fresh ones and sauté them with a hunk of butter and a fearless amount of salt in a second *cocotte*.

I'd love to add garlic and ginger, because onions, garlic, and ginger are a flavor triumvirate, but this soup is meant for Margaret, who dislikes "anything spicy." So I restrict myself to a goodly amount of chopped parsley. Finally, I roll out the noodle dough, cut it into long thin strips with a paring knife, and spread the strips out to dry on the cutting board.

It's really not hard.

For a couple of hours I'm so engrossed in putting together my soup that I forget my life is falling apart. Or at least transforming in some radical, as yet unpredictable, way. Meanwhile, Margaret continues to slumber. Manu is, I assume, once again doing the lunchtime deliveries on his own. William, despite the fact he obviously came to Paris to see me, remains as remote as the sun. And the whole apartment smells like home.

But it's not my home.

I make myself a second cup of tea and take it to the room-that-is-no-longer-my-room, where my phone is on the nightstand, powering up next to the Waterford crystal clock. That's yet another item that doesn't belong to me. Margaret presented it last May with great affection and fanfare. But surely it's the rightful property of Sophie, like the room and the clothes and the apartment and Margaret herself, whom I now feel slipping out of my grasp like a dropped silk scarf fluttering to the ground.

Nothing stays the same. Nothing lasts. I put down my cup and pick up the clock, weighing its heft in my hand. It's heavy for its size, but small, and would easily fit into my trusty tote bag. I could take this one little memento of my time here. No one would ever know.

Except for Sophie. She would know. She would want it back. She wants it all back.

Anyway, what would I do with an elegant clock with Roman numerals and thin delicate hands like Tinkerbell's wand? If things go as I anticipate they will, I'll soon be on my way back to life in Phoenix, Arizona, to my marriage, to William—who uses his phone to tell time.

Speaking of which, my phone is now at one hundred percent power, which is more than I can say for myself.

OK. William has been in Paris for nearly forty-eight hours. And he has to be awake by now.

I carry the phone to the window and click on "Favorites." Kat's still there. She's at the bottom of the list, when for so many years she was at the top. I haven't been able to delete her, even though every time I see her name it's like a dagger through my heart.

Nowadays, Manu heads my "Favorites," followed by Margaret, Hervé, and William.

Who picks up on the fourth ring. "Finally," he says.

Finally? That's my husband's first word to me, after months of no words.

"Will. Hello." I almost say *bonjour* but stop myself in time. He would find it affected, and it probably would be.

Our greeting hangs in the air. I guess we're both remembering our last phone conversation, which ended in the rupture of our marriage.

"So you're in Paris," I say before the pause becomes any more awkward than it is.

"Yeah." He clears his throat. "I'm—I'm staying in your old hotel."

Here's a cool thing: William has an unusually beautiful speaking voice. It's rich and melodious, despite the fact that William himself is not musical. His manner of speech is one of the many things that first drew me to him. Something about the precise way he pronounces the first and last letter of each word sends ripples of pleasure throughout my body. Even now.

"Did you solve your work emergency?"

"What?" He sounds surprised I would care. "Oh. Yeah."

"Good. Great." I gaze out the window. The clear sky has now turned to silver, the buildings are ivory, and the pavement is the color of a charcoal briquet. The only spot of color is a brightly painted *porte-cochère* across the street. Most doors in Paris are a serious and sedate bottle green. The door to Margaret's building is. But the people who live opposite us broke what may very well be a rule and painted their entrance an incandescent hot pink. Kat's favorite color.

"Anyway," I say when he doesn't elaborate. "You're here. We should get together."

A woman emerges from the hot pink door, attaches a chain to the collar of a honey-colored poodle, starts down the sidewalk, and is halfway to the end of the block before William responds.

"If you want to."

Wait. What?

William is the one who got on a plane and came all the way to Paris. To see me, I assumed. Yet he talks as if getting together is all my idea. It makes no sense. But often I don't understand William, what he thinks or doesn't think, what he feels or doesn't feel. His interior life is like *The Matrix*. You can't see it; you have only a sense of a vast universe existing beyond your sight and control. I've always found this intriguing as well as unsettling.

"Well, we have to meet. It's why you came, isn't it? It would be the right thing." I need to make an effort to maintain a neutral tone. "Don't you agree?"

"Yeah."

I wait for him to continue, and when he doesn't, I pull the window open and lean out. It's raining. The cool drops feel heavy and purposeful against my face. "Listen," I finally say. "I can meet you later this afternoon. We can have coffee. I have some news for you."

Without intending to, I'm using my former human resources voice. It was effective at managing troublesome employees and may be equally useful for dealing with William. Maybe I should've tried this approach years ago.

"What time?" His voice cracks on the "i" of "time."

I turn my back on the window, on Paris, step to the nightstand, and again pick up the crystal clock. It's just three. I need to finish the soup, take a bath, and wash my hair.

"How about five?" That should give me plenty of time, plus by then Manu will surely be back and able to watch over Margaret.

"Fine. Good. I have something to tell you too."

I'm about to ask what when three short beeps tell me he's hung up.

I'm glad. My first conversation with William in more than four months is over. It wasn't so terrible. The sky didn't fall. But I'm not any less freaked out than before, nor have I done much to prepare him for my "big news."

Meanwhile, my big news is growing, growing, growing, right here in my belly. Whether or not either of her parents is ready, she will burst upon the scene in only sixteen, or seventeen, short weeks.

Seems like a long time.
Seems like no time at all.

fourteen

I DO NOT CHOOSE the Café de la Poste as the venue for my meeting with William.

Nor do I select the ever-popular pizza joint. Or the stand-up coffee bar at the bakery with the red-and-white-striped awning. Or any other familiar establishment where people might recognize me.

Instead, I pick a small, darkish, no-name café Margaret and I don't frequent, on a street we rarely walk down. I wear Margaret's capacious Burberry and arrive early so that when William comes I can be sitting down, coat flaps arranged to conceal my baby bump. The news of Catherine is not news I want to deliver by accident.

"*Merci*," I say to the unsmiling man who delivers my *thé au citron*. Ordering tea with lemon instead of milk earns greater respect from French waiters, who seem to feel you should add milk to your tea only at breakfast, if ever. At least that's my impression. Possibly they just don't like the hassle of bringing the pitcher. Or they believe the proper destiny of milk is to be made into cheese. Either way, today feels like a lemon day.

My hand trembles as I lift the hinged lid of my stainless-steel pot and peek inside. The tea is very black and has a kind of oil slick on the top. I probably should've ordered a non-caffeinated tisane instead.

"Hey."

I let the lid drop. William is standing less than six feet away, wearing a magenta hoodie I have not seen before and carrying a tan plastic grocery bag from Albertsons. He made it right on time. I was wondering if he would, because he hung up on me before we could settle on a spot to meet and I had to text him the address of this café.

"Hi," I say.

You know that scene in the movie *Psycho* where the violins go *wreek-wreek-wreek* while Janet Leigh is being stabbed in the shower? That's the soundtrack playing in my head right now.

"Hello," I add, lifting my chin and trying to imitate the rich velvety purr of a Parisienne.

I don't succeed, but William doesn't seem to notice. He just stands there and stares, a muscle working in his jaw. Do I look different? Better? Worse? A few days ago, before all this insanity began, I was thinking how great my skin looks now that I'm in my second trimester. In fact, I've never had a smoother, clearer complexion in my entire life. Margaret tells me I look radiant. But then Margaret would.

William takes three steps forward. I hold my breath. Then he takes two steps back. I'm wondering what the problem is when it occurs to me he's registering my new appearance. Since having my hair bobbed, I've kept it this way, learning to enhance the look with smoky eye make-up and apricot lip gloss. The cut was Margaret's idea, but truthfully, I didn't need much urging. I've always yearned for short hair that bounces when I walk. Now I have it.

He squints as if he can't quite put his finger on what's different about me, obviously forgetting that he's seen this new hairdo twice before. The first time was here in Paris when he came in pursuit of me and we had a big fight. The second was in Phoenix when I went in pursuit of him and we had another big fight. You know—the one I thought was the final one.

Finally, he shrugs and slings the Albertsons bag onto the tabletop. "Here. I brought your mail."

I scooch down in my chair to peek into the bag. "Huh."

Only William would methodically collect someone's snail mail, including advertisements, then hand-carry it all the way from Arizona to France. But this is a man who rotates his socks and underwear so they wear evenly, and who tracks our Costco shopping list on an Excel spreadsheet. He even recalculates the transactions on our bank statements every month to make sure the computers did a good job.

And yet, perhaps crazily, I appreciate these qualities, especially that last one. Dad was haphazard with money. Kat didn't care about it at all. To her, money was never a thing to spend energy worrying about. She always figured it would be there when she needed it. And in the end, she didn't. It outlasted her.

William shifts his weight from one foot to the other. "You look different." His voice is low, as if maybe he's already figured out that French public spaces are quieter than American ones.

"So do you." I eye his new stubble beard. It's the first time I've seen it up close. Does he have one of those special razors that leaves a fashionable scruff, or does he shave at night so he'll have a five o'clock shadow by morning? Both seem too intentionally voguish to be like William.

Also unlike William is that when he finally does take a seat, he swings his chair around and straddles it backwards. Not how Granddad, or the military, taught him to sit in a public place. Or any place.

"You subtracted hair." He smiles crookedly. "I added it."

Ah. So he does realize what the difference is. I toss my head, for the bounce, and feel lighter. "How are you? How's Granddad?"

He takes his phone out of his hip pocket and places it face down on the table. "Good. He's good."

"Good," I repeat, idiotically. "So you're in Paris."

"Yeah. I came—I came to see you."

"I'm glad."

His eyebrows rise. "You are?"

"Yes. I've been wondering about you. Worrying even. Did you receive my texts? Emails? Voicemails? I even mailed you a postcard."

"*Vous désirez, monsieur?*"

We both jump in our seats. The unsmiling waiter is standing at William's elbow. Americans like to go on about "rude French waiters," but the truth is service in Parisian cafés, even seedy no-name cafés like this one, is generally excellent. Within a couple minutes of arriving, you can expect to be approached and asked what "you desire." Sometimes this question catches me off guard. It's so vast. So philosophical. I'm not always a hundred percent sure I know what I desire, to be honest. I wish I did.

"A beer," William says, and I take advantage of the distraction to make sure Margaret's coat still camouflages my stomach. Hang in there, sweet Catherine. We'll get through this, together.

We sit in silence as the waiter fills a tall thin glass with amber liquid, carries it over to our table, and places it between us. William grabs it as if he's dying of thirst and holds it up. "Cheers."

When he puts his glass down, empty, I say, "Well?"

He licks his lips. For a guy, William has very full, soft lips. I picture them on my lips. "Well what?"

"My texts! Emails. Etcetera. You ignored them."

He frowns. Looks at the floor. Fiddles with his phone. "Yeah. Sorry about that."

I hate it when people apologize by saying, "Sorry about that." It's not a true apology. People who say it aren't really sorry. They just want you to overlook whatever they did or didn't do, and move on as if nothing happened. "No harm, no foul," William often says. It's another expression I don't care for.

But since someone has to be the adult in the room I come straight to the point. "Will, I've got something important to tell you." I speak slowly and clearly. I don't want to have to repeat myself. That would be unbearable.

Yet, unbearably, he doesn't even look at me. Instead he picks up his phone and starts to scroll. I don't believe he's doing it to be annoying, per se. I just think he doesn't know where to put his hands.

"Will?"

He scrolls a bit more before looking up. His normally chocolate brown eyes have turned coal black, and his expression is alert. Yet at the same time I have the sense that a significant portion of his brain is elsewhere. William is here but not here.

Still, William's brain is often only partially available to me, and I can't stop now. I don't want to. William needs to know about Catherine, and Catherine needs William to know about Catherine. I take a deep breath.

"Will. Listen to me. I'm pregnant."

Wreek-wreek-wreek.

How many times in the history of planet Earth has a woman delivered this exact same news to a man? Billions? Trillions? It's the oldest headline in the world. Yet, as far as I know, not one of us has ever found a smooth way to go about it.

Even so, I expected more of a reaction. Or at least some reaction.

"Will, did you hear what I said?"

He grips his phone. The muscle in his jaw twitches. His inky eyes flick from my face to my abdomen to my face again. Two, three, four seconds go by, and then he chokes out three words. "Is it mine?"

All I can do is sit and stare. Perhaps this is a valid question. Perhaps I shouldn't be surprised. But you know what? I am surprised.

"Is it *yours*?" My voice is too loud. "Are you kidding me?"

His upper lip curls. "I'm only asking."

"It's yours, Will. You know it is."

For a long moment we glare at each other across the table. I think he's going to argue his point, but when he shrugs, glances at his phone, and returns it to his hip pocket, smirking, I realize he's playing a game. William doesn't truly believe I could, or would, be pregnant with someone else's child. Not so soon after our break-up, which after all was less than six months ago. I'm not that kind of player, and he knows it.

So I take pleasure in watching him watch me as I lean back in my chair, casually flip open Margaret's coat, and run my hands over the firm swell of my belly, arching my spine to make my stomach look bigger than it really is. His cheeks turn a satisfying shade of purple. I'm glad I took the trouble to put on something attractive—not my favorite long baggy sweater or even the loose red Christian Dior tunic from Hervé, but a stretchy black mini dress that fits snugly over my torso and shows off my developing cleavage. It's Sophie's. So is the black, white, and tan Hermès scarf draped around my shoulders. The clothes I'm wearing are sophisticated, flattering, and make me feel stronger and smarter than I probably am.

William leans forward and grips the edge of the table. A flicker of something electric—desire, confusion, anger, excitement—travels the space between us. "How many months?" His voice is hoarse. "When?"

Good. Catherine and I have his full attention now. "Almost twenty-two weeks. And you know the 'when.' It was the same night Kat died."

Oh, that crazy night. After Kat closed her eyes for the last time I drove straight from the hospital to meet William at a downtown Phoenix hotel restaurant. His suggestion. We didn't talk about what happened. We didn't talk at all. We ate too much and drank too much and ended up having to get a room where we had sex I barely remember. But now he frowns as if he doesn't recall the occasion. "April fourth," I add.

"April fourth." He frowns. "I didn't know."

He's staring at my stomach when a phone pings. Not my phone. It sounds nearby, close enough to be William's, but he doesn't move to take it from his pocket. His hands are still gripping the edge of our table.

"How could you know? You've never answered any of my attempts to reach you. To tell you the news. You were shunning me."

He looks up at me. "Is it a boy?"

I flinch. "A boy? What the hell kind of question is that?" I rewrap the lapels of Margaret's coat over my belly.

Here I was just getting ready to tell him some fun things about Catherine. How, for example, the first time I saw her image on the ultrasound she looked like she was clapping her tiny hands. How she turns joyful somersaults while I'm walking downstairs or riding the Métro. How certain music—like Margaret's beloved Chopin—makes her fall right asleep.

He shrugs. "What I mean is—do you know the sex?"

I lace my hands together and place them like a package on the table before me. Even before the ultrasound I knew the child I was carrying would be a girl. I just knew. I'd already decided her name would be Catherine. After Kat, but with the French spelling. I couldn't help myself, though I'm sure William would

never want any child of his to be named after Kat. To put it
mildly, they did not get along. Kat rubbed him the wrong way
from the start.

"Amy. Please." He maintains his death grip on the table, his
knuckles blotchy.

I sigh. He'll have to know eventually. He's Catherine's father.
Always will be. "It's a girl. A daughter."

A scowl forms on his face, then clears. "A daughter?" Before
I can react, he leaps to his feet, his mouth curving in the
beginnings of a grin. His killer grin. "Wow. That is—" He
searches for a suitable word. "That is really something."

The only other time I've seen William have so much trouble
expressing himself was the first time I told him I was pregnant,
before we were married. Together William and I must be insanely
fertile. When I think back on it—the speed of our courtship and
wedding—it seems like it happened to someone else.

He paces, then returns to sit in a different chair, one closer to
mine. In fact, his right knee bumps against my left knee. The
coin-sized spot where our bodies touch is warm, almost hot.
Physical contact with William has always had this mesmerizing
effect on me, and I don't move away. Maybe I should. But I can't.

I can't.

"Ames, are you OK? I mean, how do you feel?"

His eyes have returned to their normal chocolate brown, the
same color as Kat's. And I think I see—yes, slipping out of the
outer corner of his right eye, a single tear.

Which would make this the first time I've ever seen William
cry. It feels momentous. In our few years as a couple I've done
the weeping for both of us. Even when I had the miscarriage,
soon after our hasty wedding, all he did was look grave, and then,
days later, inform me in a neutral tone that "one third of first
pregnancies end in miscarriage."

Facts and data. They can serve you, and you can love them,
but they'll offer little love or solace in return. Anyway,
information isn't the same thing as knowledge. I said this to
William once, not long after we started dating. He just looked at
me.

But I need to keep a clear head so I move my knee away.
"I'm fine, everything is fine."

He notices neither my change of position nor tone, because the nearby phone is pinging again. It has to belong to him.

And it does, because this time his hand goes to his pocket. "Listen." He doesn't look at me. "I'm beat. Jetlag is kicking my butt. You look tired too. Why don't we call it a night?"

"Call it a——?"

"Go home and get some rest," he interrupts, slapping a ten-euro note on the table. "We can meet again tomorrow morning, when we're both better able to talk. How about nine?"

Before I can say yes or no or what-the-hell, he leaps to his feet. Smiles his killer smile. "I won't ask you any more questions now."

I get up slowly, conscious of the intent way he studies the shape of my body. His fingers flex, as if he's thinking about reaching out to touch me, and I wonder what it would feel like— the sensation of his hand cupping my belly. No man's hand has cupped my belly, or cupped any part of me, for quite some time. Since April fourth, specifically.

Instead, he puts his hands to work zipping up his new magenta hoodie. "Should we meet here? Is this a convenient place for you?"

"Um. Sure." Both the time and place would be perfect. The café is nearby, and tomorrow is Saturday. That means no lunchtime deliveries and Manu will be available to watch over Margaret, if need be.

William is already halfway to the exit. "Great. See you then. Take care of yourself." He reaches for the door and pauses. "Yourselves," he corrects himself.

Catherine tickles my ribs. My darling girl. "Yeah. I will. You too."

I'm buttoning my coat when he swings back around and hurries over to me. Before I realize what he's up to, he grasps me by the shoulders—cupping them—and lightly presses his lips to my forehead. My body flares like a flame. But William has no clue. He turns and leaves the café without looking back.

I sink back into my chair and watch him through the window as he strides down the narrow sidewalk, phone in hand. It's over. Our first meeting is over. William never asked how I've been spending my time in Paris or what I've been doing for money. Or where I've been living or what my plans are. Or even where I got these great clothes.

He does, however, possess one salient piece of data. He knows my big news.

Me, I only have a plastic grocery bag full of snail mail.

fifteen

WHEN I RETURN to the no-name café the next morning, William is already there.

"Hey," he says, glancing at my stomach.

"Hey."

I take a seat. He chose the same table we had last night. Today it's bathed with sunshine and is clearly, I now see, the best one in the place—not too close to the door, enough out of the traffic path to be private, as far as possible from the noisy electronic game machine in the corner, yet near a window so you have a good view of the street. Choosing your table in a Paris café is an art.

This morning, however, it's hard to appreciate our primo location. Despite the fact that Sophie slept at Manu's last night and I got to stay in my own comfortable room, I was so freaked out about William and Margaret and Sophie and what in the world will happen next that I lay awake until well past three. When I did drift off, I slept too deeply and too long, leaving me no time this morning to wash my hair or even slap on lip gloss. My head pounds. My eyes burn. I have a pillow wrinkle embedded into one cheek.

But William isn't looking at my dirty hair or my naked lips. His focus is on my cabbage-sized stomach. I squirm, because this morning, instead of a chic mini-dress and Hermès scarf, I'm wearing a baggy-at-the-knees pair of leggings and a size extra-large T-shirt from the flea market that says "I ♥ Paris" in big red letters across the chest. My permanently rumpled black fingertip-length trench coat is draped around my shoulders. My black boots that were shiny new last April are dirty and scuffed. When I threw on these clothes, I believed I was choosing them at random. Now I realize this is a defensive outfit. Like when you purposely don't shave your legs before going out on a date.

Because you just don't trust yourself.

"I got breakfast." William nods at the basket of *croissants* and the pair of *café crèmes* positioned on the table between us. Unlike me, he is groomed and alert, not knowing or caring that in Phoenix it's past one in the morning and he should be the sleepy one.

I sip my coffee, wishing it were tea, and reach for a *croissant* while he talks.

And talks.

Last night William seemed barely able to utter a complete sentence, but today he overflows with conversation. Granddad sends his love. Summer in Phoenix was hotter than normal, setting a record for number of one-hundred-plus-degree days in a row. The new job is going well. His promotion to chief engineer has doubled his workload, and the T-30 prototype program was cancelled, but he enjoys being a supervisor, and a new project is already in the pipeline. His work buddy Robert has split up with his wife, Jennifer, but they claim it's only temporary. I picture the delicious baby girl they had last January and ask myself how anyone could walk away from a child. Even if it's only temporary.

I don't contribute much to the conversation. I don't need to. William does all the talking, glancing in the vicinity of my midsection from time to time but not mentioning it. Nor does he seem to recognize how uncharacteristic his chattiness is. Instead he rambles on, projecting a determined good cheer and an air of prosperity personified by new jeans (a better-fitting brand than usual) and the hip ankle boots from the other day. That promotion must have come with a big raise.

Or perhaps he somehow found out about the news from Kathryn. That was the sole item of interest in the sack of snail mail he delivered to me last night—a letter from Kathryn, the aunt Kat was named after and the executor of her estate. "Remember last spring when I said Kat made you her sole beneficiary?" she wrote in her big loopy old-fashioned longhand. "When the estate is settled, I'll mail you a check. Get ready! I think you'll be pleasantly surprised."

I've always known Kat had a nest egg—her grandmother left her stocks and bonds in addition to a set of Noritake china—but not how much. All I know is she was always ready to take time off from her website design business to go surfing or skiing or run a 10K somewhere. I used to nag her to save more and worried she wasn't providing enough for her old age. "Joke's on you," she would say now. "Har har."

While I wonder whether William is the kind of person who would steam open an envelope to read someone else's mail, he continues his monologue. "The house is fine, not as clean as when you're there," he confides with a wink, forty-five minutes later.

The *croissant* I've been nibbling drops from my fingers onto my plate. No way can this be true. William is ten times better at housekeeping than I am. He never leaves dirty dishes in the sink, not even a water glass. He squeegees the shower every day, then meticulously dries the walls and fixtures with a special microfiber towel purchased for that purpose. He vacuums or mops the floors on a set schedule maintained on his phone calendar. He regularly disinfects sinks and toilets. He power washes the exterior walls of our house twice a year. Before we were married he used to send his Egyptian cotton sheets and pillowcases out every week to be laundered and ironed by hand.

For sure he's returned to that last routine. He was never satisfied with the way I iron sheets.

Yes, I ironed our bed linens. Table linens too. I didn't even mind. It's relaxing.

I sip my now-cold coffee, again yearning for tea—specifically a big mug of hot strong English Breakfast laced with milk and sugar the way Margaret makes it. But when I left this morning she was still zonked out. "Do not worry about her," Manu reassured me as I sped out the door. "I will be here all the day." He returned to the apartment late last night and spent the night there, sleeping on a cot we found behind Margaret's armoire and set up next to the dining table. He didn't say where he'd been all evening. I assume with Sophie.

"So you know what I'd like to do right now?" William sets his empty cup on the table with a sharp clack.

My arms move to shield my stomach. It's a reflex. Yesterday he said he had "news." Here it comes. "What?" I ask, my voice husky.

"I'd like it if you'd show me some of your Paris."

I lower my arms. "*My* Paris?"

"Yeah. Why not? By now you must know your way around pretty good. We could start with a long walk." His gaze flickers to my belly. "Assuming, you know, that it would be OK. For you."

"Of course." My pregnancy has gone super smoothly. I know how lucky I am. I barely had morning sickness, and not at all after the first few weeks, which is probably why it took me so long to accept the possibility that I could be pregnant. The whole experience has been completely different from the first time. Kat would say it's meant to be.

He's staring at my stomach, and again I tense, waiting, if not for the promised news, then for the interrogation I've been expecting since I told him about Catherine. It's weird. I assumed he would begin pelting me with questions right away. The William I know would not only be furious he didn't find out he was going to be a father until now, the middle of my second trimester, he would insist on getting up to speed on all the details as soon as possible. "You can't make a plan until you have all the facts," he always says. And I can't argue with that.

But instead of quizzing me he shifts his focus to paying the bill, overtipping the waiter even more egregiously than he did last night. I guess no one told him restaurant prices in France already include a service charge, and I don't say a word. He likes to be the one to tell people things, not the other way around.

"Ready?" He pushes back from the table.

I gobble down the remainder of my *croissant*, gulp a couple swallows of coffee, and get to my feet. If William and I had come on a trip to Paris together, just the two of us, it might have gone like this—*croissants* for breakfast, a day of sightseeing. Today it's the three of us, and he and I are tippy-toeing around each other. I suppose he's as freaked out about everything as I am.

We exit the café, William holding the door for me, and I pivot left, pretty much at random. A huge part of the pleasure of walking in Paris is that, no matter which direction you choose, you're guaranteed to encounter something beautiful or amazing or confounding or funny. Maybe William has already figured this out because he doesn't ask where we're going. He just strides along at my side, matching his pace to mine, the way he did during our honeymoon in San Francisco.

On that too-brief trip—unbelievably, one of the few times I'd been outside the state of Arizona—we walked all day and made love all night. The memory curls my toes. It's been ages since I've thought of San Francisco, the hills, the bay, the sourdough, the big square bed in our tiny hotel room. My happiness felt complete. I assumed there would be more vacations to more lovely cities, preferably lasting longer than four days. But William would never agree to being away from his job for too long. "You don't want the brass to figure out they can function without you," he once told me.

Without any specific plan I head for the same destination Margaret selected on that eventful day I met her—the Pont de Sully, the bridge that connects the Right Bank to the eastern tip of the Île Saint-Louis. Just like me on that first ramble with Margaret, William doesn't realize he's walking over a bridge until we're a third of the way across.

"Hey. First time I've seen the Seine." He leans over the stone balustrade and gazes down at the choppy water. Exactly the way I did last April. Unlike me, however, he pronounces the name of the river the way most Americans do: "Sane." But I don't correct him and tell him "Seine" rhymes with "men." Let him enjoy it on his own terms.

He swivels his head from one side to the other. "I thought the river would be wider."

"It is in other spots. This bit is just the part between the Right Bank, where we were, and an island, where we're going."

"Island?"

"Yeah. There are islands in the Seine. We're about to get to one."

"You mean that there?" He frowns as he squints at the mass of white stone five-and-six-story buildings ahead. "Doesn't look like any island I've ever seen."

Of course it doesn't. The heavily developed islands in the Seine sure don't resemble the bushy green clumps dotting the Mississippi River in southern Minnesota, where William grew up.

I decide he'll have to see it to believe it and lead him the rest of the way across the bridge into a long narrow street. Like many Paris streets it's solidly lined on both sides with buildings. No vegetation or open spaces. No indication you're anywhere near a body of water. You're cognizant only of a cramped urban neighborhood teeming with many pedestrians and few cars. In other words, the polar opposite of Phoenix. And, I guess, Minnesota.

William hunches his shoulders and jams his hands into his pockets. San Francisco was an exception, I learned later. William doesn't go for cities or crowds or closed-in spaces. His idea of a good vacation is a camping trip to some untrammeled wilderness or a road trip through the empty expanses of the American West. Not that we ever went on any such trips. That would have involved taking time off work. And I can't imagine William ever coming to love a big city, much less understand why anyone else would love it.

But I have to hand it to him; he seems determined to try. "Hey." He's come to a halt in front of a display window. "Look at the chocolate."

I know this chocolate shop well. It includes a café, and Margaret and I come here often to share a pot of the thickest, smoothest, richest, creamiest hot cocoa you could ever imagine. It's another of the voluptuous pleasures of Paris—indulging in an hour of casual delight on a random weekday afternoon. At first, I felt guilty being so decadent, but decadence is an easy thing to get used to.

I study the window display. I suppose Margaret will soon be coming to this chocolate shop with Sophie instead of me. Everything will change. *Has* changed.

William reaches for the brass door handle. "Wanna go in?"

"Chocolate? Now? We just had *croissants*."

I half wish I did feel in the mood for something sweet, though, because William's offer is so unprecedented. Here he is volunteering to accompany me into a chocolate shop, a cramped one crowded with low tables he'd be sure to bump his shins against, and tiny hard chairs he would find uncomfortable to the point of offensiveness. I struggle to understand. Perhaps his plan is to seduce me back to Phoenix with a steaming cup of *chocolat*. Perhaps it's simply that even he is falling under the spell of the enticing aromas emanating from the shop. But my stomach is telling me the next thing I eat needs to be protein, not sugar or carbs. "No. Thanks. Maybe later."

"Your call." He shrugs and walks on ahead of me.

I follow, asking myself where this new William came from and if he's here to stay. If he were, would that make all the difference? Would that be the game changer? It may well be the right thing. For Catherine. For me.

A hundred yards later we emerge from the narrow street shaded by buildings into a small square shaded by trees. A sprinkling of sidewalk cafés gives it a village feel. William's shoulders lower, and I sense him starting to breathe easier.

"You're about to hit your second island of the day," I tell him as we saunter across the open space. The cornflower blue Paris sky, punctuated with cumulous clouds, arches high above us. The light breeze that ruffles our hair is cool but not cold. Another weird thing is William hasn't mentioned how radically different this weather is from what he left behind in Arizona, where it must still be in the hundreds. At this stage of the year most Phoenix residents would be thrilled to escape the oppressive heat, even for a day. At the very least, they wouldn't be able to stop talking about it.

"What? Two islands?" he exclaims instead. We're already crossing the second bridge, this one narrower than the first and affording a more expansive view of the slate-colored river, which he scans from bank to bank, nodding. I'm starting to think he might actually be impressed. "How many are there in total?"

"Islands? Several."

How I wish I knew the exact number of islands in the Seine. It would be fabulous to astound William with the depth and specificity of my knowledge. Instead I am—as I tend to be even when not made stupid by the lack of sleep—vague. "A long time ago there were quite a few small islands in this section of the river," I say, "but they combined some of the littler ones to make bigger ones."

I watch as William tries to wrap his brain around this engineering feat of yore. "When?"

"In the 1700s and 1800s, I think."

His eyebrows lift. "How do you know all this stuff?"

"From reading."

From high school all the way through my twenties, instead of going to Paris, I read books about Paris. Hundreds of books. Fiction as well as nonfiction. Even academic works. So I do know stuff, just not numbers.

He shoots me a look of grudging respect.

"Anyway," I continue, "the island we're coming to next is called the Île de la Cité and is the heart of Paris. Of France really." I pause to rack my memory banks for an enticing detail. "In fact, the kilometer markers on all the highways of France are measured from a spot on this island."

"Cool."

I nod, accepting the praise. William loves any kind of fact, no matter how random or arcane. He likes them for their own sake and to use them to impress others. I don't tell him that Notre-Dame Cathedral is also located on the Île de la Cité, because I want him to be surprised. Most Americans have heard of Notre-Dame, but many don't realize it's on an island. I'm willing to bet William doesn't. He's not a reader. He doesn't care about literature or architecture or even geography. So I hoard this bit of trivia and allow the tidbit about highway markers to soak in.

We encounter a street performer costumed to look like a marble statue—this one is dressed in the flowing white robes of a Roman centurion, his skin heavily caked with white greasepaint, his eyes bloodshot from holding them open without blinking. But William doesn't even glance at the guy or register the tin can at his feet half filled with euro coins. Possibly he thinks it's a real statue, out there on the sidewalk for no reason. I smile to myself. I'm being elitist, but it's a treat to know things William doesn't.

"You don't need a map to get around, do you?"

Our elbows bump, and I catch my breath. It's our first physical contact since last night, when his knee touched mine and later when he briefly brushed his lips across my forehead.

My voice is shakier than I mean it to be. "Map? No, not

here."

He shakes his head. Faced with navigating a foreign city, William would absolutely equip himself with maps, guidebooks, websites, and apps. He'd never just wing it. He'd never, say, take up with a random stranger he met in a café and end up living with her. He wouldn't go on an expedition into forbidden catacombs with a bunch of guys he'd just met.

Yet those are two of the most exciting and fulfilling things I have ever done.

"You'd learn your way around in no time," I add. "You've only been here for a couple days."

I point him down a long, straight street, the right side featuring a row of gaudy souvenir shops. The left side is the north wall of Notre-Dame Cathedral, but William doesn't even glance at it. "You're the boss," he says. He is absolutely aiming to please. This reminds me of when we first met. He would cook me cozy dinners at his house, take me up to Sedona for elaborate picnics, and plan whole weekends around what I like to do. Like those four short days in San Francisco. And four long nights. The memory sweeps through me like a wave sluicing across the beach. I almost groan.

"This is an island, huh?" He tips his head back to take in the upper stories of the souvenir-shop buildings on our right. "I'm guessing these structures are solid stone. They must deliver a huge gravity load. I wonder what the weight per unit area is." He pulls out his phone and starts to punch numbers into the calculator app.

William is an aeronautical engineer, not a civil one, but as we dawdle along he's effortlessly lost in the land of x and y, of knowns and unknowns, of quantitative not qualitative. Catherine flutters, reminding me that in our sweet little equation of one plus one I'm supposed to be the responsible adult, the parent who needs to be calculating and hypothesizing, and most of all, thinking rationally.

Oh, but it's not easy. Just as when I followed William around on his first morning in Paris, just as when we met in the no-name café last night, nothing is happening quite the way I thought it would happen.

At the end of the street, we veer left into a vast open plaza.

His shoulders again relax, a sign he's happy to be in an unrestricted space despite the masses of people swarming all around us.

"Where to now?" He pauses and starts to look around.

"No! Keep going. Don't look back." I grab the sleeve of his jacket and tug him forward. I don't want him to see it too soon. We reach the middle of the plaza before I stop and allow him to turn. "*Voilà*. There it is. Notre-Dame de Paris."

His mouth drops open as he gazes up at the iconic façade. William is not religious and doesn't much care about art or history—or at least any history besides American—so I don't expect anything like actual awe. But for a few seconds he gawks in respectful silence. Then he glances at me. "Isn't this one of the seven wonders of the world?"

Facts and data.

"Dunno." I shrug. "Maybe."

He stares up at the two square towers. "It's smaller than I thought it would be."

I wince. True, the towers aren't skyscrapers. A lot of the impact from the cathedral comes not from its size but from the fact that it stands at the heart of France and has been doing so for more than eight hundred years. I mean—it's *the* Notre-Dame.

"Do you want to take a picture of yourself with the cathedral in the background?" I ask to paper over my annoyance. "It's kind of a must-do."

"Photo. Good idea."

When he gets out his phone I step back, expecting him to whip out the selfie stick I saw him with the other day and add to his William Does Paris series. But before I realize what's happening he slings his arm around my shoulders and pulls me to his side.

After months of zero physical contact with a man (unless you count the obligatory cheek kisses with Manu and Hervé), I find myself pressed up against a very solid, very real man. The muscles in my arms and legs seem to emulsify, and I forget how to breathe.

"Smile." He holds out the phone with his free arm. I grin foolishly at it. Our heads are tilted, almost touching. The only part of Notre-Dame visible in the background is a section of one of the three Gothic arches. None of the scores of people milling around pays us the slightest bit of attention. We're just another pair of tourists conscientiously documenting our trip to the City of Light.

Île Saint-Louis, check.

Notre-Dame, check.

William is as oblivious as all the other tourists. He doesn't realize that if I turned my face toward his, our noses would touch and our lips would be less than an inch apart. He doesn't hear my heart leaping around like a baby goat in my chest. He snaps a series of pictures, as one does, and then shows them to me. I barely glance at them. His arm is circling my waist. His breath strokes my cheek. Oh God.

"Are you hungry yet? I am," he says as he drops the arm he was holding me with and returns the phone to an inside pocket of his jacket. He's not wearing the magenta hoodie today but a lightweight tan blazer that fits as if it had been tailored for him. Unlike me, William has dressed to impress.

At this point we've been wandering for more than an hour, and I'd like to eat something too. But more than that I need to sit down. I consider guiding us back to the Île Saint-Louis, to the small mahogany-paneled restaurant Margaret took me to for our first lunch. Then I decide the Latin Quarter, the Paris most people think of when they think of Paris, would be better. Besides, there's a bistro in a glass-roofed *passage* near the boulevard Saint-Germain that I want to try. It's small and quiet and looks like it would be a good place to talk.

It is. Over our warm goat cheese salad starter, William finally asks what I've been up to the last four months. I recount the highlights of my summer, saying I've found an apartment and a job. I spend nearly an hour describing my mad adventure in the catacombs, which I guessed would intrigue him. I'm right because he asks a ton of questions: Are they like sewers (no), are they dangerous (yes), how were they built (no idea, but I do know they were originally quarries), was it cold (sort of), why did you go down there (because I wanted and needed to have a fabulous adventure).

I don't mention Margaret and Manu. Certainly not Sophie or Hervé. That world, my French world, must never be allowed to mix with William's. The two universes are diametrically opposed, if not mutually exclusive. They are, as William might say, like matter and anti-matter.

As we finish the main course—poached salmon with sorrel sauce—William puts down his fork and looks over at me. "Wow, Ames. You are über brave."

I flush. "What? Me?" I don't want to admit that a significant portion of my Paris adventure has been more desperation than bravery. Often, courage is just the feeling you have no other real options.

"Hell, yeah. I don't think I would have the guts to do what you did."

"I expected you to think it was stupid," I say, and clamp my lips together, not sure if we're ready for this level of honesty.

But all he does is sip his sparkling water and stare past me out the window. Again, I have the sense he's as reluctant to truly open up as I am. Or perhaps he simply doesn't know where to begin. He hasn't even asked about what medical care I've been receiving or brought up the subject of my phone bills. He doesn't start to share his news, whatever it is. And I don't ask. Things are going so well.

"I think coming to France, like you have, is damn cool," he remarks.

"You do?"

Wow. Last April, William was royally pissed off about my coming-to-France. Now he's declaring it "damn cool."

"And, obviously, you're surviving." He grins. "What next? Are you up for more walking?"

I am, and as always, Catherine is too.

After settling the bill—which I insist we split—we follow the cobblestone *passage* to where it opens onto the broad and busy boulevard Saint-Germain. We wander until we reach the medieval garden behind the Musée de Cluny, where we stop to sit on a bench. Usually this mini park is teeming with tourists, but today it's been taken over by old people, seated side by side on the benches or ambling hand in hand along the raked gravel paths. They're at such total ease with each other they don't even need to speak.

I know I should just ask William why he's come to Paris. But

PARIS EVER AFTER

when he takes my hand as we leave the park I go mute with gladness. I remember our first date, nearly five years ago at a Mexican restaurant in Phoenix, and how he related his whole life story. I picture us decades from now, an old couple strolling along in comfortable silence. It isn't for many blocks, at the rue Soufflot, that I'm finally able to find my words.

"Let's turn." I tug at his arm. "There's something I'd like to show you. It's not far."

He follows me willingly.

In my wanderings over the summer I couldn't help but notice Paris has a ton of monuments to science and math. Streets are named after guys like Newton and Ampère and Poincaré and Einstein and Descartes. The names of seventy-two scientists, engineers, and mathematicians—also all guys—are inscribed on the Eiffel Tower. I guess being married to William has had its effect on me. I notice these kinds of things. The first time I happened upon the pendulum at the Panthéon, a former church and now mausoleum, my immediate thought was how much he would love it.

Now I see I was right.

"It's a Foucault's pendulum! Whoa!" His eyes shine as he spots the volleyball-sized brass bob suspended from a long wire hanging from the dome high above our heads.

"The plane of the pendulum's movement is consistent," he continues as we watch the bob swing back and forth, back and forth. "However, if we stand here long enough, we'll see the trajectory of the swing appear to change." He draws my attention to the markings on the platform beneath the brass bob. "But it's not the pendulum's direction that's changing. It's the Earth beneath it. Foucault's pendulum proves Earth rotates on an axis."

I gaze at the brass bob, half-hypnotized by both the slow magisterial swing and the steady drip-drip-drip of William's detailed commentary. Though it's a Saturday, the Panthéon is not crowded—there wasn't even a line to get in—and the vast space absorbs the presence of the dozen other onlookers. It's lovely. I can almost feel as if we're the only ones here. Just us and the ghosts of Voltaire and Descartes and Marie Curie.

William turns to face me, his cheeks rosy. "Did you know you can use a Foucault's pendulum to calculate latitude?"

I can't help smiling. "Nope. I did not know that."

He launches into a lengthy explanation, during which, yes, the trajectory of the pendulum's swing does appear to alter.

"You see it?"

"Yup. Science in action. Super." I've never really understood these sorts of explanations and have always wished I did.

I should be far more interested in learning what our future is going to hold or if indeed we even have a future. And yet, this moment in the company of Foucault's invention feels complete. Pure and simple and whole. William is so happy to be where he is, with me and the pendulum. I can't bear to break the mood.

It's his phone that breaks the mood. When it rings, it turns William's face as white as the grease-painted Roman statue guy. He reaches into his pocket and silences the phone without even looking at it, his eyes black.

"Work," he says before I can ask. "My department's in the middle of a big proposal, and they have a lot of questions. But you're probably bored. Let's get going."

William has always been honest to a fault. I can't in a million years imagine him telling a lie to spare someone's feelings. Not even mine. Or, maybe, especially not mine.

Anyway, I feel I need to cut him some slack. Less than six months ago I took off for a week in Paris without even telling him first. It'll take me a while to live that down. So I don't question him. I allow him to lead me from the cool building into the warm sunlight, where again he lets me choose our route.

Eventually, however, I do ask, as we thread our way through a maze of mostly empty streets, "If you're needed at work, shouldn't you be calling them back?"

He glances at me and grins. "I'll do it later. Right now, I'm with you." He takes my hand, and his touch sends zings of delight up and down my body. He's choosing me over work. I can hardly believe it.

In this past half year, so much in my life has changed. Kat died. Catherine was conceived. Sophie returned. Perhaps something huge about William is changing too. I imagine Earth tipping on its axis, sending landmasses sliding and crashing together, forming new continents, new oceans and seas. I imagine a new and bright and shiny world.

"Will. I want to apologize."

"For what?"

"You know. For going off to Paris last spring. Without saying anything."

"Oh. That's OK."

"It's OK?" I've been feeling guilty about this all summer. "I thought you were really mad."

"Yeah."

He doesn't elaborate, and we lapse into another comfortable silence as we return to the bustling boulevard Saint-Michel, emerging at a point opposite one of the gates to the Jardin du Luxembourg. Parks in Paris tend to be fenced. This one is enclosed with a particularly impressive grille-style barrier, fifteen feet high and fashioned of black wrought iron trimmed with gold.

William's face brightens. "Let's go in there." The sight of so much nature—even caged French nature—quickens his step.

We walk the entire considerable length of the garden, around the big fountain with the galloping horses, and then all the way back again, to the large octagonal pond that glitters in the shadow of the Sénat building. Only a few weeks ago this area was overflowing with baseball-cap-wearing tourists. Now, in September, it's returning to its normal French self. Quiet and orderly and controlled. For me, the tall, black wrought iron fencing doesn't represent a cage. It's a sign that, like Hervé's secret garden, herein lies a place of repose. Refuge.

I steer us toward the pond. This portion of the Jardin du Luxembourg feels especially cozy because the statues all around us are of queens and female saints—no kings or male scientists— and because there are many living women here too, mothers with babies and toddlers.

Or maybe they're nannies. Either way, I'm grateful when William locates a couple of the green metal chairs scattered all around and positions them facing the water. We sit side by side, loosely holding hands, watching a small boy playing with a toy boat. He's wearing crisp blue shorts and a spotless white shirt, and is wielding a long pole to propel the boat across the rippling water. His mother, or nanny, isn't helping him. He's managing it all by himself.

William's behavior since he reentered my life has been

surprising, titillating, mystifying, and even disturbing, but here in the elegant and airy Jardin du Luxembourg I feel secure. I feel on home ground.

"Did you know," I say, returning to tour guide mode, "they've been using these same toy boats here for more than eighty years?" It hardly seems plausible, but Margaret assures me it's true.

"Cool."

The little boy reels in his boat and re-launches it. If Catherine and I stay in Paris, one day she'll be old enough to play with these boats. She'll dig holes in the nearby sandboxes and laugh at the puppet shows, perfectly understanding the French. She will become French.

If I return to Phoenix with William, she will become someone else. As will I.

William stretches out his long legs. His movements are easy and casual. "The boats are great. I can see our little one playing like this someday."

"You can?"

He chuckles. "Sure. In Minnesota I had my own little rowboat."

sixteen

AS I UNLOCK THE DOOR to Margaret's apartment, I ask myself if it's possible for a person to truly change. Kat always said no, but Margaret might offer perspective. By now she should be up after her long sleep. I've missed her. While she can be dippy at times, she often has wise, even shrewd, insights into human nature. She's older and has seen more of life. She has compassion for people. She doesn't expect them to be anything other than who they are, even if who they are is less than ideal.

But when I push the door open and step inside, I realize I'll never get the chance to ask.

Sophie's back.

She, Margaret, and Manu are huddled around an unlit fireplace. Margaret is wearing her pale pink cashmere dressing gown and is settled into her customary chair. Her usually perfect silver hair is perfect again, and she's put on lipstick. Manu looks the way he always looks—calm and kind.

Sophie, on the other hand, is a bit of a wreck. She's wearing a white spandex dress that I tried on once and found too tight but that on her is way too loose. Her hair is wet, her enormous round eyes are glassy and bloodshot, and her skin is ashen. She sits hunched over, elbows on knees, eyes closed, and is speaking in a low voice. Manu and Margaret listen with rapt attention. No one notices me standing next to the coat rack, breathless and sweaty from sprinting up the stairs.

An alarm bell ding-dongs in my head. Not just because a fresh box of Godiva chocolates someone procured is already half empty, reminding me of Margaret's sugar binge the day Sophie returned, but because the sitting room has been transfigured for three. The maroon velveteen loveseat occupied by Sophie and Manu (they are sitting almost close enough to touch) never used to be here; it had been wedged into a corner of Margaret's office. The nut-brown leather armchair that I like to call my own is standing off to one side, as if declared surplus. Unnecessary.

To think I was in such a huge hurry to get home.

I take off my coat and crush it to my chest like a favorite stuffed animal. I, too, look the worse for wear. My "I ♥ Paris" T-shirt is sticking to my armpits, my leggings sag around my hips, and my boots are caked with dust. What I really need right now is a nap, a bath, and a change of clothes.

"*Mais non!*" says Margaret. But no.

She's talking not to me but to Sophie. Her green eyes are shining, and she leans forward to take her daughter's hands and bring them to her lips.

I'm about to get back into my coat when Manu spots me. "*Aimée! Te voilà!*" There you are. "Come. Join us."

I hesitate. "I don't want to intrude."

Margaret looks up and waves her free arm. "Don't be a goose. Come and sit, dear. Have a piece of chocolate."

By this time Godiva's irresistible perfume has reached my nostrils so I'm forced to obey, dragging my abandoned armchair to the outer perimeter of their cozy half circle. Sophie watches me help myself to a chocolate and sling my legs over the arm of the chair. Margaret watches Sophie. It's weird. The whole dynamic is the exact opposite of yesterday. Margaret is calm and warm, and Sophie seems to be on the verge of a breakdown. Manu is the same as always.

Margaret pats Sophie's knee. "*Ma pauvre.*" You poor thing.

Sophie places her hand over her mother's and resumes her monologue.

I listen but as usual comprehend little, which frees my mind to wander. What an unlikely couple they are, Manu and Sophie. He's measured and calm; she's jittery. He's considerate and kind;

she's self-absorbed, from what I can tell.

Not only that, they don't look alike. Kat subscribed to the theory that we're attracted to people we physically resemble. Study the wedding photos in any newspaper, she claimed, and you'll see how often the happy bride and groom share the same smile or brow line or chin. I tried this. It's true.

Nevertheless, some of us still irrationally insist on falling in love with people who look nothing like us and are probably our antonyms in every other way. Like Manu, who is dark-haired and amiable, and Sophie, who has flaxen locks and thin skin—both literally and metaphorically. The Manu-Sophie couple makes me nauseous, but I have to stop dwelling on something that isn't any of my business. I need to focus on my own future.

"*A l'université?*" asks Margaret. It's one of the few things I've understood. Some days I feel my French is improving, and I'm proud. Other days are like this.

Sophie nods. "*Oui, Maman.*" Her hair is wet not from being just washed, I now notice. It's wet from sweat.

I concentrate hard for the next few minutes, but the only additional words I'm able to pick out are *un mariage* and *le Maroc*. Since I can't imagine what "marriage" and "Morocco," much less "university," have to do with each other, I return to thinking about William. Our outing ended too soon, for me.

We were sitting by the pond in the Jardin du Luxembourg. The late afternoon sun was casting long shadows across the gravel pathways. He was holding my hand and telling me how tides exist in all bodies of water, even ones as small as this pond.

"In this case the movement would be infinitesimal. Impossible to measure," he was saying. Then his phone rang, and he dropped my hand. "I should take this," he said, holding up the phone to show Robert's face grinning from the touchscreen. Work. It's never far from William's mind. Even in San Francisco he took work calls. "Hey," he said into the phone, standing up. "Yeah. Uh-huh."

I was planning to just wait when he pantomimed to me to call him later, using a two-fingered "Call me" gesture like a character out of *Sex and the City*. I've never seen William do that before—it's the kind of cutesy thing he scorns—but today he pulled it off like a pro. It took a little of the sting out of being dismissed. I giggled, he grinned back, and I felt life was full of promise. Possibility.

"*Vraiment?*" Manu says now. Really?

I reach for the golden Godiva box. A couple more chocolates, then I'll take a bath. It's not like I'm contributing anything to the conversation. Afterwards, maybe I'll even have a nap. Then I'll call William, as he said I should, and set up our next meeting.

For tomorrow. Not tonight. So much has happened in the last twenty-four hours. William's behavior has careened from surly to charming to mysterious to enticing to reassuring. I owe it to Catherine, and to myself, to take the time to consider everything carefully. No more harebrained moves for me.

I'm popping a chocolate into my mouth when Sophie lifts the skirt of her white dress to reveal a long red scar curving across the top of one milky thigh.

"Goodness gracious!" Margaret's face turns greasepaint white, and she leaps to her feet. I reach out, worried she's headed for a relapse of yesterday's craziness. But before I can steady her, she sits down and again gathers Sophie's hands between her own. Both she and Manu listen intently to what I assume is the story, which looks pretty shocking. Of this account I glean but a single word, "*couteau*"—knife. And only because Sophie repeats it five times. Also, it kind of goes with the topic of scar.

After a few minutes Manu gets up to crouch beside my chair.

"Do you remember when I told you Sophie said she was kidnapped?" he whispers to me. I nod, unable to take my eyes from Margaret's pale face. "Evidently, that was not the whole story. She tells us it started with a man she met at university. He was from Morocco. They fell in love, she says. It was an *amour fou.*"

I glance at him and nod again. *Amour fou* means crazy love. Listening to Hervé has given me the impression that, for the French, "crazy" love is the best kind. When it comes to affairs of the heart (he likes to explain with a world-weary shrug), we must accept we are irrational beings. Infidelity is inevitable. Permanency is not paramount. What matters most is our experience of a mad romantic passion, to be fully enjoyed in the moment and looked back upon with fondness. It sounds a little frivolous, and I could be generalizing here. Perhaps only barons think this way. I have no personal experience with French romance because I've never stuck my toe in French dating waters. And it doesn't look as if I'll ever need to.

Manu, still kneeling beside me, continues his explanation. "This man, he take—he took her to his home. In a small village in *Maroc*. They move in with his mother. And then he—I mean his *caractère*—it changed completely, she tells us. He wanted her to be a traditional woman. A wife."

I study Sophie's scar. It has a hook on one end, like a candy cane, and goes from her knee almost to her hip. Her tale of captivity is bizarre and melodramatic, but something about it feels familiar to me. Not because I've ever been carried off to Morocco by a medieval-minded male. Or, um, stabbed.

But I do know the sickening sense of the rug being pulled out from under you, as the universe suddenly shows itself for the capricious jokester it really is. I do know what it's like to be on the losing side, having lost both my parents and my best friend. A wave of empathy washes over me as Margaret pulls the white dress over the red scar and enfolds Sophie into her arms, crooning softly.

"He took her passport," adds Manu. "He did not allow her to use a telephone or to mail a letter. The mother, she watched Sophie all the time." He shifts his weight from his left knee to his right. "When this man was obliged to take her to the hospital for her injury, she was able to—what is the word—*échapper*?"

"Escape," I translate, surprised I know the word.

"*Merci*. At the hospital she found transport with refugees and was able to cross into Europe at Gibraltar. It took many hours."

Well, that would explain why she looked so dirty and bedraggled when she got back. "She escaped from her husband," I say more to myself than to Manu.

"*Oui*," he agrees, but then holds up a hand. "Er—*non*. Perhaps not indeed her 'husband.' She says the *mariage* may not have been correct. Not official." He frowns and tilts his head. "*Quelle histoire, n'est-ce pas?*"

His eyes are sparkling. Yes, it's quite a story. I picture Sophie bumping along in the back of a truck, using that filthy daypack for a pillow, subsisting on the dry crusts of discarded sandwiches.

I shrug. "Sounds like the plot of a made-for-TV movie."

"*Pardon?*"

"I mean—lured into a sham marriage? Held captive in Morocco for two years? Do you believe all this?"

Manu squints at me, and it's clear he does indeed believe all this. William wouldn't, not in a million years. Even Kat would have her doubts, and she normally always sided with the woman.

And yet—while browsing through Paris bookstores I've run across numerous novels, memoirs, and even comic books recounting similar narratives of modern-day abductions. It seems to be a popular storyline. We may never really know if it happened or if Sophie just made up a tale she knew couldn't be verified.

Or, rather, a tale her mother wouldn't choose to verify.

Because I'm sure Margaret will never go to the police to seek justice for Sophie's wrongful imprisonment. She'll want to cover it up and forget about the whole thing. She'll want to go back to a "normal" life as soon as possible. Manu will naturally bow to Margaret's wishes. And to Sophie's. Even now he's left me to kneel at her feet and gaze up at her with troubled blue eyes as she sobs on Margaret's shoulder.

The teakettle starts to sing. I didn't even know it had been put on. When no one takes notice, I get up to make the tea and bring it out to the sitting room. I place the tray on the hammered copper side table beside Margaret's chair. She looks up at me and mouths, "Thank you" but doesn't relinquish her embrace of Sophie. Nor does Manu budge from his post at Sophie's feet. I stand off to the side for a minute, looking down at the three of them.

Who am I trying to kid? Margaret and Manu and Sophie belong to each other, belong to Paris, in a way I never will. Or could.

I turn my back and retreat to the room-that-is-no-longer-my-room. More than anything, I need a nap. But I don't lie down. Even though I slept here just last night, the bed—like the whole room, the whole apartment—feels remote, indifferent, empty, foreign. Nothing here belongs to me.

Or at least very little. The majority of my clothes are in my carry-on, and that's still over at Hervé's. Here, only the few maternity items hanging in the armoire, the two pairs of shoes peeking out from under the bed, my underwear, and half a dozen English-language novels picked up at flea markets and secondhand shops are really mine.

Which is good, because at this point in my life I need to be easily portable.

"*Aimée?*"

Manu is in the doorway. His face is the color of chalk, and the corners of his eyes droop. Poor guy. While I was out wandering Paris with William, lunching on salmon with sorrel sauce and learning about Foucault's pendulum, Manu was here dealing with Margaret and Sophie.

"Margaret seems to be doing a lot better," I remark as he silently stands there.

"Yes. She slept till past noon o'clock."

"Good. Does she remember yesterday?"

"I think no. When she woke she asked for Sophie. We will take her to the doctor on Monday."

That's soon enough. It's already late Saturday afternoon. "Well, I'm glad she's doing so well."

He takes a half step into the room. "Would you—do you mind to stay *chez moi* tonight? Margaret desires to have Sophie here with her."

"Sure. No problem."

He smiles at me. "*Merci.*" He hasn't asked about my day with William. But my relationship with William has got to be the last thing on Manu's mind right now. "It won't take me long to pack my stuff," I mumble, reaching to pull the maternity tops from their hangers.

Fifteen minutes later, my clothes and shoes are stuffed into two shopping bags. Toiletries and vitamins fill my trusty tote. The money belt is strapped around my ever-expanding waist. I leave the novels behind. Who knows—they might help Sophie improve her English. Not that Sophie strikes me as the bookish type; she seems more like the shop-till-she-drops-and-then-go-for-mani-pedis type. She certainly could use a mani-pedi. I bet Margaret has noticed the same thing and has already made appointments for them both.

I'm careful to not take anything I didn't bring from Phoenix

or buy here in Paris. The diamond bangle bracelet, the butter-soft
leather jacket, the blue-and-white-striped silk dressing gown and
its matching nightie, the Waterford crystal clock—they all stay
here where they belong. Besides, I don't need silks and diamonds.
I like them, sure. But I don't need them.

My last act is to fold up Hervé's red Christian Dior tunic,
wrap it in tissue paper, and lay it on top of my clothes in one of
the shopping bags. I'll return it to Hervé when I go over there to
get my carry-on. Funny. He hasn't called me, or Margaret, since
yesterday morning. But that's Hervé. You see him, then you
don't. You never find out what he was doing in the interim.

When I reenter the sitting room, carrying my worldly goods,
Manu is perched on the arm of my empty chair. Sophie and
Margaret are sitting side by side on the loveseat with their arms
looped around each other's waists and their cheeks almost
touching. I can't help admiring the scene. Margaret has her
beloved daughter back at her side, which is a good thing.

She looks up. "Ah. Amy dear. Thank you, darling, for being
so understanding. It's just for tonight. We'll get everything sorted
tomorrow."

"Sorted?" I look at Manu, then back to Margaret, before
remembering Margaret knows nothing about what's happening in
my life right now. No one has told her about William's arrival in
Paris or what I am in the process of deciding I must do next. Her
world is all Sophie, all the time. As it should be.

"Um, sure," I say. "Tomorrow. We'll talk then. Have a lovely
evening. Don't get up. See you soon. Mwah mwah." I
pantomime cheek kisses and stride to the door.

Margaret laughs. "Your *soupe de poulet* was magnificent, by the
way. We had it for lunch."

"Good. Great." I smile over my shoulder at her. Soup is
always better the next day.

"*Aimée!*" Manu catches up to me. "I will accompany you."
He reaches for my shopping bags.

"No need. Just give me your key."

Maybe this sounds rude, but my mind is filled with images of
him spending the night here at Margaret's. With Sophie. In my
former bed. It shouldn't bother me. At least not anymore.

"Are you sure?" He glances back at Sophie, who is munching

down another chocolate and ignoring me. She doesn't need to act so sulky. She's won. She's getting back her clothes, her room, her mother, her boyfriend, and her life. If she ever saw me as competition, she doesn't need to worry now.

At the door, Manu plucks my trench coat from its hook and helps me into it as no American man has ever done but as French men always seem to do. I sort of wish he wouldn't. The brush of his hand on my shoulder makes me blush, which is stupid, and I can't meet his eyes as I accept the key to his apartment.

"Call me when you arrive."

"Sure," I say, stepping out of his reach. "Thanks for letting me stay at your place. Again."

"Manu!" Margaret is waving her arms. "Don't forget the soup, darling."

"Ah. Right. Wait here." Manu hurries into the kitchen and returns bearing a white plastic food container. "For your supper," he says.

"Oh. OK. Thanks." As I accept the container, I realize all this must have been determined in advance. They discussed me and decided that soon after I returned I'd be dispatched elsewhere. Maybe William has reappeared in my life just in the nick of time. Maybe it's all meant to be.

"You can heat it in the microwave."

"Yes, I know." I wedge the container into my tote and gather up my various bags. It's my own soup. I do know how to heat it up.

"You have the code to get into the building, correct?"

I nod. What is his problem? I've been to Manu's place dozens of times, including the night before last, when I slept on his clic-clac.

I open the heavy front door of Margaret's apartment before Manu has a chance to do it for me and turn for one last look. Honey-gold parquet floor, butter-pat yellow silk wallpaper, heavy clove-dark beams striping the cream-white ceiling. For a few blissful months this home was my home. Margaret was my mother. Manu was my friend and boss. Paris was the city where I lived. It was a real-life fairytale come true and a whole lot more than many people get. I'm grateful for it all. I really am.

"*A plus tard,*" he calls as I hurry down the stairwell.

"Yeah. See you later," I answer without looking back.

In the courtyard, I look down at my belly, where Catherine remains perfectly still.

Not to worry, sweet child. I'm going to get a grip on things. Soon. Promise.

seventeen

IN THE FRANCE I'VE COME TO KNOW, Sunday is a day of rest. Shops close. Traffic dwindles. Pedestrians consist mainly of families walking off the effects of their midday meal. The entire atmosphere is one of repose, ease, and equanimity.

During the months I lived with Margaret we always slept in on Sundays. The rest of the morning we frittered away sipping tea and nibbling *croissants*. Later we'd go out for lunch, sometimes with Manu. We never felt we ought to be doing something more productive with our day. It was always just enough to enjoy the food, the conversation, and each other—a delightful way of passing the time that Margaret told me is called *art de vivre*.

On this Sunday morning, William's fifth day in Paris and surely one of my last ones, I wake before six. Our rendezvous isn't until nine-thirty, but I can't sleep. And neither can Catherine; she's been bouncing around all night.

At nine twenty-eight I show up at the Hôtel du Cheval Blanc, showered and lotioned, hair shining, make-up flawless. The day is warm, so I wear the cotton navy blue and white polka dot chemise dress Margaret found for me on sale at the BHV department store and insisted I buy. With sandals. No socks.

I even shaved my legs.

In our brief phone call last night, William proposed we meet at his hotel and go from there to breakfast. But when I enter the lobby the only people present are an elderly woman and the deskman. The woman leans on a purple metal cane and speaks French with a foreign accent I don't recognize as she supervises the transfer of her immense amount of luggage from the lobby to a waiting taxi outside. I help with the lighter bags, wondering if I'll have the gumption to be traveling alone when I'm this lady's age and if I'd carry this much stuff.

Everyone has a story to tell. It could be outlandish, like Sophie's tale of being held hostage in a remote Moroccan village for two years. It could be mundane, like my entire narrative from birth until the day I left Phoenix and landed in Paris (when my life became very fabulous indeed). This lady looks like she opted for the solo-travel adventurous road. She smiles at me as she gets into the cab. *"Merci,"* she says, pronouncing it "murr-see." I smile back.

When the woman and her luggage are gone, the deskman turns to me. He's the same one who was here last spring, when I stayed at this hotel. He doesn't show signs of remembering me even though he should. He called cabs for me, stored my bags, let me use his phone, and even bought me breakfast one day. I was a tremendous pain in the rear. But perhaps I am completely transformed; perhaps I have turned into Amy 2.0.

If I return to Phoenix with William, will I remain this way? Or will I revert to the often-dithery (and too-often weak) Amy? I hope not.

"Numéro soixante-et-un," the deskman says when I ask, in pretty good French, if *Monsieur* Brodie is here. *"Merci,"* I reply, and head for the stairs. Not a lot of security measures in place at the old Hôtel du Cheval Blanc. You can walk in and be given any information you request.

Room number sixty-one is on the top floor. William doesn't enjoy surprises—he likes to be the one with the superior facts and data, remember—but I'm determined to go up anyway. My husband needs to start getting used to the unexpected. Babies are full of surprises. Kids too. And, I guess, spouses.

As I trudge up the worn wooden stairs, I think about the other time William and I encountered each other in a Paris hotel room, last April when he found out about my "break" and came in pursuit. He was angry. He ranted and shouted and accused and slandered. He even kicked over a chair.

Since then I've tried to tell myself, "Well, it was only a chair—at least he didn't kick me," but that's not very comforting. Dad never abused the furniture. He never yelled or cursed. He was never violent in any way.

By the time I reach the sixth floor I'm out of breath, but I don't take the time to compose myself. William's proximity has me on high alert. I step straight to the door labeled with a six and a one and rap on it.

I wait. Listen. All is silent. Maybe I should've texted or phoned first instead.

"Will?" I call through the door.

Still no answer.

I knock again, louder this time, because maybe he's in the bathroom. Two seconds later I hear a crash and a muffled "Shit."

When the door swings open I see why he wasn't waiting for me downstairs. He overslept. "Sorry," he mumbles. "Jetlag." He wears a sheepish smile, a pair of white cotton boxer shorts, and nothing else.

My cheeks and chest go oven hot.

Here's the scenario I was expecting: William greets me at the door, jacket on and ready to go. He apologizes for running late and laughs at me for climbing six flights of stairs for nothing. Then he escorts me to a nice café for a nice breakfast of buttery *croissants* and hot *café crèmes*, after which we set out on another ramble around Paris. Eventually we talk about the things we need to talk about. We settle the things we need to settle. We do the right thing. For Catherine. That's the way it was supposed to go.

Surprise.

"Sorry." He steps back, holding the door open for me. "Come in."

I pause. No one knows I've come here—not even Manu. I didn't call him last night, even though he asked me to, and he didn't call me. No doubt he was busy with Sophie. How quickly the beautiful life I lived this summer with Margaret and Manu has faded into soft-focus, like a dream. Now I'm wakened from that dream and facing the reality that I'm five months pregnant. I have no real job. I've been living in a foreign country with no papers— Margaret's promise to help with a residency visa probably won't happen now. Why should it? Margaret has Sophie back. She has her real daughter.

"Ames? Are you going to just stand out there?"

William yawns, still barely awake. I straighten my shoulders and walk past him into the room. The bed is unmade, but nothing else is out of place—no clothes or shoes are strewn about, no potato-chip bags or empty water bottles litter the floor. The only non-shipshape element is William's battered canvas briefcase, lying on its side and spilling out a half-dozen plain manila file folders. That must be what he tripped over on his way to the door. Typical of William to bring along work stuff on a personal trip.

The door clicks shut behind me. I move a few feet farther into the middle of the room, where I stop and slowly turn around. William stands about a yard away, his arms dangling at his sides, seemingly unembarrassed to be next-to-naked in front of his estranged wife. Sunshine streaming through the one window gilds his bare skin gold and divides his face in two so that half is illuminated and half is in shadow. His smooth chest swells as he takes a long deep inhale. I realize I can hear the wild clatter of my own heartbeat, and I wonder if he can too.

A full five seconds tick by. Yes, I count.

When I get to number six, I hold my arms out to him. "Hey," I whisper. He doesn't pause. He steps forward, grasps my forearms, and pulls me into him.

Somehow, we move from the middle of the room to the bed. Somehow, my sandals fall from my feet, my loose dress is swept over my head, and William's boxers slide down his legs.

Somehow, my body unfolds beneath him. The echo of my soft "Hey" hangs in the dusty air over our heads. No other words enter my brain. My arms and legs and all my other parts perform without specific instruction from me. I am pure instinct, pure desire.

OK, for one tiny instant, just as he lowers himself onto me, I do waver. I do wonder if this is happening too quickly, too easily, too unthinkingly. But then the sensation of William's warm firm mouth closing over mine drives away that thought too. It's been so long.

Too long.

He falls asleep immediately afterwards. As usual. It's all I can do to keep from laughing out loud. William is predictable. He's a known quantity. Except for the scratchy new beard, our lovemaking was the same as always—familiar, comfortable, like slumping on the couch to watch a favorite movie or re-read a familiar book from childhood. I lie flat on my back beside him, my body still thrumming, and listen to the rumble of his light snore. In a little while he'll wake up. Maybe we can go again. I'd like that. Now that I've come this far, I see no reason to deprive myself. It's been, as I say, a long time.

Meanwhile, I wiggle my toes and look around. When I was staying at this hotel last April, my room was decorated entirely in variations of red. The walls, and even the ceiling, were covered with a wallpaper design of scarlet cabbage roses the size of dinner plates. The carpet was a dark fuchsia. The sheets were the color of steamed salmon, and the duvet cover was printed with enormous crimson poppies. It was a riot of reds and pinks.

William's room is a requiem in brown. The sheets and bedspread are tan, the curtains are taupe, the furniture is muddy mahogany, and the carpet is a faded cinnamon. The walls are upholstered floor to ceiling with the same carpeting as the floor. I have never seen carpeted walls before. But then, before last April, I'd never seen a wallpapered ceiling.

Brown. My least-favorite color. Even now, as relaxed and gratified as I am, the drabness of the room tugs at me, tamps down my buzz.

William stirs. His face is turned away, but I can tell he's awake.

"Hey," I say, nudging him with my foot. "Isn't this room driving you crazy?"

"Huh?" He twists around to stare at me, the muscles of his back rippling. "Whaddaya mean?"

"You know. The color."

He frowns.

"Your room is the color of dirt." I hold up a corner of the dun-colored sheet and wait for him to laugh.

"Oh." He rolls away. "Never noticed."

Obviously, he didn't. The room is clean and cheap, and that's all he cares about. I tell myself it's not important, because it's not, and play my fingertips across his satiny skin. William has a particularly beautiful back, broad with a narrow waist, lean but not gaunt, and well muscled. The valley of his spinal column is absolutely smooth—no bumpy vertebrae mar its perfection. Some women look at men's butts. I look at their backs.

His shoulder twitches, and I think he's about to roll over to face me—I prepare to welcome him—but instead he sits up and swings his legs off the bed. "Just a minute," he mutters. Halfway to his feet he sits down again, and to my disappointment, reaches for his boxers and slips into them before heading to the bathroom.

As he always does, he closes the door behind him. We're not the kind of married people who feel free to pee within sight or sound of each other. Kat and I, on the other hand, were always too busy chattering (usually about nothing) to completely close the bathroom door. I had to make a real effort to get into the habit when I married William.

Margaret would say that's a big part of what marriage is—making an effort. Adapting. Compromising. At times it's seemed harder than it should be. But how would I know? My main example was my parents' somewhat dysfunctional marriage. My brief romantic relationship (yes, there was that) and then deep friendship with Kat was one of those lightning-bolt, once-in-a-lifetime things where everything feels easy and right and relaxed, as if touched by a sorcerer's wand. I know nothing about how ordinary non-magical couples function.

One thing I do know is this bed, despite the fact that the sheets are hideously brown, is ten times more comfortable than Manu's clic-clac. I feel contented, calm, sated, and drowsy. "Count your blessings," Dad always used to say to me. Well, maybe I'm learning to do that. Maybe—just maybe—this will be my last Sunday morning in Paris. Lying here, so snug, so relaxed, I'm coming to think this could be the right thing. It can work. If we make it work.

William takes his time in the bathroom, giving me the chance to fan my hair over the pillowcase and arrange the top sheet so it lies smoothly over my body. My baby bump makes a nice visible mound this way. For years I used to lie on my back and admire how flat my stomach looked when I was supine, at least during my thin times, and perhaps I'll do so again someday. But right now, I treasure the delicious roundness and firmness of my growing belly. Right now, it's my most fetching feature, which is why I was a little disappointed when my dress first came off and William's eyes didn't go straight to my abdomen, as I expected. He did take care not to put too much weight on me, true, but the whole time we made love he kept his gaze fixed on the wall above the bed.

I tip my head back to peer up at said wall, but there are no pictures or posters or even flyspecks to attract anyone's attention. The nightstand is bare, too, except for William's phone, which I now reach for. We may not be the kind of married people who leave the bathroom door open, but we've always felt free to check out the pictures on each other's phones. Now's my chance to examine the shots he took of us together in front of Notre-Dame yesterday. I don't feel I'm doing anything wrong or underhanded when I type in his password. We've always shared our passwords.

Odd. I expected the pictures from yesterday to be the most recent ones. I know he took at least three. Yet the last photo to appear is of William standing in front of the bakery with the red-and-white-striped awning. I fold a pillow in half, prop up my head, and proceed to scroll. William beside the window of a wine shop. William in front of a florist's. William holding a *croissant*. These are all from Thursday, the day after he arrived in Paris. The ones he took of us yesterday in front of Notre-Dame aren't here.

I'm thumbing backwards through the images, again thinking how uncharacteristic it is for William to take so many selfies, or any selfies really, when I come across a close-up of a woman I've never seen before. My thumb halts, poised in mid-air over the touchscreen. She's more a girl than a woman, and is wearing a tight white T-shirt, a purple Arizona Diamondbacks baseball cap, and a wide relaxed grin. I sit up straight, wrapping the sheet across my chest.

This is certainly one of William's co-workers. It has to be. The office is where he spends all his time. Work friends are the only friends he has. A group of them must have gone out for a team-building baseball night. But further scrolling doesn't reveal other images of other baseball-hat-wearing colleagues. Only more pictures of this girl.

Many more pictures. She's super pretty, with masses of long blonde hair, almost-black eyes, and fair skin. Her eyebrows are fashionably thick and as black as her eyes, which makes me think the hair color can't be real, but the overall effect—very light hair, very dark eyes and brows—is appealing. Arresting even.

I zoom in on one of the close-ups. She has a flawless complexion and could be twenty-five, thirty, or fifteen. It's impossible to tell. The dimples in each cheek make her look younger than maybe she is, as do the freakishly white teeth. The whole effect is what Kat would call "excessively pert." In this particular photo, her expression is not only pert, but saucy and provocative. Not the look of a co-worker.

I press my lips together and swallow back whatever is rising from my stomach. "What do you really know about this guy?" Kat asked me more than once between the holiday party where William and I met and the brilliantly sunny March day when we so hastily wed, me pregnant and overwhelmed and drunk with love. "Don't you ever wonder why such a hunk of man sandwich hasn't already been snatched up?"

No, I never have. "He's an introvert," I assured her, and myself. "He's an engineer." One über-focused on his job. I never worried about him cheating on me during his frequent business trips. William's the kind of guy who would rather stay home working on a jigsaw puzzle than go out to a party. That's the face he's always shown to me.

The photos of this girl go on and on, and so do I. I can't help it. But when I come to one where she's standing in a kitchen, my scrolling stops for good. Because it's my kitchen, and she's wearing one of my aprons. Nothing else. Her left hand is propped on the smooth curve of a bare hip. Her right is gripping a spatula, my favorite lightweight super thin stainless-steel spatula that was a birthday gift from Kat, and using it to make a mock military salute. She is smiling a wide, wholesome smile. If she weren't topless, she'd look like a USO entertainer from a World War II poster.

William has been quiet in the bathroom all this time, but now the toilet flushes. I take the last thirty seconds while he washes his hands to click over to his text messages, where I see his current text thread is with someone named Samantha.

Her most recent text to him was:

Tell her today. Do it, do it.

Before that it was:

You can get through this! Be brave.

Before that:

I miss you! ☺

And before that:

When are you coming home? ☹

William's replies are, if possible, even more nauseating:

I love you, pumpkin.

Miss ya babe. ♥

Don't fret. ☺

Coming home soon. ♥♥

"What are you doing?"

That last one wasn't a text. That was real-life William, standing at the foot of the bed. He's still wearing only his white boxer shorts but no longer looks like a golden god. His skin is pasty white, except for two spots on his cheeks, which are scarlet. The only warm color in the room.

"Give it," he says, holding out his hand.

I don't. I sit perfectly still, pressing the phone between my palms like a tortilla. It's strange. All our best and worst moments have been in hotel rooms. Our four-day honeymoon in a San Francisco hotel was a high point and felt magical. Our child, my child, was conceived in the Phoenix business hotel we ended up staying in the night Kat died. Our fraught chair-throwing encounter last April, at the Paris hotel where William booked a room when he followed me here, exposed the cracks in our marriage.

And now here, at the good old Hôtel du Cheval Blanc, the cracks have deepened into chasms.

"Who is she?" I ask. Just to see what he says.

"She's nobody," he mumbles.

I snort and toss the phone to the floor. "Seriously? You have a lot of photos of nobody."

His jaw twitches, and I know his brain is operating at maximum capacity, assembling the pieces of what has just taken place. William is good at puzzles, and he's a devotee of game theory. For a fleeting instant I wonder if he left the phone on the nightstand on purpose, hoping—or perhaps knowing—I would pick it up and browse through the photos.

Thereby relieving him of the burden of having to "do it," as Samantha said.

"She's a friend," he says. His eyes are like dull dry black stones.

"Oh, you can do better than that, William. How did you meet?"

He grabs a pair of jeans and starts to pull them on. I can smell the cheap hotel soap he used to wash his hands. His customary vanilla scent has been completely obliterated. "She's from Minnesota."

"Minnesota?" It's the last thing I expected him to say. "Do you know her from there?"

"No, but Granddad does."

"Granddad? Are you kidding me?" I can't imagine what William's grandfather, whom I adore and respect, could possibly have to do with this next-to-naked *person* cavorting in my kitchen.

"She's the grandniece of one of his buddies. She wanted to move down to Phoenix. Get a job. Granddad asked if she could stay with us till she got settled." William delivers this information in a robot-like fashion. Facts and data.

"Stay with *us*?"

He scoops up the phone from the floor, stuffs it into his back pocket, and doesn't answer.

He doesn't have to. I get it. William didn't want to admit to his grandfather that we were separated, so he let this random girl come down to stay. The two of them were alone together in the house. One thing led to another, I expect under the influence of booze. That's when William is his least guarded and most impulsive self. We were both more than a bit tipsy when we first met at that holiday party.

Still, I'm seized with the unhealthy compulsion to hear every last excruciating detail. "Tell me the rest, Will. Are you sleeping with her?"

An amazingly stupid question. Of course he is. Her bare boobs in my kitchen testify to that. No wonder he ignored every single one of my calls, texts, emails, and postcards all summer long.

He strides over to the armoire and pulls out a shirt. Good power move, William. Soon you'll be fully dressed, and I'll still be sitting here wrapped only in a wrinkled brown sheet. Bravo.

"Let me go at this another way," I continue when he just stands there, holding the shirt and staring at the carpet. "How long has this pathetic little fling been going on?"

He glowers. "I don't like how you're talking, Amy."

"You don't like how I'm talking? I don't like how you're acting! When were you planning on telling me? About—her?"

As I speak these words I put the last pieces of the puzzle together. William came to Paris to finish what he started last April, when he told me he never wanted to look at my face ever again. He probably even brought along divorce papers for me to sign.

But finding out about Catherine threw him for a loop. Hence our tourist day yesterday. Hence the sex that happened here today. But all this time the excessively pert Samantha was texting and calling and putting the pressure on.

"Are you in love with her?" I ask.

It's another stupid question. Of course he is. Or thinks he is.

He shrugs into his shirt, buttons it, and tucks it into his jeans. "Christ, Amy, where do you get off sounding so high and mighty? You haven't given me the time of day for literally years! All you ever cared about was yourself. And Kat."

I look away. It's true that when Kat got sick I poured all my time and energy and love into her. For three intense and painful years. But she was dying. And then she died. You'd think William would get that.

"People at work were right about you," he adds.

"What? What people?"

His mouth twists into a sneer. "You don't think the whole company wasn't onto your wonderful 'friendship' with Kat?"

He uses air quotes around the word "friendship." William never uses air quotes. At least he never used to. Barely ten minutes ago, this man I suddenly don't know at all was in my arms. In my body. I shudder.

"Phoenix is a small town, Amy," he says as I sit there, clutching my sheet. "You probably don't remember, but someone from work knew you in college. Or knew of you."

I glare at him. Phoenix isn't a small town, but I do recall that
Jennifer, Robert's wife—possibly soon-to-be ex-wife—went to
ASU around the same time I did. She might have remembered
that Kat and I were a couple for a while, and she might consider
this a juicy-enough bit of gossip to pass on.

My humble version of sowing wild oats. I've never been
ashamed of it or regretted it. Our love affair was sweet and good.
But not permanent. Not real, not for me. For Kat it probably
could have been—I will always feel bad for rejecting her
passion—but we stayed best friends in spite of it all.

What's more, this happened more than ten years ago. It's old
news.

"Do you have a point?" I ask. I couldn't be to Kat what she
wanted me to be, but I did honestly adore her. She was my first
love and my best friend.

And I've never missed her more than I do right now, this
minute.

William snorts. "My point is that I work for a conservative
company."

"Oh please, Will. It's the twenty-first century. Even in
Phoenix. What you call my 'friendship'"—I do the air quotes—
"was a long time ago, was not a big deal, and was between me
and Kat. Period. End of story."

Literally the end. Kat, my friend, my sister, my one-time
lover, is gone forever. It's a fact I need to get used to, but suspect
that, at the deepest level, I never will. I pinch the web of skin
between my thumb and forefinger because I read somewhere it's
a good way to keep from crying.

William crouches to zip his boots, then begins to pace. He's
not a large man, but he's several inches taller than I am and looks
massive right now. Intimidating.

"You, on the other hand," I add in a louder voice, "appear to
be carrying on an extramarital affair. How 'conservative' is that?"

His answer is to kick over the suitcase standing beside the
window. If there were a chair in the room, I suppose he would
throw it.

Fear skitters through me, like dry leaves being blown over a
patio. It's a keener fear than when I was down in the catacombs,
wading through knee-deep water in black-as-India-ink tunnels.

Or when Dad died while I was still in high school. Or when I first came to Paris, alone and grieving. But I can't afford to be afraid right now. I've got tiny Catherine right here with me, needing protection, needing shelter, needing her mother to step up and be Amy 2.0.

So as William continues pacing I wrap the sheet more tightly around my body and try to act as if I'm not sitting naked in a strange bed in a hotel room in Paris having a marriage-ending fight with my husband.

"What do you really want, William?"

He pauses to stare at me. The question is existential even for a person like me, who never tires of existential questions. For William, it's too much. He stands motionless, his lips parted. I think he's ready to speak. But no. He spins around, strides to the door, and stomps out of the room. His hipster ankle boots bang down the uncarpeted stairs like gunshots.

Every muscle in my body is quivering—as if I've run a marathon or climbed fifty flights of stairs—but I leap from the bed and stumble out to the landing.

"Coward!" I yell as loud as I can. "Coward!

eighteen

I DON'T PURSUE WILLIAM down the stairs. I'm pregnant and not about to chase a man all over Paris.

Also, I'm wrapped in only a sheet, have started to cry, and need to pee.

I shuffle back into his room, where I slam the door, lock it, drop the sheet, and head to the bathroom. There the walls aren't carpeted, but—true to the room's color scheme—they're painted a dark dispiriting tan. I sit, bawling like a two-year-old and despising myself a little more with each hot tear that drips down my face.

Because I should have known.

The ironic stubble beard, the hip ankle boots, the strange selfie series—those were all major clues that William was under a new influence. Kat would've guessed right from the start. Along with most people. I mean, we weren't exactly together anymore. Not too surprising his interest would turn elsewhere.

Yet I've always needed to believe William was someone with firm principles. Smarter and steadier and saner than I am. Certainly above infidelity to his lawful wife. Perhaps even incapable of it. After all, he's not only an introvert, he's painfully shy around women. "Women are an indeterminate value," he once said to me in what I thought was a joke. "You cannot solve for them."

Twenty minutes later I blow my nose and stand up. William mustn't return and find me still in his room, sitting naked on the toilet, and sniveling like a toddler. I hurry out of the bathroom, pull on my clothes, and start to hunt around for my sandals.

"Damn it."

I say this out loud because I've just stubbed my toe on William's suitcase, still lying on its side where he kicked it over.

"Damn," I repeat. "Double damn. Triple damn." On the final "damn" I sink to my knees and start to beat the canvas suitcase with my fists. Just because it feels so very, very good.

Wait. The bag shouldn't be this solid. I heft it. It's nearly full. This isn't like William, who's super-conscientious about unpacking and hanging up all his shirts and pants immediately upon arriving anywhere. The military instilled in him an aversion to appearing rumpled. But I guess it's a clue he wasn't intending to stay in Paris for long. Jet to France, tell the dingbat wife he wants out of this joke of a marriage, then jet home to Samantha's well-toned arms.

Sounds like the sort of efficacious plan William would devise. He would want to get the legal bits ironed out as soon as possible. And it would be like him to come to Paris to break it off in person, face to face. In his mind, that would be doing the right thing.

He had no way to predict I would surprise him with Catherine.

I'm about to get to my feet and go wash my face when I spot an orange object poking out of the partially unzipped suitcase. For a while I just stare. It's not a piece of clothing. Besides, William would never wear such a bright color. I don't touch it. Normally I wouldn't go through his stuff. We don't have that kind of marriage.

But what's normal here? Screwing Samantha? Showing up in Paris, with no warning, to ask for a divorce? Then falling into bed with the person you came to ask for a divorce from?

I unzip the bag the rest of the way and flip open the lid.

The "something orange" is an Hermès box. Flat, square, about the size of a trivet—the kind of box high-end silk scarves come in. I should have recognized it right away because only Hermès uses this distinctive shade of mandarin and because

Margaret has a collection of identical boxes stacked on top of her armoire. An Hermès scarf was one of the first items she lent me, when she was dressing me up in her and Sophie's clothes.

A fist closes around my heart. In the early months of my marriage to William I expected him to bring me home trinkets from his business trips. Maybe it was silly, but television and the movies taught me that's what newlyweds do. When he never brought me a single thing, not even a used swizzle stick, I was hurt.

It took a bit for me to figure out William gives presents only for occasions such as anniversaries and birthdays. Only because it's a kind of rule. In truth, he doesn't much like giving gifts. Nor does he like receiving them. "They are an inefficient reallocation of resources," he once told me.

Again, I told myself he was joking. I was in love.

But love can make you stupid. Just yesterday William and I had what I thought was a great time exploring Paris. This morning we fell into bed and had what I thought was great sex. Yet all the while he's been carrying on an intense romantic relationship with someone else. What could he be thinking?

I know what Kat would say: "Women spend more time thinking about what men think than men actually spend thinking."

I reach for the box. The narrow ribbon, chocolate brown and imprinted with the word "Hermès," falls away with a single tug. The lid slips off smoothly, easily. Inside lies a folded pink and orange scarf. The vivid colors of an Arizona sunset.

The scarf, pure double-ply silk, glows invitingly. I pluck it out, shake it open, hold it up, and sigh. Exquisite. Perfectly square. A hand-rolled and hand-stitched hem. Signed by the artist. Probably cost at least three hundred euros.

I admire its beauty. Then I use it to blow my nose.

When the gods of fashion fail to send down a bolt of lightning to strike me dead, I get to my feet and walk in circles around the small room, the defiled scarf balled up in one hand. On the third lap I stop at the window and rest my forehead against the cold glass. Six stories below, a family of four hurries down the sidewalk. The mother carries a white *pâtisserie* box. The father grips a *baguette* in one hand and a bouquet of long-stemmed white roses in the other. The two little girls, wearing white cotton dresses and shiny black patent leather Mary Janes, are trailing behind. They're probably on their way to *grand-mère's* for Sunday lunch.

Margaret once described for me the grand French tradition of family Sunday lunches. The meals last for hours, involve many courses and multiple generations, and are sadly falling out of fashion. I pull the window open to watch the second little girl disappear around a corner.

Family. A thing I don't know much about but will have to build for Catherine. Whatever it takes.

I again blow my nose into the Hermès scarf, which doesn't make for a very absorbent handkerchief, and prop my forearms on the black wrought-iron railing. A crisp autumn breeze strokes my face. That's what cool weather does—it cheers you. It bucks you up. Hot weather just makes you want to lie down in the dark and die. I never learned to tolerate summers in Phoenix even though I lived there my whole life. Every day of these past months in Paris has been like a death-row reprieve. Sometimes I felt guilty, like I was getting away with something by not suffering through the annual inferno with the rest of my fellow Arizonans.

Little did I know that all along it was William who was getting away with something.

I dab my nose with the scarf. Then I lean out as far as I safely can and fling it upwards with all my might. The breeze catches it, and I admire how it billows, the bubblegum pink and clementine orange showing up brilliantly against the dove gray Paris sky.

But its moment of glory is fleeting. Inevitably, inexorably, like an expiring ballerina at the end of act three, it wafts and slithers and ripples to the pavement six stories below. There, it is promptly run over by a bus.

Too bad. A waste of perfectly good Hermès.

Nevertheless, the sight of the scarf lying flat in the street, vanquished, is gratifying. Even inspiring. I need to get going, but when I turn I spot William's suitcase again. It's splayed open at my feet, nearly full of perfectly folded shirts, Dockers, and underwear. No more Hermès boxes, as far as I can tell. Just regular William-type stuff. I use my bare foot to flick the top item—a crisply starched blue Oxford button-down—out of the bag onto the none-too-clean carpet. It lands on its side but stays folded. I stoop to pick it up, bringing it to my face. Like everything associated with William it smells of vanilla, an aroma I've always found to be fatally irresistible and one of the main ingredients to the recipe that has brought me to this point— married, pregnant, and now betrayed. I take a good long whiff, rubbing the smooth cool cotton against my cheek, and turn again to the open window.

"Do it!" Kat would say. "He deserves it."

Yeah, he kind of does. So I shake open the shirt and hurl it skywards.

Unlike the scarf, however, the shirt doesn't flutter and billow, as if yearning to take flight. It drops like a rock. It lands awkwardly, sprawled with one sleeve on the sidewalk and one in the gutter. It looks like someone's dropped laundry, and, as I watch, a bicyclist veers to avoid it. Pitching Samantha's Hermès scarf out the window was poetic. But sending William's Oxford shirt to plummet to the street was pure prose.

I guess that's the difference between silk and cotton, between Hermès and Lands' End, between Paris and Phoenix.

nineteen

I STEP BACK and shut the window. I won't be flinging out any more items of clothing today. It's not worth the bad karma, and after the initial thrill, it doesn't make me feel much better.

If only I could talk to Kat. Sometimes I forget she's gone forever. I'll be walking down the street or sipping a cup of tea, everything normal, and I'll realize as if for the first time that Kat is dead. That she's never coming back and that I'll never talk with her again. How could such a horrible thing happen? It feels so wrong.

Catherine stirs beneath my ribs. Yes, sweet child. I do remember I'm not totally on my own. You're always here with me, inside me, and in four short months, you'll make your entrance into the world. It's exciting. Also terrifying.

Straightening my shoulders, I cross the room to my tote bag, still lying beside the bed where I'd dropped it, and hook it over one arm. I hop around on one foot to strap on my sandals because I don't want to sit down on the bed, which smells like sex.

That's everything. I can go now. But on my way to the door I slow to look down at my wedding ring. It's a thing I do quite often. Not just because it's beautiful, but because it represents what I thought was a lifelong commitment. Yes, I'm sounding so old-fashioned, but my dad stayed true to my mother when things got tough. He even remained faithful to her after her death, though perhaps he may have acted differently if he hadn't been in a wheelchair. From the outside, you never know what a marriage is like.

I pull off the ring and massage the indentation on my finger. It's probably significant that I've never taken it off. And that now my hand looks bare without it. Empty. Catherine, who so often seems to be trying to communicate with me, remains still. If she could speak, what would she say?

I think I know. Of course I know. Catherine would want what all children want: parents who love each other.

The ring glitters in the palm of my hand. It's simple, one tiny diamond, but it was William's mother's, the only thing he has that belonged to her, and it would be horrible if I lost it. One thing I've really learned is that losing things—parents, friends, homes, jobs—is way too easy. So I slip the ring back on, and then—without giving myself any more time to think—I open my tote bag and take out my phone. Maybe it sounds crazy. But it may not be too late for our marriage.

Because here's the thing: William is Catherine's father. This is an empirical truth, like the speed of light or the circumference of the Earth. No one can change this truth, not William, not me, certainly not the excessively pert Samantha. We can agonize and agitate. We can argue for our various desired outcomes. We can deceive, like William and Samantha. We can dither, like me.

But the fact is—and it's the biggest, fattest, scariest fact of them all—I need to get my act together and seriously start to build a life worthy of Catherine.

Whatever it takes.

He picks up on the fourth ring. "Yeah?"

"Will. What are you doing?"

"Walking."

When William's upset he needs to take physical action. "Are you coming back?"

"Back?" His voice is raspy, and I can't help wondering if he's been on the phone with Samantha, telling her everything that's happened and receiving instructions. "Back where?"

"To your hotel room."

"Oh." He clears his throat. "Are you still there?"

"Of course I'm still here."

I struggle to sound calm. Mature. He doesn't need to know I've spent the last thirty minutes crying and throwing his stuff out a sixth-floor window.

"We need to talk," I add.

"Yeah. I know." His tone is mild. Which isn't surprising. William never stays mad for long. Anger is a waste of energy, he often takes pleasure in telling me. It consumes resources that could be used on things like work or baseball.

"I'll wait here for you," I say, needing to place a palm on the wall for support. Possibly it would have been better to arrange to meet at a café or in a park, on neutral ground, but at the same time I don't want to talk in public. Our conversation is not going to be easy. The image of Samantha in my kitchen wearing only an apron—one of my aprons—has been burned into my brain. I don't know what it will take for me to forgive William.

I only know I owe it to Catherine to try.

So I return to the bathroom, splash cold water on my face until it looks less puffy, finger-comb my hair, and apply an extra-thick coat of apricot lip gloss. Back in the bedroom, I gather up the sheet I'd dropped earlier and make the bed, then sit down on the brown carpet to repack the suitcase. Eventually he'll notice the scarf and one of his shirts are missing, but there's nothing I can do about that now.

I'm positioning a stack of shirts into the center of the bag when I spot a tin box tucked into a side pocket. It's William's first aid kit.

An actual smile comes to my face as I pull out the tin and cradle it in my hands. This is the first aid kit William carried with him in his daypack on that long-ago Saturday we drove up to Sedona for a picnic. The fateful picnic that resulted in my first, unsuccessful pregnancy, the pregnancy that started it all. After a leisurely lunch of cold chicken and kale salad, we hiked among the red rocks, jumping from boulder to boulder and laughing like idiots.

When I inevitably slipped, badly scraping both knees, William whipped out this tin and bound up my wounds. I was touched. Since Dad died, only Kat had made me feel so cared for. So safe. In the three years since college I'd dated nothing but needy jerks and loser man-boys. I never thought I'd find anyone as capable and decent and adult as William. Maybe all we have to do is make the effort, as Margaret would say, and he and I can find our way back to that early infatuation and grow it into something real. Bigger and better than before.

I clasp the first aid kit to my heart. Perhaps even now William is deciding to get his act together and start behaving more like the man his granddad raised him to be. Like an officer and a gentleman. After all, he's been yearning to start a family since day one of our relationship. Sure, he's confused, angry, resentful, and probably embarrassed. But when he gets past that, he might realize what he has with Samantha is a ridiculous rebound thing.

And what he has with me is a child.

Our child.

No time to lose now. Today may be, as Dad always liked to say, the first day of the rest of my life. I'm returning the tin to its spot in the suitcase when I spy a small object stowed inside the adjoining side pocket. At first, I think nothing of it and continue tidying up the suitcase. Then I notice the tissue paper wrapped around said small object is smooth and un-rumpled, too un-rumpled for it to have traveled all the way from Phoenix. No, it has to be another item William purchased here in Paris.

This time I don't hesitate to snoop. The tissue paper, as if eager to assist, falls open the second I touch it to reveal a white cotton drawstring pouch. I wonder if the pouch holds naughty lingerie for Samantha. But the white cotton looks too pure, too innocent, too virginal, for anything X-rated to be inside.

"Amy. What the hell?"

William has returned. He's standing in the open doorway. His left hand still grips the knob. His right is clenched in a fist.

I don't stop to wonder how he managed to open the door without me hearing. I hold up the white cotton pouch.

"What's this?"

His normally brown eyes glint like wet charcoal. "Put that back."

"I don't think I should. Aren't we supposed to be coming clean with each other?"

He just stands there, flexing his fists. I cradle the pouch in both hands and give him time to respond. I do that for Catherine.

But when he continues to wordlessly stare at me I insert my fingers into the pouch and loosen the drawstring. Inside is a tiny folded garment. Huh. Well, it is sleepwear. Just not the X-rated kind.

It's pajamas. One-piece footie baby pajamas.

Size newborn.

Color blue.

They are soft. Plush. Darling. "William. Who are these for?"

Even as I pose the question, I'm aware I already know the answer. No math is needed to solve this problem. William learned about my pregnancy on Friday evening, after most shops have closed. He spent all of Saturday with me—breakfasting, lunching, visiting Foucault's pendulum, walking the Jardin du Luxembourg. Today is Sunday, when most shops are also closed. Anyway, when I got here he was still in bed.

Meaning that William had to have purchased these baby pajamas before finding out about the existence of Catherine. Meaning they can't possibly be intended for her.

I spread the little garment over my thigh and run the tip of my pinkie finger around the perimeter of the tiny breast pocket. It's always seemed curious to me that infant wear has pockets. After all, what would babies keep in them?

"Tell me, Will. Tell me what you came all the way to Paris to say."

During the time I give him to answer and in which he does not, I note that the pajamas have a tiny Eiffel Tower hand-embroidered on one lapel of the Peter Pan collar. I also slip the ring from my finger and place it on the floor next to the suitcase. Everything is happening fast.

"Will," I say. "I want to hear you speak the words. At least do that. Can't you do that?"

He glares.

"You surprise me, William. You really do."

twenty

ON MY WAY OUT of the Hôtel du Cheval Blanc I pause at the reception desk. The deskman, tipped back in his chair and reading a battered paperback, looks up at me.

"*Bonjour, monsieur.*" I extract a small white rectangular card from my tote bag. Like an older French person, I carry "calling cards" printed with my name and phone number. Manu made them for me, at Margaret's behest. "*Voici mon numéro de téléphone. Pouvez-vous s'il vous plaît me contacter dès que Monsieur Will Brodie se prépare à partir?*"

My voice sounds as if it's coming from a distant planet, but I manage to speak grammatically, even remembering to use the reflexive.

The deskman nods and replies that he would be delighted to give me a ring when *Monsieur* Brodie makes a move to check out of the hotel.

It's a precaution. I don't really think William will sneak out of Paris before we've had a chance to talk and start to settle the things that need to be settled. But you never know.

Meanwhile Catherine and I need food. Now.

As I step out into the Sunday-quiet street I scan the pavement for the Hermès scarf and Oxford shirt, but they're nowhere to be seen. Perhaps someone recognized their worth and scooped them up. Or William himself saw them and took

them with him. Whatever. It doesn't matter. I head straight for
the nearby Café de la Poste, sit at my favorite table in the corner,
and order an omelet, fries, green salad, and a gigantic *café crème.*

As I wait for my food, I gradually start to relax. In Phoenix I
never went out to eat by myself. In Paris I love eating in cafés and
restaurants alone. For one thing, you appreciate the food more
when you have no distractions, and for another, there is just no
snugger or more settled feeling than sitting at a tiny table for one
and being waited upon.

This time, though, the food seems tasteless. No pleasure, no
pain—apparently that's my sweet spot, where I need to be.

Afterwards, I cross the street to the bakery with the red-and-
white-striped awning. Not because I'm still hungry but because I
have so many things to forgive and forget and ponder and
arrange and do. I didn't have a Plan B, and now I'm going to
have to scramble. Maybe a little something sweet will help.

"*Une de vos petites tartes aux framboises,*" I tell the thin unsmiling
girl behind the counter. "*S'il vous plaît.*"

How curious that my French is fantastic today, when I feel
so numb and stupid, and frankly, flattened. In fact, it may be the
only sector of my brain that's functioning. When the girl hands
me a raspberry tartlet wrapped in white paper, I murmur "*merci*"
with just the right intonation and recall my first morning in Paris,
last April. This same girl waited on me in this same bakery, and I
couldn't remember the French word for "sandwich." Despite the
fact that it's "*un sandwich.*" Obviously, straight A's in French class
don't necessarily translate to fluency in actual French. Just as
book smarts don't translate to life smarts.

I carry the tartlet to the little park behind the Hôtel de Sully,
which is not a hotel but a private mansion with a public garden. I
come here often because the garden's a bit of a secret one—few
tourists seem to find their way in even though it's adjacent to the
popular Place des Vosges—and because it's so austere. No
flowers, no fountains, no statuary, no ponds. But the pebbles in
the gravel pathways are always raked smooth, and the box hedges
outlining the grass parterres are always precisely pruned. Like
most French gardens, it's restrained, precise, and assured.

The way I'll need to be from this point going forward.
Because—and this is what robbed all the flavor from my omelet

lunch—I'm going to have to go back. To Phoenix. Alone. Even before William showed up in Paris I knew this was my most likely next step, because it's the best chance I have of establishing a stable life in time for Catherine's arrival. Still, it's amazing how quickly my list of options has narrowed down to this very one.

I find a bench, sit down, unwrap the tartlet, and take as big of a bite as I can stomach. No one in the whole wide world knows where I am right now. I am flying solo. Last spring, when I got here, it was scary, but over the past few months I've come to love this untethered feeling. It means freedom. Adventure. But today the sweet, delicious food in my mouth tastes like sawdust. The late-summer sun on my face is thin and unsubstantial. My stone seat is cold and hard.

Because while I'm free, yes, it's in the way an orphan is free or a released convict is free—alone and adrift in a world where what I thought was true is untrue, and what I thought was mine is not mine. I set the tart on the bench beside me, tilt my head back to gaze up into the pale sky, and remind myself that none of what took place today should be surprising.

Not long after William and I got married I accidentally knocked one of his jigsaw puzzles to the floor. It had been almost complete, and though I spent the rest of the day trying to reassemble it, the puzzle was still mostly a mess when he came home from work that night. But, to my astonishment, he didn't get mad. He didn't even seem surprised. "Things fall apart," he said, shrugging. His non-reaction, weirdly, hurt my feelings. As if he didn't even care enough to get mad.

But the fact is he was right. Things do fall apart. All the time. Every day. I pick off one of the raspberries from the tartlet, roll it around in my mouth, swallow it, and get out my phone.

"*Allô?*"

Channeling Amy 2.0, I come straight to the point. "Hervé, I'm wondering if your offer of a place to stay still stands."

We haven't spoken since Friday morning, when he got into that weird argument with his housekeeper, or whoever she was, and I had to leave without saying goodbye. But he responds to my query without missing a beat. "*Absolument,*" he says.

"Thank you. Thank you. You are totally saving my life. Can I come this afternoon?"

"But of course."

He doesn't question my change of plans or ask what I've been up to the last couple days. No doubt his intention is to pump me for information when I get there. Little does he know my intention is to excuse myself, go straight up to my room, and log on to his Wi-Fi. I need to email people to arrange a place to stay when I get back. Also make reservations for my one-way airplane ticket. Also contact Kathryn about the details of Kat's will. Also, maybe, even start to scout around for a job. I used to volunteer at the local library, and before I left Phoenix, was offered a position there. That would be a start.

But I don't forget my promise to make him a meal. "This afternoon we can discuss a menu for tonight. I'd love to cook dinner for you."

"Ah, but Amy. That is not necessary."

"Oh, but I want to. Truly. Anyway, we'll talk soon. Thank you again. *Ciao*." Yeah, people in Paris say *ciao* for goodbye, even though it's an Italian word. It's another habit I'll be giving up, as it could seem pretentious. In Phoenix.

I end the call and drop my phone into my tote bag. Calling Hervé was step one. It was easy.

Step two—going over to Manu's to get my stuff—should also be easy because he's sure to be out, ensconced in some fancy restaurant eating his way through a massive French Sunday lunch with Margaret and Sophie. Margaret would insist on observing this custom, especially on Sophie's first weekend back in the fold. But this is a good thing because I have no idea how I'm going to tell Manu what's happened and what I've decided to do next.

It's going to be hard. Since almost the first day I turned up in Paris, Manu has been my best buddy. More so than Margaret, who's a bit like a zany fairy godmother, full of fun and light-heartedness but also unsteady, unstable. Manu, on the other hand, is just always—Manu.

But now, regardless of what I do or where I go, our relationship has got to change. Like Margaret, he's returning to his former Sophie-centric life. Even if he wanted to continue our friendship, Sophie surely wouldn't stand for it. I wrap up the remainder of the raspberry tartlet and hurl it into a trash receptacle on my way out of the garden.

Yet I don't head directly to Manu's. No. I choose the long way around, walking slowly past the greengrocer's where Margaret and I get our fruits and vegetables, the florist's where she has a standing order for a weekly bouquet of fresh flowers, and the cheesemonger's where you can buy any one of three hundred different kinds of *fromage*.

Catherine hops about, happy I'm up and moving. Perhaps she likes wandering the streets of Paris as much as I do. After all, since shortly after conception, her air and water and food have all been French. The sounds she hears are French sounds. The vibrations she feels are French vibrations. In a way, Paris is home to her.

I need to burn it all into my memory banks. I need to remember that no matter where I end up, Paris will always go on and on. It will be here, even if I'm not. Eternal Paris. Paris ever after.

A ping coming from my tote bag announces the arrival of a text. It can't possibly be William (too soon for him). When I take out my phone, I see it's Manu, wondering where I am. I picture him seated in a white-tableclothed restaurant, surreptitiously thumbing out a quick message, in violation of Margaret's no-devices-at-the-table rule, but I don't smile. Nor do I reply to the text. In fact, I power down my phone completely.

I don't quite understand why. It's almost as if I'm angry with Manu or jealous of his newly rekindled love with Sophie. Which is ridiculous. I should be glad for him. He deserves to be happy. After all, I have no claim on Manu, just as I have no claim on any other person, place, or thing in the French capital. I had borrowed this life for a while, that's all. Or, better said, it was lent to me.

And now, poof, it's disappearing. That shriveling sense of having found something wonderful only to then lose it wraps around my heart like a boa constrictor.

When it starts to rain I quicken my steps and turn the next corner onto Manu's street. Here, there are no greengrocers or florists or cheese shops to beguile or distract me. At the door to his building I punch in the code, enter, and mount the six flights of stairs as rapidly as I can. My calves are weak in spite of the omelet and fries and salad. It'd be great to linger at Manu's cozy place for a while. Maybe even take a nap. I sure could use one. Last night I was excited about meeting up with William and didn't get much sleep.

As I unlock the door, I visualize the sensation of my hot cheek coming to rest on a cool pillow. Just for a half hour.

"*Aimée.*" Manu is standing in the middle of the compact room, holding his phone in one hand and his jacket in the other. "Did you receive my text?"

I pause to take in the sight of him. He's wearing the denim shirt we picked out together at the flea market up at Clignancourt. The one that makes his eyes look even bluer.

"Um, yeah," I say, a lump forming at the back of my throat. I'm not prepared to say goodbye. That much is obvious to me. "I thought you'd be doing the long Sunday lunch thing. With Margaret."

"No. We went for brunch earlier. Then I come here to look for you."

Believe it or not, brunch is a thing in Paris. Margaret loves it. I think it reminds her of the massive English breakfasts of her youth.

Manu has stepped closer and is studying my face. I feel myself redden. Despite all my cold-water splashing and lip-gloss applying, I'm sure he can tell I've been crying. Manu really looks at people. He listens, too, and notices what you don't say as well as what you do. Even more than Kat, Manu has the ability to see into my heart. I've always known this. Today, for some reason, I know it more. If that makes any sense.

"Margaret tells me to tell you she hopes you passed a good night. She has not forgotten about helping you find a more permanent place to stay."

I focus on the floor. Margaret is another person I'll have to say goodbye to. Another important, significant person, like Kat, whom Catherine will never get to meet.

Manu eyes me as he pockets his phone and hangs his jacket on a hook. "You have been with William, have you not?"

Bingo.

"Yes. Good guess." I head for the clic-clac and sit down. My legs won't hold me up for another second.

Manu nods, then strides to the kitchen alcove. "I make tea.

Yes?" Normally he finds my devotion to tea a subject for humor, but this time he doesn't crack a smile. Ever since Sophie returned, he's been solemn, worried, distracted. He's changed. Like everything else. Things fall apart.

I start to shake my head no—I had a big coffee less than an hour ago—but he's brandishing a royal blue box of Tetley, my favorite brand of tea. It wasn't here this morning. At least I don't think so. I was so freaked out about my rendezvous with William I might not have noticed it.

Manu fills the kettle, switches it on, and looks at me over the kitchen bar. "You have something to tell me. Do you not?"

Oh, he is good.

"Yes." My voice quavers. The words I have to say will be painful. Embarrassing. I've hardly had a chance to get used to the idea myself. But maybe it's better I don't have too much time to think. I reach for the orange and white pillow, and cradle it against my chest. "Something has happened. I mean, I discovered something."

Manu circles around the bar and perches on a stool. "I think I know. William, he has found another lover, yes?"

I jump to my feet. "How did you guess?"

He shrugs. "He is a man."

"Yeah he's a man! A married man. To me." I turn and hurl the pillow across the room as hard as I can. "At least he was."

The pillow-hurling felt good, and fortunately, I missed sending Margaret's African violet crashing to the floor. But my outrage sounds flat even to my ears. Expecting William to be faithful to me all summer was unrealistic. I should've been expecting something like this all along. But I was too wrapped up in my own little dream world, here in Paris. With Catherine.

Manu shrugs again, and his thin face crinkles into a wry smile. "*Mais, chère Aimée*, you did leave him. You came to France."

The kettle starts to whistle, a welcome interruption as I'm on the verge of looking around for something else to throw. Because while William hooking up with Samantha, or someone, was more or less predictable, the baby pajamas signify a twist even Manu might be surprised by.

Size newborn. Color blue. I guess William's getting his boy.

"Yeah, I did come to Paris," I agree after an awkward silence.

"I'm not sorry."

But that was then. This is now. Now everything has changed. Catherine is on her way, and I have to move forward into the future. I can't muck around in the past, in the should-haves and the what-ifs.

While Manu is fiddling with the tea, I round up my two shopping bags full of clothes, station them next to the door, retrieve my money belt from the desk drawer where I'd hidden it, and step into the bathroom to strap it on underneath my dress. Along with my tote bag, this is everything I brought with me when I moved out of Margaret's yesterday. Step two is almost complete. Step three, going over to Hervé's, is next.

As I emerge from the bathroom Manu is placing a tea tray on a small, round, yellow plastic table he moved to a spot in front of the clic-clac. The tray holds two tall white mugs, a fire-engine-red teapot, a white porcelain pitcher of milk, two dainty demitasse spoons, and a small dish of individually wrapped sugar cubes. No American man has ever served me tea this way. No American woman either.

"*Voilà*," he says.

"*Merci*," I say.

We sit side by side on the clic-clac as he pours out the tea, adds milk and sugar the way I like it, and passes me a cup. Our elbows bump, and I picture what his arm would feel like around my shoulders, how warm and welcome it would be. I wipe the corners of my eyes with my knuckles. It seems incredible I can still produce tears.

"Manu, listen. I have something else to tell you." I take my gaze to the ceiling, where in two places the paint is peeling in arcs, like raised eyebrows. Unlike William, Manu doesn't repair things five seconds after they break.

"*J'écoute.*"

Also unlike William, Manu doesn't command me to "just spit it out." He simply tells me he's listening. I'm going to miss that.

"I've made a decision. I'm going back to Phoenix," I say.

His mouth drops open. It's an un-French thing to do, and I briefly wonder if he picked it up from me.

"*Mais non!*" He sets down his cup, sloshing a little tea on the tray. "*Aimée!* Why?"

I put down my own cup and look at him. "Why? Because I have no other choice."

I didn't expect he would be so surprised. I even thought the news might come as a relief. Without me around he could devote all his time and energy to Sophie. He wouldn't have to try to balance our friendship with his relationship with her. Everything could go back to the way it was. Margaret would love that. So would Sophie.

"I've thought about it a lot," I add, though in fact I came to a final decision an hour ago, while sitting on the cold stone bench in the plain green garden behind the Hôtel de Sully.

He cups his hands around my shoulders and turns me to face him. "*Aimée*, I do not understand. It cannot be possible. You will go back to your husband? After this thing that he has done?"

"What? Go back to William? No! Are you kidding me?"

I snort. At least Manu considers William's affair to be an actual serious betrayal, not some normal "boys will be boys" behavior I have to tolerate. His shrugs and the airy "he is a man" attitude were making me start to wonder. "I'm not going back to my marriage," I say. "No way. It's over. In a way, it never really began. And now too much has happened. Is happening."

Like, for instance, the blue baby pajamas.

Ironic. William, who's been wanting to have a child since forever, is now about to have two. I wonder if he's realized the ridiculousness of this twist. Probably not. William doesn't do irony.

"But if you do not return to him," says Manu, "why do you not remain here, in Paris? Where you are happy?"

An anger I didn't know I had wells up inside me.

"Stay in Paris? Tell me, please, how I could do that. I sure can't live with Margaret anymore. Even if I found a new place that was affordable, how could I continue to live in France and have a child here? I don't have papers or insurance or a real job!"

I wriggle out of his grasp, where I've lingered too long, jump up to retrieve the pillow, and hug it to my chest like a shield. "I love Paris. You know that. I've had an amazing time here. With Margaret. With—you."

Manu's face has turned grim, but I press on because while I'm talking, I'm not thinking. And I don't want to think. Thinking is awful. I do too damn much of it. "I have to start getting serious, Manu. I'm going to be a mother. Soon." I toss the pillow onto the clic-clac and head to the door. "And, right now, I need to be on my way. Thanks for everything. I appreciate it. Really."

My voice is louder than it needs to be. My motions are more exaggerated. I pick up my two shopping bags and stand with my back to him. Manu. I'm running from him. Last spring, I ran from the grief of losing Kat. Now I'm running from the feelings I hadn't wanted to accept.

Damn. And here I thought I was done running.

He leaps up and places his body between me and the door. "*Aimée*. Please stay."

He again takes me by the shoulders, but I yank away. The warmth of his touch is confusing. Painful. Besides, I can't tell if he means, "Please stay here right now" or "Please stay in Paris forever."

Either way, it doesn't matter. Sophie awaits. She's no doubt wondering where Manu is right now.

"Manu! Please stop. Paris was an interlude. It was a—break. Don't you see that? Everything has changed. I wish you the best."

I want to mean this. I really do. Because what other choice do I have? As unlikely a couple as they seem, Manu and Sophie obviously have it going on. I need to be glad for him.

"If you mean Sophie—"

But whatever Sophie story Manu is going to launch into is cut short by the shrill ring of a phone. Not mine. His.

He grabs it and answers immediately. "*Oui. Oui. Je comprends.*" I understand. "*Oui. Tout de suite.*" Right away.

"It's Sophie," he whispers to me.

Of course it is.

While he murmurs into the phone, I slip out the door. I don't look back.

Because here's a bit of advice: When you're walking away from the person you know you can never have, you shouldn't string it out. The best thing for that person, and for you, is to move on. Kat taught me this.

I'm halfway down the first flight of stairs when Manu bursts out of the apartment, phone still gripped in one hand. "*Aimée*! Stop. Where do you go?"

I pause mid-step. Normally I'd hesitate to tell him I am going to stay at Hervé's, because Manu doesn't like or approve of Hervé.

But then I remember Manu's approval isn't supposed to matter anymore. I remember Sophie. So, I clomp down to the first landing before turning and looking back up at him. "Don't worry about me. I've arranged to stay at Hervé's for a couple of days. Just until I leave for Phoenix."

I relay this information as neutrally as I can. Facts and data. When you have nothing else, you have those.

The frown on his face fades. "Ah," he says. "You do not depart for America immediately then?"

"Um, no."

I'm baffled. I assumed the mere mention of Hervé's name would annoy Manu, as usual. But he seems more interested in the timing of my departure than in the fact of it. He even looks relieved.

I lean my hip against the banister for support. "I have a lot of things to do before going back. Plane tickets, sorting, packing. Money stuff."

And I want to say goodbye to Margaret. Thank her for everything. She has been a wonderful friend and mother substitute. She's been amazing.

I have to say goodbye to Paris too. Maybe for forever. You can stay in France without a visa for only three months, and I passed that mark weeks ago. When I go through passport control at the airport, they might notice and put a black mark on my record.

Manu nods, and I have the sense, as I so often do, that he's been reading my mind. "*Aimée*, will you call me tonight?"

He sounds entirely calm. Normal. Un-traumatized. Well, I should've known Manu would quickly regain his equilibrium. He's like one of those weighted dolls that, when knocked over, immediately rights itself again. He never acts out of panic or haste.

Lucky Sophie.

I turn to head down the stairs. "I have to get going. I'll see you tomorrow morning, for the deliveries."

Because, crazy as it sounds, that's the other thing I absolutely positively must do. No matter how awkward or painful it'll be for me, I need to help Manu with the lunch deliveries until he finds someone to take my place. This someone won't be Sophie. I'm pretty sure of that. No way would she consent to schlepping crates up and down stairs.

But then perhaps Manu wouldn't ever ask her to.

twenty-one

I LEAVE MANU'S APARTMENT BUILDING feeling like a trapeze artist who's missed the biggest catch of her performance. Swing out, swing back, swing out, and then—oh no—I don't reach forward at the right moment. I'm a hair too late or too early, my fingers slip when they should grip, the shouts and waves of the crowds below make me lose focus. And down into the safety net I fall.

The net being, in this case, Phoenix.

Halfway to Hervé's he texts to give me the door codes. It's the most encouraging development of the day so far. If for only a short time, I have access to the most marvelous space in all of Paris. I want to make the most of it while I can.

As I enter the courtyard, I almost step right onto Hervé. He's down on his knees inside the door, using a rusty pair of clippers to hack at a vine growing up between the paving stones.

"Hey." When he doesn't respond, I add, "I really appreciate your letting me stay here, Hervé."

When he finally rocks back on his heels and squints up at me, his lips pursed, I wonder if I somehow misunderstood our arrangement. It's been such a holy hell of a day.

But when he says, simply, *"Bonjour,"* stressing both syllables, I realize what the problem is. I've made one of my frequent *faux pas*. In France, you're supposed to say a proper greeting before launching into conversation. Even in a dress shop, you need to start with a polite *bonjour* before peppering the clerk with questions about size or color. *La politesse.* It's not optional.

"*Bonjour,*" I echo, better late than never. It's almost a relief to be back to annoying Hervé. Sometimes superficial relationships are the best; they're much less painful.

He scowls as he jumps to his feet and plants a chaste kiss on each of my cheeks, but when he peels off his gardening gloves and reaches out to take my two bulging shopping bags, he murmurs, "Permit me," in his usual polite way.

I have to giggle. Hervé, for whom feminism is a serious affront, would never allow a woman to carry her own luggage. So I don't insist. I follow him through the garden, glancing back at the clippers he left lying on the ground. Hervé doesn't seem like the type to do his own weeding. But maybe it's a hobby. Both clippers and gloves look well worn.

He leads me directly to the wisteria tunnel where, as on my first visit, I linger and gape. It's so verdant in here. Even the air seems tinted green. Next spring, the vine will be festooned with purple blossoms the size of bunches of grapes. I'll never see them. I'll be bracing myself for another Phoenix summer. On the bright side, Catherine will have arrived. I'll have a daughter, a child to love and to love me. I'll be the mother I never had.

"*Allez, viens,*" Hervé says to hurry me along. "Your *valise*, she waits for you. Upstairs."

We move single file through the open door of the castle, across the shining black and white tiles of the mahogany-paneled foyer, and up the spiral stone staircase.

I look around, shaking my head. No, I didn't dream up this place. It is real. It exists.

"You perhaps are fatigued? You can repose yourself before dinner. I think that is a good *idée.*"

It's unlike Hervé to make grammatical mistakes in English or to sprinkle in French words. But today he seems distant, distracted. He hasn't even looked over his shoulder to see if I'm still following.

"Yes, good idea. Thank you." He leads me down the long, carpeted corridor and into the same suite of rooms we looked at the other morning. My *appartement*, he called it, and the term thrilled me a little. I went straight from my childhood home, an inner-city stucco bungalow, to living with William, in a just-built house, and have actually never lived in an apartment. "Thank you. A nap was part of my plan actually."

"*Parfait.*" He places my bags on the floor next to the fireplace and glances around the room, narrowing his eyes as if he expects to see something or someone who doesn't belong. But all is as it was. Which is to say fabulous. And, just like the other day, the house is hushed and still. The contrast with the hubbub of the Paris streets outside—a near-constant din of motorcycles, sirens, and street cleaners—is stark.

"I leave you then." He hurries for the exit, possibly embarrassed at hosting a member of the opposite sex. Hervé is antiquated. Stuffy. I can't imagine him having sex. With anyone.

"OK. Thank you." I close the door behind him and move my bag collection to the bedroom, where my trusty carry-on still stands beside the armoire. Along with my stomach, my possessions have expanded during the months I've been in Paris. I'll have to decide how much I'll be able to carry back to Phoenix.

Sorting, culling, organizing, packing. Saying goodbye goodbye goodbye. I have a lot to do, and it will all need to be done in the next few days. Stringing things out would be unbearable. I need to get on with it, as Margaret would say.

I gaze with longing at the majestic bed, which looks super comfortable, but I don't lie down there. I go straight to the bathroom, peel off my clothes, turn on the shower, and step under the pounding jets.

Because this is important: I want and need to wash off the scent of William. The whole time I was in Manu's apartment, talking with him, sitting near him, I was conscious that only a few hours earlier, I'd had sex with William. I even worried Manu would be able to tell. Not that he'd care, I guess. He has Sophie now. But I care. I don't want Manu to know I had sex with William barely ten minutes before finding out William had been busy having sex with someone else. Just picturing it makes me cringe. It makes me want to never have sex again.

Sounds over-dramatic, but it's how I feel. I let the hot water run over my body for a long time, reveling in the spaciousness of the shower stall, and when I've dried myself and used some of the scented lotion I find on a shelf above the tub I put on a clean T-shirt and leggings. The polka dot chemise dress would be more suitable for an evening *chez* Hervé, but I can't wear it because that, too, carries the scent of my last encounter with William. At least in my imagination. I wash it out in the sink, along with my underwear.

There. Now everything William touched has been cleansed. He's gone. Forgotten.

If only forgetting about Manu could be so easy. I wonder when I started to care for him. It all came on so gradually I didn't realize it was happening. My brain was too full of thoughts and worries about William, I guess. And Catherine. Meanwhile Manu took root in my heart and grew there, slowly and steadily, like a wisteria vine in a secret garden.

Stop. These thoughts are not going to help. What's going to help is tackling everything that has to come next. I settle onto the bed and take out my laptop. It's a hand-me-down from one of Manu's clients. Booting up takes forever, so while it's whirring and clicking, I get up to wander around.

At Margaret's I had one room with one window. Here, my domain features three rooms with five windows. Two of them open out to balconies, one of which is furnished with an iron bistro chair and matching round table. I can't resist stepping outside.

I rest my belly on the carved stone balustrade, breathing in the vegetal perfume of the garden. From this vantage point I have an aerial view of the wisteria tunnel and the whole of the luxuriant greenery beyond it—the plum trees, the rose bushes, the hydrangea hedge, and two octagonal flowerbeds I didn't notice before. In contrast to the Hôtel de Sully's sober parterres, Hervé's private Eden burgeons with blossoms. I stretch out my arms and look up. There's the Eiffel Tower. I am still in Paris.

A silky wave of gratitude washes over me. Yes, the last few days have been an incredible bust, as well as ridiculously eventful, but the last few months have been an amazing adventure.

I arrived in France ignorant and raw, grieving from the loss of Kat and clueless as to what my life should become. Clueless in a bunch of ways, to be honest. But on day two I met Margaret. Her motives for befriending me may have been selfish at first—

she was lonely and I reminded her of her lost daughter, remember—but her affection was always pure-hearted and true. She introduced me to Paris. And to Manu. She shared her *joie de vivre* and showed me how to take pleasure in the good things in life. Like food.

All in all, I've been insanely lucky. Not many Americans come to Paris knowing no one and end up staying in a sort-of castle, if only for a few days.

"Amy? Do you sleep?"

I sit up. Look around.

I don't remember coming in from the balcony and lying down on the bed. But I must have done so, then conked out. The computer is on the floor, also in sleep mode. The sun has set, and the room is in shadows.

"Amy?" Hervé says again. His voice is crisp and clear. And nearby. As if he's right in the bed with me. This thought sends me leaping to my feet and lunging for the light switch on the wall, where I look all around and suck in a deep breath. Thank God. Hervé isn't there. Just his voice.

"It is late," the voice says. I search for its source and spot a red LED light blinking on the bedside table. An intercom. I see no buttons on the device. Is it voice activated? I picture Hervé listening in on me talking in my sleep or snoring. Creepy.

"Yes," I say to it. "I mean, no. I mean, I'm awake." Yikes. I must have slept for hours.

"*Bon.* Come to the library when you are ready."

"OK. Yes. Sure."

Long naps in the afternoon make me groggy. I walk around my rooms, rubbing my face to try to wake up. Too big of a nap also cuts the day in two, making everything that took place in the morning feel like it happened yesterday. Which I guess is a good thing. An awful lot took place this morning, very little of it nice, and I need to put all of it in the past as soon as humanly possible.

My one good dress is still damp from the quick wash I gave it earlier. So I change into my cleanest jeans and least-wrinkled T-shirt. In the bathroom I brush my hair and apply some apricot lip gloss. That will have to do. Anyway, it's only Hervé.

I find him in the grand salon where we had coffee the other day. It doesn't have books, so I wonder why he calls it a library. If

I had a room like this, it would be lined from floor to ceiling with books.

"Hervé. I can't believe I slept so late. I was going to cook you dinner."

He shrugs.

"I had an amazing nap though." I flop down on the brocade settee opposite him before remembering that flopping is not how one comports oneself in France—especially in elegant surroundings. I scoot to the edge of the settee, where I position myself with knees together and ankles crossed. "It's so quiet here. I was out like a light."

His eyes widen. "You went out?"

"What? No, I mean, I slept very soundly."

He sips some champagne. "Ah."

Like the other day, a small fire flickers in the fireplace. Unlike the other day, orchestral music is playing softly, and a sweating bottle of Moët et Chandon presides on the low table between us. He knows I can't have champagne, but it's still odd he started drinking before I got here. Hervé is always such a stickler for protocol. "You find your bed is comfortable?" he asks.

"Yes. It's fantastic. Thank you." I watch the columns of tiny bubbles travel up the tall, thin flute in his hand. My tongue tingles. Of all types of alcohol, champagne is the one I enjoy most.

Ha. It's just as well Hervé isn't offering me any; after everything that's happened lately, I'd be tempted to gulp down a glass. Or two. "I love the room. Rooms. You're really helping me out here, Hervé."

I want to be sure he knows how truly grateful I am. Ever since I came to Paris people have put themselves out to help me. It's been incredible. I don't want to leave without recognizing and thanking each one of them.

"Amy. Stop." He flutters his hand in the air, revealing what looks like a new Rolex on his wrist. He must have a whole collection. "It is not necessary to display obligation. I insist."

He takes another sip of his champagne and stares into the flames.

I sit on my hands. Not only is Hervé not plying me with alcohol, he's not pumping me for information. I expected him to start off by asking about Sophie's abrupt reappearance, Margaret's investment potential, or the reason I changed my mind about staying with him. He is, for Hervé, peculiarly incurious.

But this is another good thing. I've no desire to add to the day's tally of fraught conversations. It's Sunday night. One of my last evenings in Paris. I am totally up for some banal chitchat.

I'm about to ask Hervé the name of the composer of the music he has on, or if he knows how to play the concert grand piano that forms the focal point of this room, when a bell chimes. I look for the source, this time knowing to search for a red LED light.

Hervé follows my gaze to the blinking intercom half hidden behind a cloisonné vase on the side table. "It is time. Do you wish to go in?"

"Sure." I hop to my feet. Nine p.m. is late to eat dinner, in my opinion, but I'm starving. Catherine needs nourishment. And it's better to think about food than about Manu, and how after I leave Paris I'll never see him again.

"During the week I take an early supper," Hervé adds. "But it is your first evening here, so we must celebrate."

He escorts me across the cool foyer into a dimly lit dining room. I can't help but chuckle at the sight of two formal place settings positioned at the far ends of a long mahogany table, miles apart, like in one of those BBC period-costume dramas. An enormous flickering candelabrum commands the center of the table. A floor-to-ceiling tapestry depicting a hunting scene, complete with horses and hounds and ladies with conical hats trailing veils, dominates one long wall. The opposite wall features a life-sized oil painting of a stern-looking gentleman wearing a lace collar, thigh-high black boots, and a pointed goatee. I look for an echo of Hervé's features in the scowling face but find no resemblance.

"This is fabulous," I say as Hervé pulls out one of the chairs for me. Margaret would be able to tell if the china and crystal arrayed on the table is Limoges and Baccarat. It probably is.

He shrugs. "I confess to you that typically I take my meals in the kitchen. The breakfast table there is more—what is the word?—*convivial*. But it is also pleasant to dine properly, as Margaret would put it."

I nod. "She would."

"I called her and invited her to join us, you know. But she declined. I even invited her daughter. Sophie? But they had other plans."

I nod again. I'm not surprised. Sophie is, rightfully, taking all of Margaret's attention. Her priorities, like Manu's, like William's, like mine, are realigning. It's like a game of musical chairs. The music has stopped, and everyone is grabbing for a seat. It would be easy to get caught between chairs and land on my butt on the floor. I must be careful not to let this happen. Because it's not just me anymore—it's Catherine too.

Hervé picks up his ivory-handled knife and fork. "*Bon appétit, chère madame.*" Again, he doesn't offer me any beverage, not even water, and I wonder if this is some baronial thing. Maybe nobles don't serve others; they wait for others to serve them. It's weird though. I'm thirsty.

"*Bon appétit,*" I echo as I look down at my sliced red tomatoes drizzled with a tarragon vinaigrette.

Salade de tomates à l'estragon is a starter that pretty much anyone can produce, which makes me wonder who produced it. After all, the bell that summoned us to dinner didn't ring itself. The tomato starters didn't travel from the kitchen to the dining room on their own. Yet I haven't seen a single domestic servant, unless you count the angry woman from the other day. But maybe Hervé has armies of people to cook and clean for him. Maybe what comes next is a perfectly executed *sole meunière* with lemon wedges and butter and chopped fresh parsley.

What comes next, however, is the same scowling lady from the other morning. She's bearing an enormous stainless steel tray and wearing a black shirtwaist dress with a white apron—not a maid's outfit, but almost. The temperature in the room seems to drop as she removes our empty plates and replaces them with small cups of a thick pink soup.

"*Et voilà,*" Hervé murmurs as the woman exits backwards through the swinging door. He doesn't say thank you or introduce her to me. He doesn't even look at her. He's too busy brushing imaginary lint off the sleeve of his blue blazer, which— like a lot of his clothes—looks a little too big for him. Even the Rolex watch hangs slack on his wrist. For the hundredth time I think how little I really know about Hervé.

The soup is a fish bisque. This, too, can be an easy dish to pull off as you can actually buy ready-made *soupe de poisson* in any Paris grocery store. It comes in clear glass jars and isn't bad if you add croutons and a dollop of garlicky mayo, which tonight our cook didn't bother to do. Still, the smell tells me it will be edible—*correct*, as the French would say—and I lower my eyes as I dip in my spoon. I might as well enjoy being fed and waited on like a lady of the manor. It certainly won't happen in Phoenix.

"This is fun, Hervé. But I hope my being here isn't causing you a problem."

He glances up. "You mean Odile. She is not a problem. She doesn't enjoy to do any extra work, that is all."

I don't answer, because the extra work is obviously me. We've returned to sipping our soup in silence when Hervé looks up. His pointy nose twitches like a Pomeranian's as he stares at the heavy mahogany door that opens to the foyer.

"Expecting company?" I ask, though I don't believe it's possible. As far as I can tell, Hervé has few friends. Or maybe it's that I can't imagine uptight, prissy Hervé having the kind of pals who would just pop by. He's the sort who makes and then loses friends, in some way cursed to alienate people before relationships have time to solidify. Not that he doesn't have good qualities. He does. Otherwise, why would Margaret and I spend time with him? He can be witty, quirky, and almost too generous. But sometimes I feel sorry for him. He never seems to relax and allow himself to be real.

Before I can ask any more questions, I hear a metallic click and the murmuring of voices. Hervé puts down his spoon and purses his lips to emit a soft whistle. It sounds like a signal, and indeed, a sound that could be an answering hiss comes from the direction of the kitchen. Then the foyer door bursts open, and a tall, heavy-set, elderly man wearing a camel hair coat and carrying a black and tan plaid umbrella sweeps in. He has a full head of Brillo-pad-gray hair, matching eyebrows, and a hooked nose. His expression is aggrieved, as if someone switched out his morning *café au lait* with decaf, and the rest of the day went downhill from there.

Hervé and I sit as if affixed to our chairs as the elderly man's dark eyes move from the flickering candelabrum to the shining array of china and crystal and silver on the table to the cups of soup in front of us. When he gets to the Rolex peeking out from beneath Hervé's sleeve his umbrella falls and clatters to the floor.

The spell broken, Hervé leaps to his feet. "*Monsieur!*"

Monsieur moves the umbrella aside with his foot and steps farther into the room. He's twenty or so years older than Hervé but clearly the alpha male here. "*Qu'est-ce qui se passe ici?*"

As Hervé begins to explain "what is going on here," *Monsieur's* bristling eyebrows pump up and down like frightened caterpillars. Hervé wrings his hands and stutters through what sounds to me like a series of inadequate explanations. *Monsieur* continues to work his eyebrows. He is not appeased.

I could live in Paris for decades and still not be able to understand French people when they talk to one another, much less argue. Soon it won't matter though.

Two minutes later a woman about the same age as the man—but with nicer hair—enters the room. Hervé rushes to her side. "*Madame,*" he purrs, and pulls out a chair for her. But the interruption doesn't help his case. *Monsieur* shrugs out of his luxurious coat, tosses it onto a chair, and begins to fire off a series of follow-up questions.

No one takes notice of me—not even *Madame,* who sits and watches the two men as if she's at a play. So I seize the opportunity to finish the rest of my soup. Catherine and I need to eat, after all, and I'm pretty sure dinner is now over. When my bowl is empty, I push back from the table as unobtrusively as possible. I have an overwhelming desire to call Manu. I shouldn't do it. He's probably with Sophie. But, I tell myself, he would find this whole story so much fun.

I'm halfway to my feet when *Monsieur* pauses his interrogation and redirects his piercing gaze to me. "Ah." He bows slightly from the waist. "*Mademoiselle.*"

I sink back down into my chair. "*Bonjour, Monsieur.*"

"*Bonsoir,*" he corrects, and inclines his head in a cordial manner. I'm trying to think of an intelligent-sounding way to introduce myself when he returns to berating Hervé, which I'm sure is what's happening, though I don't know why or what for.

At first, I assumed these people were Hervé's parents and

they were angry with him for, say, failing to appear at an aunt's hundredth birthday party or denting the fender of the family Bugatti. But now I'm not so sure I'm getting that dynamic. The vibe here isn't familial. It's commercial.

Madame joins in, leavening the men's harsh tones with a sweet low voice, but I understand her French only a little better than I do theirs. I catch a word now and then—*maison* and *travail*—"house" and "work." But otherwise they may as well be speaking Martian.

Hervé is standing with his back to the wall tapestry and holding up his hands like an outlaw in a TV western when I again dare to rise from my chair. *Monsieur* is speaking in crisp tones. *Madame* is nodding her agreement. Seems like a good time to make my getaway. I'm halfway to the door when *Madame* turns and smiles at me, her eyes widening as she notices my baby bump.

I smile back, suppress an impulse to curtsy, and scuttle away.

twenty-two

IN MY ROOM, which likely isn't going to be my room for even the short time I need it, I curl up on a brocade loveseat and struggle to rein in my galloping heart.

Phoenix is small. Ordinary. In my opinion, boring. All my life I dreamed of a place that was bigger and more beautiful, a place filled with excitement, glamour, adventure, beauty, history, and character.

A place like Paris.

Yet there have been plenty of times when the experience threatened to be overwhelming. Like the catacombs. Like tonight. "Be careful what you wish for," Dad used to tell me. "You just might get it." I've never much cared for this expression, but I've got to admit there's truth to it.

What I should be doing is calling around to hotels to find a room. But it's past ten p.m. This has been one extremely draining and depressing day. How great it would be if Hervé explained to *Monsieur* and *Madame* who I am and asked them to let me stay here just for the night. Unfortunately, I'm pretty sure Hervé's focus is on looking out for number one.

I sit up and reach into my pocket for my phone. Again, I yearn to talk to Kat. For ten years, fully a third of my life, she was the one I went to with all my problems. She wasn't perfect—who is?—but she always listened, always helped me see the funny side of things. Anyway, when you've lost someone, you don't think of the ways they might have failed you. You think of the ways you failed them.

I can't call Kat. But I can call Manu. In fact, I can't stop myself, even though the recollection of his dropping-everything response to Sophie's phone call this afternoon makes me cringe.

But, as should probably not be surprising, he doesn't answer. I hang up. Two minutes later I try again and leave a voicemail ("Call me! Even if it's late"). For good measure, I type out a text too, and am hitting "Send" when I hear a light tap-tap on my door.

"*Mademoiselle?*" I jump to my feet as *Madame* peeks in. "May I chat with you?"

She speaks in heavily accented but perfectly understandable English. Thank God. I'm really not up for struggling through my imminent eviction in French.

"Yes. Please come in." I watch as she heads for one of the *bergère* chairs positioned in front of the fireplace and seats herself with care. She moves as if every muscle in her body pains her, and lightly places her palms on the padded armrests, as if for support. I take the opposite chair, my feet flat on the floor, my hands balled up into fists on my lap.

Maybe I can spend the night on a bench at a train station. They're open twenty-four hours.

"Don't worry, I'm going to leave as soon as poss—," I begin, but *Madame* waves her hand.

"First, I must apologize to you, *Mademoiselle*, for the terrible incident you have just witnessed."

I'm surprised she would apologize. The incident downstairs wasn't that terrible. It was confusing and even amusing.

She continues before I can respond. "But now I must ask you. What do you do here?"

This makes more sense. Naturally, *Madame* and her husband are wondering what the hell a random pregnant American woman is doing holed up in their guest suite. *Monsieur* has probably sent her up here to—as Margaret would say—suss me out. And then kick me out.

"Hervé is the acquaintance of a friend of mine." My voice is smaller than I would like it to be. "A lady. I've been living with her these past few months. But then her daughter returned and needed her room back so Hervé offered to let me stay here. As a guest. Just for a couple days. I don't know him that well, really. We met in July. I'm going back to the States in a few days."

Madame cocks her head to one side and creases her forehead as if maybe she's wondering whether her English is up to this conversation. I'm about to rephrase my explanation, more slowly and less colloquially this time, when she winks. "You perhaps ask yourself who I am, no?"

"Yes," I admit. "I do."

She lifts her chin. "I am Elisabeth de Villiers. The gentleman you saw with me downstairs is my husband, Jacques de Villiers."

"Ah," I say, as if this information makes perfect sense to me. So these are Hervé's parents after all. But it's still a little hard to believe. In the argument downstairs, they were using the formal *"vous"* and not the informal *"tu"* when addressing each other. Granted, they were speaking so rapidly I could have misconstrued the verb conjugations. Or perhaps noble types say *"vous"* even to their own children. Who knows?

I unball my hands and straighten my back, endeavoring to match a little of *Madame's* dignity. "How do you do. It's a pleasure to make your acquaintance. My name is Amy Brodie. I'm from Phoenix, Arizona. I've been staying in France, but I'm leaving soon."

There it is, my life to date, summed up in three sad sentences.

Madame nods and glances around the elegant room as if she hasn't seen it for a while. "This is our home."

"It's lovely." To say the least.

"Merci." She leans back and sighs, her small, satisfied smile telling me she's well aware of the glories of her house and garden. "Now. You must know." She makes her mouth into a little moue. "That person downstairs. The one you call Hervé? His real name is Jean Martin. His responsibility is to care for the house when we are traveling. Or I should say 'was.' He is no longer employed here."

"Employed?" I jump to my feet. "You mean to say—he's not your son?"

Madame's china blue eyes widen. "Our son? *Mais non. Pas du tout!*" But no. Not at all.

"So—" I pause to clear my throat. "He's not a baron?"

"A baron? Oh my dear child!" She presses her lips together as if to keep from laughing out loud and runs her hands across her lap, fluttering her eyelashes.

Margaret would be able to tell if that bouclé skirt and its matching cardigan jacket are real Chanel. She could take one look at *Madame's* double-strand necklace and know if the pearls were genuine. And yet, like me, she was apparently not able to recognize a real baron from a fake one.

Unless… maybe it's *Madame* and *Monsieur* who are the imposters? It's hard to know what's real and what's fake anymore.

I begin to sidle toward the door. "*Madame*. Please. May I ask—is Hervé still here?"

"Ah." She looks up at me with a smile. "You perhaps doubt what I tell you. And why not? This story is all very, how do you say, *ridicule*."

I nod. Ridiculous is absolutely the right word. Everything that's happened today has been *ridicule* to the max. Nevertheless, I need to see Hervé. One look into his face and I'll know the truth.

"He prepares to depart." *Madame* waves her hand at the door as if to say, "Go ahead, go find out for yourself."

I dash out of the room and down the spiral stairs. As I thump onto the final landing, I spot Hervé charging across the foyer. He's wearing a wrinkled navy blue raincoat I've never seen before and pulling an enormous rolling suitcase behind him. The surly servant follows, a large tan duffle bag in her arms. I don't know if she's going, too, or is just helping Hervé with his bags.

"Hervé! Wait up."

He doesn't wait up. Instead he yanks open the front door with enough force to send the shining brass knob crashing against the interior wall, and plunges out into the night.

"Hey!" I sprint across the black and white checkerboard tiles. "What's happening? Where are you going?"

Clouds cover the moon, but golden light streaming from the open door of the house illuminates the two fleeing figures. It's like a scene from an old movie—the elongated cast shadows, the echoing clatter of footsteps. I imagine violins playing minor chords.

Only when I yell "Hey!" a second time does Hervé slow and glance over his shoulder.

It's then that I halt my pursuit. He's hardly recognizable. Hervé—or, I guess I should say, Jean—looks inches shorter and years older than just an hour ago. His whole appearance is beaten down, defeated, broken, like the middle-aged men I see drinking cheap cognac at the Café de la Poste at eight in the morning.

"You're not a real baron, are you?" I shout as he disappears into the inky black mouth of the wisteria tunnel. When he doesn't look back, I know it's true.

In retrospect, everything makes perfect sense. All this time Hervé, with his aristocratic sneer and almost comic snobbery, has been playacting at being a baron. Margaret and I totally fell for it. People believe what they want to believe, Dad always used to say.

The only person who may have suspected the truth was Manu. It would explain his deep dislike of Hervé and vice versa. Here I thought Hervé disdained Manu, looked down on him. But I bet it was really fear. He sensed Manu saw through his act. What a crazy twist of events. I can't wait to tell him about it. Surely Sophie wouldn't begrudge me that.

"*Mademoiselle?*"

I turn. I was lingering out in the empty courtyard, appreciating the crisp air and the solitude, but now *Monsieur* is standing behind me, silhouetted in the doorway.

"I most sincerely apologize," he says. "You must be at some inconvenience."

Monsieur's English is great. In fact, his speech is as flawlessly British as Margaret's. I picture him as a young man going to school in London to perfect his English and returning here to ever after wow people with his BBC-like vowels.

"Please." He holds out his hand to me. "Come in."

I take a last lungful of cool night air and follow him into the house.

"*Monsieur* Martin tells me you knew nothing of his— pretense. Is that true?" *Monsieur* asks.

My cheeks burn with mortification. "Yes. It's true. I thought this was his place. We weren't close friends. I didn't know him that well at all."

I keep stressing this because the last thing I want is for these people—the real baron and baroness—to think I was sleeping with Hervé. Or Jean. Whatever.

"The woman with him," I add. "Your cook?"

Monsieur grimaces. "Odile. His wife."

I'm taking in this new factoid when *Madame*, who followed me downstairs, glides to *Monsieur's* side and links her arm through his. He looks down at her, clasps her hand, and kisses her forehead. I wonder if I'll ever be part of a sweet old couple like this.

It's unlikely. Not at the rate I'm going.

"Oh. I see. Well," I say, heading for the staircase, "I'm so sorry for the intrusion. But you don't have to worry. I'm leaving right now."

That's all I want—to get the hell out of here as soon and as gracefully as I can. I'll figure out where I'm going later.

"*Mais ma chère enfant!*" *Madame* holds up her small, white palm like a traffic cop. Again, I notice how thin she is. Margaret would admire her slenderness, but in my opinion, she could stand to put on a couple of pounds. "You must be *fatiguée.*" She glances again at my baby bump.

It's funny because *Madame* is obviously the one who's fatigued. Her face is the color of rice. Her pale eyes have a hollowness behind them.

"Please, you must stay here for tonight," she adds. "It is late."

I'm extremely tempted, but I shake my head. "That's most kind of you. I appreciate the thought. But I couldn't impose."

After all, I've just met these people. Sweet as they seem, they're complete strangers. My mother always told me not to make a nuisance of myself. But as I'm about to explain that I have to be on my way, my stomach growls. Loudly.

Not again. Despite the fish soup and tomato salad, not to mention the huge omelet lunch I forced down earlier, plus part of a raspberry tartlet, I'm starving.

Monsieur chuckles. "Ah. You perhaps would like something to eat. *Oui?*"

Food. It's been my Achilles heel my whole life. Loving it, hating it, fearing it, and obsessing over it have taken up much of my time and energy. Too much. These hang-ups have begun to fade away under Margaret's influence and as my priorities realign around Catherine. Still, I guess it's fitting that hunger—simple, human hunger—is now the subject that breaks the ice.

"*Bon.*" *Madame* smiles, showing dimples. She must have been pretty when she was young. She still is. "We, too, would like a bite. Let us go into the kitchen and see what is there. Then you may tell us all about yourself."

Before I can think of another word of protest, she takes my hot hand into her cool one and leads me across the foyer, down a short corridor, through a swinging door, and into the most beautiful kitchen I've ever seen.

"Whoa. What a fantastic kitchen." I run my fingertips over a granite countertop. Admire the oak cabinetry. Note the double sinks.

The kitchen is spacious enough for an antique oak breakfast table and four chairs, one of which *Madame* now sinks into, closing her eyes and massaging her temples. *Monsieur* looks around the kitchen, seeming a bit lost. So I head for the refrigerator. It's full size, not the usual dinky counter-height model you see in Paris. Yet the only items on its shining glass shelves are a dozen eggs, a couple of fist-sized chunks of butter, and two unopened cartons of thick cream.

No onions or garlic. No jam or cheese or yogurt. Not even a jar of mustard or olives. After months in Paris I'm used to the French custom of daily grocery shopping, but it's astonishing how little food is here. Especially since my meal with Hervé had been interrupted—had he not planned to serve anything after the soup? Maybe the duffle bag Hervé's wife carried was full of purloined edibles. It seems petty, but today anything feels possible.

I open cupboard doors, discovering impressive quantities of china and crystal, but I find no canned goods, no bags of rice or packages of pasta, no breakfast cereals, no crackers or chips or nuts. Not even a spare bottle of fish soup. Only a little oil and vinegar, some sugar, and a Tetley box containing five tea bags. A lower cabinet holds a sack of flour and a few other baking supplies.

Madame and *Monsieur* watch me in silence. I get the impression they don't spend a lot of time in their *cuisine*, which is crazy. This place is awesome. It's five times the size of Margaret's, with workspace for two or three cooks. It has an actual dishwasher, another uncommon sight in Paris. Pots and pans hang from a stainless-steel rack mounted on one wall. A rustic iron chandelier, festooned with ropes of clear glass beads, dangles from the ceiling. All this is lovely, but what's even more fabulous is the five-burner cast-iron La Cornue range with side-by-side dual ovens.

"Well, we can always have scrambled eggs," I say, unable to take my eyes off the range. It's the size of an executive desk and is the most beautiful shade of periwinkle blue I've ever seen.

"Can we?" *Madame's* voice is small. "That sounds wonderful."

"*Ça va, cherie?*" *Monsieur* reaches for her hand and cradles it as if it were a Fabergé egg. "*T'es fatiguée?*" he murmurs to her. Tears prick my eyes. This man and woman are old enough to have been married forty or fifty years, yet they still cherish each other. They still care.

I guess it's how marriage is supposed to be, yet so seldom is. I try not to think of Manu and wonder what might have been.

"Let me cook you a light supper," I say. "It won't be fancy, but it will be hot and nourishing and will make us all feel better."

Monsieur's face brightens. "*Bravo, Mademoiselle! C'est une excellente idée.*" He jumps to his feet and holds out his hands to his wife. "Come, *cherie.* Let us allow this young lady to work."

I have to hand it to this couple. They arrive home from an extended trip to find a strange woman in their house but are still game to set her loose in the kitchen. I'm amazed at how trusting they are. At the same time, I'm relieved they're not planning to sit there and watch me. It freaks me out when people hover while I cook. William did it all the time, doling out advice, remarks, opinions, suggestions, and criticism. The last couple of years of our marriage I always made sure to get dinner completely done before he came home from work. "Why do you let him bully you?" Kat asked once.

Excellent question. Maybe I just didn't know how a marriage was supposed to be. If I'd grown up with *Madame* and *Monsieur* as examples I might have realized that things like respect and solicitude are the rocks on which lasting relationships are built.

Or perhaps these are not the foundations, but the fruits, of love.

Anyway, I'm delighted to take charge of the kitchen. Especially one as divine as this. But first I get out my phone and again try to call Manu. Still no answer. Maybe he turned off his phone and went to bed. Maybe he's spending the night with Sophie.

I place my phone face down on the table. Well, tomorrow is Monday, our second-busiest day. I can tell him all about my adventures while we do the deliveries. It'll make for a good distraction from Sophie-related, or William-related, subjects. All subjects, come to think of it.

After washing my hands, I open the refrigerator and get out the eggs, butter, and cream.

I'm searching for a bowl when I notice the kitchen has a back exit—a narrow glass door, partly concealed in an alcove and opening onto yet another cobblestone courtyard. I can't resist unlocking it and stepping outside. The snap of cool autumn air soothes me. While I'm breathing in the freshness, I notice a half circle of waist-high flowerpots. The pots are made of white stone and filled not with geraniums and ivy, as one would expect, but with culinary plants.

It's funny. Neither Hervé nor his wife struck me as back-to-the-land types. Yet earlier he was weeding, and here someone has cultivated masses of chives, parsley, thyme, tarragon, mint, and a few herbs I don't recognize. Even better and more amazing, three of the pots hold flourishing tomato plants. Late-season tomatoes the size of tennis balls weigh down the leafy branches.

Score. Halved and broiled tomatoes, seasoned with fresh herbs, will be perfect served alongside my special recipe of super creamy scrambled eggs.

I'm reentering the house, my hands full of freshly harvested produce, when *Monsieur* pokes his head into the kitchen.

"*Mademoiselle?* May I trouble you to prepare a spot of tea for my wife?" His expression—humble and apologetic—reminds me of Dad when he interrupted my homework to ask for help buttoning his shirt or tying his shoes. Dad stayed as independent as he could as long as he could, but eventually his MS meant I had to take over everything. I never minded. Being needed can be awesome. I was lucky enough to learn that at an early age.

"Of course," I tell him.

I set the tomatoes and herbs in the sink, switch on the electric kettle, and ponder the problem of bread. In France, a meal without bread is unthinkable. Unfortunately, bakeries are closed at this hour, and I didn't see any bread in the kitchen.

But we do have flour. We even have a packet of *levure chimique*, the French version of baking powder. And we have tons of cream.

Which means—ta-da—I can make cream biscuits. I hum a few bars of Bach as I pull a tea set from the top shelf of a corner curio cabinet. *Madame* and *Monsieur*, certain to be familiar with scrambled eggs, have probably never had anything remotely resembling cream biscuits. In fact, quick breads like biscuits and scones are not typically French, making me wonder what the *levure chimique* is doing here in the first place. But I don't care. Light and tender cream biscuits will be the perfect accompaniment to my eggs.

Monsieur returns as I'm pouring boiling water into the teapot. "*Mademoiselle*. You are an angel."

I grin at him. Dad called me "angel." It was his pet name for me. Here I am in a foreign country, far from my humble upbringing in inner city Phoenix, but suddenly, I feel totally comfortable, totally at home.

"Is everything all right?" I ask as I fit the lid onto the pot, which is English bone china—I checked earlier. "With *Madame?*"

"She is just tired. But this will help," *Monsieur* says as he picks up the tray.

The tea smells tempting, but it's time to start the meal. I approach the range with both reverence and trepidation. It's the first La Cornue I've seen in real life. But I've studied enough cooking magazines and websites to be pretty sure it will have at least one burner with an ultra-low simmer setting. Perfect for my slow scramble.

Before tackling eggs or biscuits, however, I power down my phone. It doesn't look like Manu will call back tonight, and I certainly don't want to hear from William. Not now. This is probably the last meal I'll ever cook in Paris. I intend to enjoy every single minute of it.

The biscuits are a little tricky because I need to guess at the proportions of flour, salt, and baking powder. Sometimes I miss my American measuring cups and spoons. But bread is "not rocket science," as William used to say. That was when we were first married, and he was still being patient with me in the kitchen. I bite my lip as I add a pinch of sugar to the flour mixture, to bring out flavor, and pour in enough of the cream to form a soft dough. William never liked cream biscuits. They were my thing. I prefer them to the regular kind because you don't need to work in hard, cold butter and because they are so meltingly tender. They are the fairy princesses of biscuits.

Since I can't imagine a French kitchen possessing a biscuit cutter, I don't bother to look for one. *Madame* and *Monsieur* may not even know that biscuits are usually round. I simply pat the dough into a rectangle, cut it into diamond shapes, set them shoulder to shoulder on a baking sheet, and slip the pan into the oven. Usually it's hard to put a meal together in a strange kitchen, but here, everything is in the place you'd expect it to be. I'm in the zone. For the eggs, I select a cast-iron skillet from the rack on the wall, throw in a slab of butter, and switch on the simmer burner. While the butter melts I whisk the eggs until the whites and yokes are just combined, dumping in a glug of cream. As the butter begins to foam, I pour in the egg mixture, toss in some chives, and double-check that the flame is at the lowest setting. Now, all I have to do is stir.

Soon, the table is set, the biscuits are two inches high and golden brown, and the eggs are fluffy and soft. I'm removing the perfectly browned tomatoes from the broiler when *Madame* and *Monsieur* appear at the door.

"*Mademoiselle?*" *Monsieur* holds up a bottle of pink crémant, a kind of light champagne, and two bottles of sparkling water. Badoit, my favorite.

"Come in," I say. "Please. Supper is ready."

"Whatever you have created, *Mademoiselle*, smells exquisite." *Madame* winks at me as she sits down.

I'm proud of how inviting the table looks, set with a blue-flowered Provençal cotton tablecloth and bright yellow china. Hervé (I will never get used to calling him Jean) was right when he mentioned that the kitchen breakfast table was more "convivial" than the stately dining room.

"Badoit?" *Monsieur* does not wait for an answer. He fills my glass with sparkling water, then refills it after I immediately drink it down. He and *Madame* exchange glances as he serves them a glass of crémant each. I see now how his baronial manners are the real thing, and Hervé's were but a cheap imitation.

As we eat, *Madame* and *Monsieur* quiz me about my background, how I came to Paris, where I've been staying, and how I met Hervé. They're good listeners, and I recount my whole story. I leave out only the parts about William's affair with Samantha and my discovery of the blue baby pajamas. That wound is too fresh, too sordid.

Eventually they get around to inquiring, with great delicacy, when my baby is due.

"Four more months."

I can hardly believe it myself. Still, there's time to get my life in order. There has to be.

"*Félicitations*," *Madame* says. "Sadly, we were not blessed with children." She breaks a biscuit in half and gazes in the direction of the courtyard, perhaps envisioning the toddlers who didn't play there.

I would hug her if I dared. *Madame* possesses all of Margaret's elegance but none of her emotional fragility. That's why I've changed my mind about refusing her kind offer to stay here tonight. Even Kat would approve of this decision. "Listen to your gut," she used to nag me. Never thinking my gut was much of a guide, I always resisted.

But in Paris, of all the crazy places, I've learned how to trust people. After a rocky start with Margaret (recall the sleepy tea incident) I found I could rely on her to be loving and generous. While I fell for Hervé's baron act, I did suspect all along he was someone to be wary of and managed to keep him at arm's length.

As for Manu, well, I knew the moment we met he was a person I could count on, one hundred percent. I didn't know what it would grow into and still find it a little incredible.

Maybe it's my imagination. Maybe it's some rebound thing. Maybe.

I help myself to a second biscuit and try to think of something, anything, else. It's ironic. I originally left Phoenix in a dishonest—some might say cowardly and selfish—fashion. Yet nothing bad happened. In fact, I was rewarded with new, wonderful people in my life. And I got to live in Paris for an entire summer, stay in a sort-of castle, and cook a meal in the kitchen of my dreams. So maybe my sin wasn't so horrible after all.

After the eggs and the tomatoes and all the biscuits are gone *Monsieur* loosely folds his cotton napkin, places it to the left of his plate, and leans back in his chair. "*Un excellent repas,*" he says, and sighs.

I feel my chest swell. Something I created in the kitchen has been called "an excellent meal."

twenty-three

I WAKE WITH NO IDEA where I am or how I got here. The white cotton coverlet resting on my cheek, the wildly ornate armoire standing opposite the bed—these objects look like nothing I recall seeing before.

But when I sit up, I remember.

William. Samantha. The blue baby pajamas.

I cover my face with my hands.

Today is Monday. William arrived in Paris last Wednesday. In that short time my life has been thrown into chaos. I'm left with only one choice: rebuild, from scratch. It feels like a huge task, but I have to do it, and quickly.

Catherine will be here in just a few months.

I'm about to hop out of bed when my phone rings. I lunge for it. Finally, Manu is responding to my messages.

But no. The call is from a Paris number, however, so I answer. Who knows? Maybe Manu lost his phone and is borrowing one to call me. Or he bought a new phone. Or he's calling from a client's landline. I yearn to tell him about the latest developments—Hervé's departure, *Madame* and *Monsieur's* kindness, that delicious kitchen.

I yearn to hear his gravelly voice.

"Manu? Is that you?"

"*Allô? Madame* Brodie?"

Well, it's a Frenchman. Just not my Frenchman. *"Oui?"* I say, not sure my language skills are up to this.

"I call you, *madame*, to say, uhh—" He hesitates, and I realize my caller is the deskman from the Hôtel du Cheval Blanc. Speaking in English. How thoughtful. "I call to tell you *Monsieur* William Brodie, he departed this morning," he says all in a rush. "For the airport."

Just when I thought my opinion of William couldn't sink any lower. He's turning out to be a real wimp.

"Thank you," I say. "I appreciate your letting me know. What time did he leave?"

But my informant has hung up. Does no one say goodbye anymore? Still, he probably doesn't relish talking on the phone in English any more than I do in French.

I set the phone on the nightstand. Calling William is the last thing I feel like doing first thing in the morning. And I'm sure he'd love to avoid our whole tawdry scene and run home to his little Samantha. Too bad. That's not how this is going to work.

I hurry to the bathroom, pee, wash my face, brush my teeth, and touch my toes ten times (this is getting harder all the time). I'm a little out of breath when I return to the bedroom and call William.

Who surprises me by picking up right away. "Hey."

"What the hell, Will? Were you planning to sneak out of Paris without letting me know?" I pace in tight circles around the room, shivering even though it's not cold. Last night *Madame* and *Monsieur* brought me a pair of portable electric heaters, because I'm a "desert flower," they said, and the weather is turning brisk.

"You said we were done," he mutters.

"We are. But I need to tell you something."

"What?" His voice is hoarse. I bet he spent the better part of the night on the phone dealing with Samantha. He's probably worn out from having to deal with women and their impossible-to-calibrate emotions.

But this is no longer my problem.

"Listen, Will. It doesn't matter to me if you want to scuttle back to Phoenix to your little girlfriend. Go right ahead. Knock yourself out. I just want you to know that I'll be there myself in a few days. Then we can settle the details of our—" I pause to swallow, "split."

The word stuck in my throat like a fishbone. But I'm glad I was the one to say it first.

There's another silence, during which I pause my pacing to gaze out the window. Outside, a pigeon lands on the balcony and struts self-importantly around the table legs. In summer this must be a lovely place to have breakfast or just to hang out with a cup of tea and a book. But my next summer will likely be spent indoors, cowering from the Phoenix heat. And I won't have time to sit around and read and drink tea. I'll be a single mother. With a job. I hope. Maybe eventually I can start to do something with food, but first I'll probably have to go back to the library. If I'm lucky. Otherwise it's human resources for me.

"You don't need to worry." His voice is so faint I barely hear him.

"Worry? What do you mean?"

"I'll pay support. For the baby. For the girl." His voice cracks on the word "girl," and he pauses to cough. "I'll do the right thing."

I can hardly believe I just heard what I just heard. "*The right thing?* You are unbelievable! You think you can screw another woman? Make a baby with her? And still get full credit for being a 'good guy' who steps up to his responsibilities? Well, I have news for you, Will. You can't have it both ways."

Bile starts to rise up into my mouth. Not morning sickness. Anger. This has been one of William's problems all along, I now realize. He wants the rewards of being generous without actually being generous.

"Anyway, I'm not worried," I add in a calmer voice. "I'm sure you'll pay your fair share." At least I assume he will. The William I thought I knew seems to have shape-shifted into a different person entirely. They say, though, you never really know a person until you divorce them.

After the call, I return to bed and pull the white coverlet over my head. Since yesterday morning, I've been bracing myself for a final showdown with William. It didn't matter where—at a café or on a street corner or even in an airport departures hall. I was ready to let him have it, face to face. Now cheating William has cheated me of that too. But I guess it doesn't matter anymore. In the long run, splitting up with William could be the best thing that's ever happened to me. I'll get to raise Catherine the way I want.

Besides, in a way, the final showdown with William already happened—yesterday morning when I showed him the blue baby pajamas. His reaction told me all I needed to know.

"*Bonjour, Mademoiselle!*"

It's *Madame*, out in the hallway. "I am sent to announce breakfast," she calls through the door. Her voice is merry.

"OK!" I leap out of bed. "I mean, *bonjour*, *Madame*. Thank you. I'll be down in a minute."

"*Dans la cuisine.*" She almost sings these last words, and I think how French is the very best language to use for summoning people to the table.

I throw on jeans and a sweater, dash off a text to Manu ("Will be at your place in time for deliveries, see you then"), run my fingers through my hair, and hurry downstairs.

Where the kitchen looks even more dazzling in the daytime.

Someone, probably *Madame*, arranged some late-summer roses from the garden in a yellow Provençal clay pot. Piano music (Chopin) wafts from one of the ubiquitous intercoms. Sunshine pours through the tall east-facing windows, flooding the space with morning light and showing that Hervé's wife, a woman I sort of feel sorry for, kept a super-clean workspace. I'm glad that before going to bed last night I washed up all the dishes from our late supper and put everything away.

"*Mademoiselle, bonjour.*" *Monsieur* looks up from the breakfast table set with green and yellow plates sprigged with red cherries. "I must apologize. There is no coffee." He holds up the box with the five tea bags and shakes it.

Before I can assure him I prefer tea anyway, *Madame* chimes in. "But this morning we have gone out for *viennoiseries*. We took a little bit of everything. I hope you will find something to like."

She waves her dainty hands over a large white ceramic platter piled high with miniature *croissants, chaussons aux pommes, brioches, pains au chocolat, pains aux raisins*, and *chouquettes*.

"Wow. That looks amazing."

I wasn't at all hungry when I first woke up, but now the aromas of yeast, butter, sugar, and chocolate kick my body into a state of high anticipation.

"Let me do the tea," I add.

Monsieur leaps to his feet. "*Mais non.* Be seated, *chère Mademoiselle.* This morning it is we who wait upon you."

He winks, pulls out a chair, and holds it for me until I obey.

"*Servez-vous.*" *Madame* watches until I have placed a *croissant* on my plate and then selects a *chausson aux pommes* for herself. Good idea. I take a *chausson*, too, which are basically turnovers made with puff pastry, shaped like the toe of a bedroom slipper, and filled with apple compote.

In Phoenix I'll be eating oat bran or shredded wheat for breakfast. So I may as well live it up while I can.

Madame smiles at me, looking years younger than last night, when she seemed ready to drop in her tracks. At the time I thought she might be suffering from some chronic illness, but *Monsieur* was right, she was just tired. "We have arrived at a grand decision." She reaches across the table to squeeze my forearm. Her fingers are cool and smooth. "We think you should stay here with us until you depart France. We would be delighted to welcome you as our guest. And it is only for a few days."

I put down my *chausson.* My mother drilled me in how to respond to wildly generous invitations like this one: "Thank you so much, but no, I can't." But these simple words will not come.

"We feel you need more consistency in your life. More security," *Monsieur* adds when I still just sit there. I want to blurt out, "You can say that again," but such language sounds way too American. Too breezy. He leans forward and peers into my face. I blush.

Finally, I succeed in channeling Amy 2.0. "That's a wonderful offer," I tell them. "Are you sure?"

Monsieur tsks. "*Mademoiselle!* We are most positive."

I look from him to *Madame.* They are both smiling. "Well, thank you. That is so, so generous."

"Splendid!" says *Madame*, lightly clapping her hands.

Voilà. The universe provides, Kat would say. I eat my *chausson* and help myself to a couple *chouquettes*, little morsels of choux pastry and pearl sugar—another item you won't find in Phoenix. *Madame* nibbles on a brioche. *Monsieur* carries the teapot to the table and places it on an iron trivet.

"Excellent! Now, shall I be mother?" he says, the way Margaret does. I manage to not giggle, and when we've all taken a sip, I say out loud what I've been thinking. Because that's the sort of thing Amy 2.0 does.

"I have an idea. Let me cook for you. While I'm here." I gaze with lust at the brass knobs and shining doors of the periwinkle-blue La Cornue range. The thing is a work of art. "I would love to. Very much."

Madame's and *Monsieur's* eyebrows rise in unison.

"You are obviously a gifted *chef de cuisine,*" *Madame* murmurs after a glance at her husband.

He winks at her. "Agreed. Without a doubt. I must add—" He smiles at us both. "We are hopeless in the kitchen. But, *Mademoiselle!* You are meant to be our guest!"

"A guest who loves to cook!" I laugh aloud for the first time in what feels like weeks. "It's kind of my thing. Seriously. I even write a food blog. And it would be a perfect way for me to pay you back. For letting me stay here."

"No need to pay us back." *Madame* presses her lips together and shakes her head, and I remember how Hervé rejected my expressions of thanks in the same way. Perhaps, in France, trying to repay favors detracts from the generosity of the gift. I don't know. All I know is that with the people I grew up with in Phoenix, it was always tit for tat, quid pro quo, an eye for an eye. There's no such thing as a free lunch, Dad liked to crack. He had a million hackneyed sayings, many of them true.

I return to the subject of food. "What are your favorite things to eat? I love to try out new dishes."

Monsieur chuckles. "We are not difficult. Surprise us."

Madame and *Monsieur* take their time over breakfast, chatting about an exhibition of Impressionist paintings coming to the Petit Palais. "It is a pity you are departing so soon," *Madame* tells me. "I think you would enjoy it."

It's like being with Margaret. She, too, likes to converse about cultural things, or fashion, or food, or history. In my family, despite my mother's penchant for classical music, conversations were mainly about chores that needed to be done around the house. But perhaps my parents would've found topics to explore with *Madame.* My mother would have enjoyed these yummy

viennoiseries, that much is for sure. She's where I got my passion
for food, for better or for worse.

I insist on doing the tidying up. In a kitchen as glorious as
this, even dishwashing is a treat. Before *Monsieur* escorts her from
the room, *Madame* informs me they'll be lunching elsewhere, but
they're very much looking forward to dining at home this evening
and enjoying whatever it is I prepare.

"Perfect," I reply. It gives me all day to work on my three
main tasks: start to organize my return to Phoenix, plan and shop
for tonight's meal, and help Manu with the lunch deliveries.

Plus one other (very big, very important) item that has been
in the back of my mind all morning: I'm going to come clean
with Manu. I have to. Because you should tell people how you
feel about them when you have the chance, before it's too late
and you regret it forever.

It's a step many people fail to take. I have, tons of times. I
never told my mother I loved her—she died so suddenly. With
Dad there was plenty of warning, but I was always too shy. I did
tell Kat, over and over during those last weeks. But for her it
didn't count because my love could never be the kind of love she
wanted and needed. I don't want to make this mistake with
Manu. If I did, I'd never forgive myself.

As I'm getting out my phone, it pings.

A text. From Manu. Finally. And—also—perfect timing.

However, the note makes no sense.

Meet me at Duroc Métro.

I type my reply:

What?

I'm starting to thumb out a second text ("When? Why?
What's at Duroc?"), but halfway through I stop and call him
directly because the old-fashioned ways are best sometimes. I'm
listening to the whirring ringtone when a second text arrives.

Aussitôt que possible.

As soon as possible.

I think for a minute. It's nearly ten a.m. Manu and I normally
leave from his place around eleven to pick up the lunches. At this
time of the morning he should be busy answering emails and
fielding phone calls from his IT clients. He shouldn't even be in
the vicinity of Duroc.

Anyway, he's not answering my call. He's obviously determined to be mysterious. But at least with Manu, you don't have to worry that a surprise will be the bad kind. And now we're going to meet. Just like that. I couldn't have planned it better if I had planned it.

Catherine wriggles with joy as I hurry out the front door, across the courtyard, into and out of the wisteria tunnel, and through the secret garden beyond. When Hervé first brought me to this place, and I still believed he was a scion of the estate, I pictured him as a small boy playing hide-and-seek in the hydrangea hedge or bumping his trike over the cobblestone courtyard. I imagined what a wonderful childhood he must have had and thought how I must provide Catherine with the same. Or something similar. Somehow.

Fifteen minutes later I emerge from the Métro tunnel, where the first thing I see is Manu standing at the top of the steps, smiling.

"*Bon. Te voilà.*"

Yes, here I am. "Manu. Hey." I pause to catch my breath. "I have something to tell you."

"Yes?" He studies me. "I have something to tell you."

"You do?" Here I was all set to blurt out my announcement before losing my nerve, but now I look around for Sophie's pale face and enormous eyes.

"*Aimée.*" His eyes are especially blue in the horizontal morning light. And he looks, finally, more rested than he has in days. "I need to talk to you about Sophie."

Of course he does. She's not here, but the sense of her hangs over our heads like the thickest, murkiest San Francisco fog.

"OK. Talk." May as well get it over with.

But he shakes his head. "Not here. Come. I also have something I want to show you."

"Show me?"

He winks. "You will see. It's not far."

Before I can argue, he sets off down a side street, giving me no choice but to follow. When I say, "*Qu'est-ce qui se passe?*" in the hopes that asking, "What's up?" in French will elicit a response, Manu waggles his eyebrows like Groucho Marx.

Fifty yards later I try again. "Hey. Aren't we forgetting the lunch deliveries?"

Manu glances at me and smirks. "No. I ask a friend to take over for me."

He must know how maddening his behavior is. If he's decided he's going to be with Sophie, he needs to own it and just tell me. And then, no matter what he says, I'll tell him how I feel—I have to, no matter what.

Amy 2.0 would do no less.

Since Manu is the one with the upper hand for the moment, I decide to let him keep it for a while and enjoy walking down a Paris street at his side. For maybe the last time. The day is spectacular—sunny and cool. Pedestrians flow around us, most of them gazing into their phones. Margaret and Hervé may deplore public cell phone usage, but they must be the only ones. In Paris, it seems all the people are on their phones all the time. Maybe it's the same everywhere, but in cities where people are on foot a lot, it's more noticeable.

We pass a bookstore, an art gallery, and a bakery before coming to a stop in front of a white stone apartment building with an ordinary dark green *porte-cochère*. Inside, the courtyard is also ordinary. No secret garden. No wisteria tunnel. Manu doesn't speak, and neither do I, as we cross directly to a second building and enter through a glass door.

I'm intrigued and apprehensive as we step into a telephone-booth-sized elevator, where we stand toe to toe, our chests and thighs almost touching. Before I came to France I never would have believed such tiny elevators existed. But they're the norm in the buildings that do have elevators, and no one thinks it's odd to stand so close together.

Although for me, with my announcement straining to burst free, it's more than odd. It's excruciating. The small space is fragrant with the woodsy aroma of Manu's aftershave. He looks good, too, wearing the navy blue cashmere sweater Margaret gave him for his thirtieth birthday in July and a crisp white button-down shirt I've never seen before.

Maybe he's turning over a new sartorial leaf, trying to improve his look for Sophie. The thought gives me a stomachache and makes me wish I were wearing something other than my ratty black trench coat. But we never dress up to do the lunchtime deliveries.

As we glide past floor two, I run out of patience. "Manu? What the hell? Where are we going?"

"Almost there."

We exit on the fourth floor, and Manu unlocks one of the doors on the landing. If I were with anyone else, I'd be feeling nervous about now. Maybe this is how Sophie managed to get herself taken off to Morocco and held captive for two and a half years. She was too trusting, too gullible, as I was with William.

I'll never repeat that mistake.

"*Entre*," Manu says and gestures me into a small entry hall flooded with sunshine and carpeted with a red kilim rug.

"Nice place," I say, just to be saying something.

"Let me give you a tour."

I want to demand that he get to the point about Sophie— because bad news doesn't get any less bad by putting it off—but Manu's face is adorably eager as he shows me into a high-ceilinged room furnished with a black leather sofa, swivel armchair, glass coffee table, and brushed chrome floor lamp. An elaborately carved marble fireplace dominates one wall. Two tall French windows look down into the small courtyard. I cross the room to get a closer look at the enormous bouquet of flowers on the mantelpiece. Stargazer lilies. That's the spicy scent that's filling the apartment and blotting out Manu's cologne.

"The bedroom is over there," he says. "And you will find also a separate kitchen."

I turn to look at him. "It's great. Who does it belong to? What are we doing here?"

"*Aimée*. First I need to talk to you about Sophie."

Here it comes. His big news. I go sit on the sofa, where I clench my fists and tell myself everything is going to be OK. Whatever happens, I'll still have Catherine. Just the two of us, forever. Maybe this is the right thing.

Manu positions a footstool in front of me and sits down. His posture is uncharacteristically rigid. "Later today I must drive her to a clinic. Sophie, I mean. Where she will stay until she recovers."

"Recovers?" This isn't what I expected him to say.

He gazes down at the gray wool carpet. "She did not want

me to tell anyone. But I want you to know."

"Know what?" I sort through possibilities at warp speed. Sophie developed an infection from the knife wound. Sophie has had a Margaret-style nervous breakdown. Sophie caught some sort of parasite in Morocco.

Manu looks up at me. We're so close I can almost see each of his eyelashes individually. "When she returned to Paris, she was not—not herself. It frightened Margaret. Very much. That was part of the reason for what happened the other day. With Margaret."

"Manu, I don't totally get what you're trying to say."

"I am trying to explain that Sophie…" He pauses and sighs. "That Sophie, while she was with this man in *le Maroc*, she was— how do you say?—*droguée*."

"Drugged?"

He nods. "Yes. Yes. *Exactement*. The man kept her all the time a little bit intoxicated. So she would be tranquil. When she left him, the absence of the drugs caused her to be ill."

"Ah. You mean she's going through withdrawal."

This explains a lot. About Margaret's crazy reaction to Sophie. And about Sophie herself. No one could be as big a jerk as she's been. At least I hope not.

Manu continues. "Last night we had to call the doctor to come to the apartment. Sophie was not in a good condition. The doctor recommended she enter a place where she can allow the drugs to depart from her system."

"Rehab," I say, again automatically providing the English word. I'll miss this.

He nods, then slides off the footstool to kneel at my feet. Our faces are even closer than they were in the elevator, and I have an overwhelming desire to kiss him.

Because that's in no way appropriate, I jump up from the sofa and walk to the window. The sky is an unblemished blue. Fingers of cool air slip through the cracks in the casement and caress my tired eyes, which still sting from all that crying yesterday. "So you're not with Sophie?" I ask.

"*With* her?"

"Yes, with her. You know what I mean. Like lovers."

"*Mais non!*" He laughs. A nervous laugh. "I am not 'with'

her."

I keep my back to him. I want to scream. All this time I've believed Manu had a thing going on with Sophie. She was always calling on him, and he was always dropping everything to be with her. If I'd known the reason behind it, I might not have put so much energy into being jealous. Not that I realized then that what I was feeling was jealousy. I was just angry and annoyed and pissed off without knowing why.

"*Aimée?*" He's standing right behind me now.

I turn to face him, and he's closer than I wish he was. Because it makes it hard for me to think.

"I wanted to show you the rest of the apartment."

What? Not this again. He backs away and heads toward the hall, but I don't follow. "Manu! What is this place?"

"*Alors.*" He pauses, then turns to face me and spreads his arms out wide like a game show host. "It is the apartment of a friend of me."

"Of mine," I say without thinking.

Normally Manu says "*merci*" when I correct his grammar. But today he turns strawberry red and hurries out of the room. When I catch up, he's standing next to the armoire in the bedroom and staring at a framed poster on the wall. A second large vase of fresh flowers stands on a chest of drawers.

"Manu?" I stay in the doorway. Being too close to the bed somehow makes me feel shy.

"*Aimée.*" The three horizontal lines in his forehead seem deeper than usual. "You like this apartment?"

"Um, sure. It's super." I'm tired of talking about this stupid apartment—it's hijacked our whole conversation—but it seems important to Manu.

"Yesterday." He pauses. "Yesterday you said you cannot remain in France because you have no place to stay."

"Yeah. That's one of the reasons."

"*Voilà.* You have a place to stay."

"What? Here?"

He grins. "*Oui.* It is available for six months. At least. My friend who owns it, he has an assignment in Sweden and has agreed to let us borrow it."

Again, I want to scream. Can he not see I am five months

pregnant? And a foreigner? And, for the most part, unemployed? An apartment in Paris for six months, incredibly cool as it is, doesn't begin to solve my problems.

His grin widens. "*Aimée.* I can see your mind operating. You also mentioned your situation in France. Your papers. I have talked with Margaret. She wants to help."

"To help?" I've been trying to get myself used to the idea of losing Margaret forever. The thought that she's worrying about me, even in the middle of all the issues with Sophie, causes me to place my hand on the doorjamb for support. "That's so sweet. It really is." I take a deep breath of stargazer lily scent. Manu, too, has been thinking of me. The fresh flowers must have been his doing. He was trying to make the place nice. Welcoming.

Now is my turn. "Manu. I have something to tell you."

His grin fades.

"Not something bad," I add. "I just want to say—what I mean is—" This is a lot harder than I thought it'd be. "You're very important to me. What I'm trying to say is… I'm really glad you're not with Sophie."

"Yes?" His face is brightening again. "I am glad too."

"Not that it matters. I mean, it does matter. To you. And to me. What I mean is I'm glad because—"

I hang on to the doorjamb as if my life depends on it. When I met Manu last April, I thought he was too short, his eyes too pale. Since then, I've come to appreciate how we're about the same height. And I've noticed how the color of his eyes changes with the light and his mood. Most of the time they're sky blue, but sometimes they look almost aqua. Right now, they're a deep periwinkle.

"Because?" He's watching me carefully.

"Because, well, I like you. A lot. Maybe more than a lot. I didn't realize until… not long ago. I just wanted you to know."

"You like me?" He swallows, his Adam's apple moving up and down. "A lot?"

"Uh-huh. I mean, yes. I do." I push off from the doorjamb and feel myself entering the room.

"*Aimée?*"

I don't answer.

I can't.

We often describe significant moments in our lives by saying, "Time stands still." Of course, time never really stands still. It flies or it drags, but it never fails to chug along, ceaselessly, mindlessly, like an infernal machine. I think what we mean is that in these times our minds pause their constant thinking. And, right now, right here, as I wordlessly and effortlessly float into this hushed, flower-scented space, that's what happens: My brain takes a break. It stops hopping around like a maniacal monkey.

A big reason for this is because Manu has taken a step toward me and is grabbing my hands. And because he's now kissing me. And I'm kissing him.

"Why," I say much, much later, when we've returned to the living room and are sitting side by side on the sofa. "Why didn't you ever say anything to me? About how you felt?"

He squeezes my hand. "I was obligated," he says. "To wait. Until I knew for sure if you wanted to return to—him."

He doesn't want to say William's name out loud. Which is good, because I don't want to hear it said out loud. It would ruin the mood.

Still. There's one more extremely important thing that needs to be said out loud. "Manu. You know. It's not just me. There's Catherine too."

He turns to me and smiles. His hair is a mess, but his arm around me is firm and steady. "Yes. *Absolument*. Catherine. You, and me, and Catherine."

"The three of us?"

"Yes."

It feels too crazily perfect. Yet I'm here. Manu is here. Catherine is here. We're all here. In Paris.

epilogue

"**MERDE.** I wanted to shop for the flowers myself."

"Yes, *Aimée*. I know. But it is easier if I go alone."

He's right, of course. Since Catherine was born, on December 12th, my outings have become as complex as lunar landings and almost as rare. Babies require ridiculous amounts of equipment, preparation, and timing.

"If I have a question I will call you." He kisses me and turns to leave the kitchen.

"Wait!" I pull him back in for a second kiss. Then a third. "Do you remember the color scheme?"

"Yellow and white."

"Don't forget we don't need tulips. We have plenty of those in the garden. Oh, and could you pick up a lemon?"

He grins. "*Oui, ma puce.*"

Generally, Manu only calls Catherine "*ma puce.*" I guess because she's tiny like a flea? *Puce* means flea and is one of those French endearments, like addressing someone as your "little cabbage," that I'll always think is weird no matter how long I live in Paris. Which I assume will be forever. But when I'm stressed, like now, Manu uses the same methods to soothe me that he uses on the baby.

It's cute and also annoying. I snap a dishtowel in his direction. "*Vas-y!*" I say. Scram.

He scrams.

Sophie, who promised to help with Catherine, isn't coming for another hour. Margaret won't be here till noon, early for a French Sunday lunch, but she wants to do the table settings. The lamb needs to be basted, and I have yet to start the white sauce for the scalloped potatoes. But I steal a quiet moment to sit at the breakfast table, cradling my cup of tea and admiring the kitchen. I never did move into the apartment Manu showed me last September. I completed my pregnancy here, under the watchful eyes of *Madame* and *Monsieur*, then after Catherine was born, Manu moved in with us. We are the caretakers of the "castle" now. Well, Manu is.

Just about exactly twelve months ago I made a rash decision. I got on a plane to Paris. And it worked out. Everything good that's happened to me since then is a result of that one action.

My tea break lasts for approximately three minutes, when Catherine wakes up, right on schedule. I zip out of the kitchen and up the three flights of stairs. When *Madame* and *Monsieur* installed a house-wide intercom system, they probably thought they were doing so for their own convenience. Little did they know they were outfitting the place with a world-class baby monitor. I can leave Catherine in her crib upstairs knowing I'll hear her slightest coo or hiccup no matter what room I'm in.

"I'm coming," I call as I hurry through the sitting room into the bedroom. "Hey there, little girl."

She gurgles as I scoop her up. I crazy-love Catherine. After she was born I worried about going through a postpartum thing, remembering my mother's chronic depression and how it hung like an acrid cloud over our tiny family. I recalled Margaret's ups and downs, and my own depths of despair after Kat died. But my fears never came true. We brought the baby home from the hospital and proceeded to live our lives.

Which is not to say that having a newborn isn't a huge deal. It is. Just as when she was in the womb, Catherine is super physical, super active. I can't remember when I've ever been so tired. Last week I cried for joy when she started sleeping for six hours at a stretch, unusual for a four-month-old, the doctor says. But I'll take it. Because what they say about babies is true. Every single second—well, almost—is amazing.

I change her diaper but don't bathe or dress her. Sophie would kill me. The reason she's coming early is to get Catherine ready for her first French Sunday lunch.

The landline rings as I'm returning to the kitchen. I don't rush. The helix-shaped staircase is slippery as well as twisty-turny, and I'm carrying Catherine. Anyway, I know who it is.

"*Mademoiselle?*"

Monsieur still addresses me as *Mademoiselle*, even though I'm a mother and soon-to-be-remarried woman—the minute the divorce is finalized. William hasn't been very communicative of late. The child support arrives like clockwork, but he hasn't acknowledged the photos of Catherine I email him every few weeks. I'm assuming Samantha had her baby and that he's busy. Perhaps even happy. I hope so. I truly do. I believe the biggest favor you can do for people is to let them be who they are. Margaret showed me that.

"*Bonjour, Monsieur. Joyeuses Pâques!*"

"Ah, yes, Happy Easter, my dear. Have the bells returned from Rome?"

I smile. "Oh, they have. Absolutely."

So here's a weird thing: In France, a bunny doesn't bring your Easter treats. Bells do. No, I'm not kidding. The story goes that on Good Friday all the church bells sprout wings and fly to Rome to be blessed by the Pope. On Easter morning, they fly back to France, dropping chocolate goodies in people's gardens as they pass (while in Rome they must also, presumably, go shopping for chocolates). It makes about as much sense as the Easter bunny, I suppose.

"The bells were very generous," I add. Yesterday morning an enormous box of chocolate eggs, hens, and rabbits arrived by special delivery. "Thanks to you both."

"*Madame* took a great deal of pleasure in making the selections."

"And she did so fabulously." Unfortunately, I can't have many of them. My weight ballooned in my last trimester of pregnancy. The doctors complained. Even now, four months later, I've only lost a fraction of it.

Madame and *Monsieur* also included a hand-knit bonnet for Catherine. They have been lovely godparents. When Catherine was born, they were even more thrilled than Margaret. Which is saying a lot because Margaret's over the moon about Catherine. She introduces her to people as "my granddaughter," and now calls both Sophie and me "*ma fille.*"

Monsieur clears his throat. "I have a favor to request, *Mademoiselle*. Will you ask Manu to contact a plumber in Beaune? We are told we have some minor flooding in the cellar."

In addition to this "castle," *Madame* and *Monsieur* own a condo on the Riviera, where they are now, and a three-hundred-year-old manor house in Beaune, in the famous wine region of Burgundy.

"Sure, I'll tell him. It's not serious, I hope."

"No, no, it will be fine. Thank you. And thank Manu for us. We know we can rely on him."

Since getting burned by Hervé, *Madame* and *Monsieur* have been a lot more hands-on in the management of their property. *Monsieur* calls and talks to one of us almost every day. I don't mind. I mean, we not only live here rent-free, we get paid to do it. Speaking of which, money matters are, so far, decent. I was able to take care of the medical bills for Catherine's birth on my own with my savings. I didn't even have to touch Kat's bequest. Health care is hugely cheaper in France than in the U.S., so that helped.

"You know you can call on us anytime," I say. I look down into Catherine's alert face and think, for the zillionth time, how much I love being part of an "us."

After hanging up I hurry to the kitchen. Hosting Easter dinner was possibly a rash idea on my part, considering how perpetually exhausted I am, but I wanted to mark my one-year anniversary in France with something special. "You can sleep when you're dead," Kat always used to say, before she got sick and this kind of wisecrack was still funny. But she was right. Sometimes you have to go for it.

My original plan was to prepare a classic American Easter dinner with baked ham, scalloped potatoes, and steamed asparagus. But the big honey-baked hams I grew up with don't exist in France, where most people serve a leg of lamb for Easter. I've never even had lamb, much less prepared it, but Manu assures me I can manage. He has more faith in me than I have in myself sometimes.

At least we can still have American-style potatoes and asparagus. And the rest of the meal will also be true-blue American. We'll have the green salad before the main course, not after it the way the French do. Yesterday, I made Parker House dinner rolls, from scratch, and decorated Easter eggs for our centerpiece. Dessert will be homemade strawberry shortcake with whipped cream. This one meal took days of prep work, but I'm on track.

"Amy! *T'es là?*"

Sophie sweeps into the kitchen. She's early, which is better than being late (with Sophie, it's one or the other).

"Hey." I was putting Catherine into her baby seat, but now I unstrap her. "Come in. Catherine just woke up."

Sophie has settled down quite a bit since her return to Paris last September, unless you count a string of questionable boyfriends. We're supposed to meet the latest one today.

"Super. I have brought her *une nouvelle petite robe adorable.* She will look *très jolie.*"

I nod. I found out Sophie speaks English as well as I do, maybe better, but half her words always come out in French. Actually, I'm starting to do that a little too. It feels natural.

"You spoil her," I say.

"It is *mon plaisir.*" Sophie not only gave Catherine all of her own baby trousseau but continues to buy new things. I've lost count of how many adorable outfits my child owns.

"Well," I reply, "I'm glad it's also your pleasure to give her a bath and dress her. I've got tons to do in the kitchen. And I was hoping to work a little on the menu for American Lunch."

She plucks Catherine from my arms. Sophie is still not my favorite person, and at first, I hesitated to let her take Catherine out of my sight. But I have to hand it to her. She really adores Catherine and seems to have a knack with babies. "American *quoi?*"

"Didn't Manu tell you? That's the name we thought of for our new catering business."

She kisses Catherine's forehead and blinks her enormous round eyes. "Ah. *Oui.* I believe he did tell me."

Manu is still a tender subject between us. When he and I

announced our engagement, Margaret was thrilled. Sophie was...
meh. I don't think it's because she wanted him for herself. I do
think she liked having the option though.

"Well, we're going to feature typically American sandwiches.
Ham on rye. Bacon, lettuce, and tomato on pumpernickel. Meat
loaf on sourdough." Sophie obviously doesn't care, but I tell her
anyway. It's what's on my mind. When Catherine keeps me up at
night I have time to cogitate and plan and even play around with
recipes. I love the thought that, instead of bringing French food
to Americans—as was my original idea with *Fun French Food*—I'm
bringing American food to the French.

"I take *le bébé* upstairs now, yes?"

"Yes, thanks. You know where everything is."

I start the white sauce for the scalloped potatoes, noodling
ideas for American Lunch while stirring the milk into the roux.
The insane success of hamburgers in Paris is what gave us the
inspiration. If the French can love burgers so much, why not the
rest of the American sandwich universe? We even dream of one
day using the money from Kat's estate to open up a little café.
But we're taking things slow. The plan is to phase out of the
lunchtime catering biz and phase into American Lunch.

"*Salut.*" Manu is back, his arms full of flowers. All in yellow
and white.

"Perfect timing! Everything's organized. Sophie is upstairs
fussing over Catherine."

"*Bon.* It is good for them both."

As I pour the white sauce over the potatoes—earlier I used a
mandolin to slice them into perfectly thin ovals—I change the
subject. "I've been thinking about American Lunch. What about
doing tortilla chips and salsa instead of potato chips with the
sandwiches?" My most recent three a.m. idea was to bring in
more of my Arizona heritage.

Manu shrugs. "Why not? It will be *exotique.*"

"I could do my own salsa. Maybe even grow our own
tomatoes? There's tons of space in the garden."

At this, he sets aside the flowers he was unwrapping and
cups my face in his hands. "One thing at a time, *Aimée, n'est-ce pas?*
First we have to find sources for the bread."

"True. I know."

Bread sourcing is still a work-in-progress. The first time I said the word "pumpernickel" to Manu he thought I was making it up. We both still learn new things from each other every day.

The doorbell chimes. It's Margaret, right on time.

"I have the funniest story to tell," she announces, handing Manu a green sack containing a bottle of champagne. She doesn't say *bonjour* first, or do the double cheek kiss thing. She's red-faced and breathing heavily.

Manu glances at me as he helps Margaret off with her coat and leads her to a chair. "Have a seat," he says to her. "Tell us."

We still worry about Margaret, though she's much more even-keeled than last September. I think it helps that she's cut back on her medication. She comes over for lunch at least once a week, and she and I are closer than ever, despite Sophie's near constant presence. In some ways she's better than an actual mother because we don't have any parent/child baggage to overcome.

She rejects the chair. "We can talk while we dress the table. You will laugh!"

She hustles us into the dining room, where I've set out stacks of china, crystal, and flatware, ready to be arranged. "You'll never guess who rang me up." Her eyes are gleaming.

"Called you? Who?" Manu asks.

"Hervé!" Margaret claps her hands with delight. "Or, I suppose I should say, Jean."

"Seriously? No way!" I put down the napkins I was starting to fold. Since Hervé disappeared that night after the big showdown, no one's heard a word from him. Not even *Madame* and *Monsieur*, who are still storing some clothes and other stuff he left behind. They're too nice for their own good.

Manu frowns. He could never, as I do, regard Hervé as a subject for amusement. "What does he want?"

Margaret picks up a shining silver spoon and gazes into it. "Do you remember how on Amy's birthday last year he told us about a vintage wine business he wanted to start?"

Of course I remember. But I'm surprised Margaret does. She retains only sketchy memories of the tumultuous week of Sophie's return. It was a crazy few days for her. For me too. For all of us.

She arranges the spoon just so beside a place setting. "Well, he has done so. Started the wine business, I mean. And it is going swimmingly, he says. So he was calling to inquire if I would care to invest. 'To take it to the next level.' Those were his very words."

"*Mais non. C'est pas possible!*" Manu's eyes are almost as big and round as Sophie's, who has just carried Catherine in and is placing her in her baby seat.

"Oh, but darling!" Margaret is laughing so hard she can barely get out her words. "With Hervé all is possible."

I take her by the hands to force her to stand still. "Is that the name he's still using? What can he be thinking? Surely he knows you know his real identity."

Margaret winks at me. "Perhaps he believes I am so dotty I have forgotten."

She squeezes my fingers, and I squeeze back. It's the first time Margaret has been able to allude to her breakdown.

"*Et alors*, what did you tell him?" Manu asks.

"I wished him the best, naturally, and told him I was certain his venture would be a marvelous success without my help." Her face is bright pink.

"*Tiens, Maman.*" Sophie is holding out a bottle of Evian. "I have brought you water."

Well, that's something. She's being thoughtful.

These past months, I've tried to see Sophie through Margaret's eyes. She did have a tough time in Morocco, then the drug rehab dragged on for weeks. The only part of her story that didn't turn out to be one hundred percent true was how she got the knife wound. The kidnapper/fake husband didn't do that—Sophie herself did, so he would be forced to take her to a hospital and she could carry out her escape plan. I never would have given her credit for such a gutsy move. But she may have a measure of Margaret's gumption. In the end, I think she'll do the right thing. Probably after doing a bunch of wrong things first.

The table is set. The flowers are arranged. The salad gets tossed. The lamb and potatoes and buttery dinner rolls come out of the oven.

"*Ça sent bon,*" Manu says. That smells good.

"Yes, and everything looks splendid!" Margaret has taken the place of honor at the head of the table. Manu and I are seated on Margaret's left. Sophie is at her right. The boyfriend didn't show up, but Catherine is parked beside her on the floor in her baby seat—my little girl's first dinner party. She's wearing a pink and white striped seersucker dress with matching bonnet and white cotton (not nylon) anklets. White socks seem to be a family tradition worth carrying on. I think about my mother a lot these days, now that I'm a mother myself. I try to understand what she went through. I tell myself not to repeat her mistakes.

"*Ça va?*" Manu is looking at me.

"*Oui. Ça va.*"

We all watch in silence, even Catherine, as Manu pops open the bottle of champagne Margaret brought.

He looks at me. "*Du champagne?*"

"Yes, please." It will be my first taste of alcohol since Catherine was born, and I love champagne. "It's a celebration."

He pours everyone a full glass. We're using *Madame's* best Baccarat champagne flutes, so fragile and thin they scare me a little.

Margaret jumps to her feet. "Wait! I want to make a toast." Her face is pink again. "Here's to babies, and weddings, and miraculous returns, and fake barons, and families, and new beginnings."

She raises her sparkling glass to each of us in turn, including little Catherine, who is saying "ma-ma-ma-ma" and pumping her fists. "May the best of our past be the worst of our future!"

Manu touches his glass to mine. "*Santé.*"

"*Santé.*" I take a sip. It tastes like stars and diamonds.

a note from k.s.r. burns

Dear Reader,

Thanks for reading *Paris Ever After*! I hope you enjoyed it. Did you know that *Paris Ever After* is actually the sequel to my first novel, *The Paris Effect*? It's where you'll find the full story of how Amy landed in Paris, as well as what happened in those mysterious catacombs.

If you did enjoy the story, I would LOVE it if you'd leave a review on Amazon.com. Just a sentence or two saying what you liked about the book can help other readers decide to pick it up. I'd be so grateful.

Want to stay up to date on my news, sales, and new releases? Sign up for my newsletter: https://bit.ly/Parisaholic. I don't send out many newsletters, to be honest. But it's a great way to keep in touch, and you'll even get a free ebook of my short story, *You Don't Want to Know*, when you sign up!

You can find out more behind-the-scenes info by visiting http://www.ksrburns.com. And while you're there, feel free to drop me a note. I love hearing from readers. It's the best part of the job!

A bientôt,
Karen

P.S. Did the book leave you hungry for *madeleines*? Try making some yourself! They're pretty easy, and I've included a recipe in the back of this book. There's also a book club discussion guide and a sneak peek of *The Paris Effect*!.

amy's favorite parisian madeleines

from Chef Didier Quémener

5 oz. butter
4 oz. eggs
5 oz. unbleached flour
½ tablespoon baking powder
3½ oz. sugar
1 oz. eucalyptus or acacia honey
3 tablespoons whole milk
1 teaspoon lemon juice

Preparation time: 15 minutes + 8 hours in refrigerator
Baking time: 5 to 7 minutes

Preparation:

Place butter in a saucepan and melt on low heat (do not exceed 165 degrees Fahrenheit).

In a small bowl, slightly whisk eggs.

In a different bowl, sift flour and baking powder together. Add sugar and mix.

Pour milk into a new bowl, then add honey and mix. Add eggs and lemon juice, then mix. Add dry ingredients mixture (flour, baking powder, and sugar), then whisk thoroughly and vigorously for 2-3 minutes. Add warm butter and whisk delicately.

Place in refrigerator in a well-sealed container for 8 hours.

Baking:

Take batter out of refrigerator. Preheat oven to 475 degrees Fahrenheit.

Butter and flour bottom of madeleine baking pan.

With a wooden spatula, work madeleine batter for 5 minutes.

Using a tablespoon or a piping bag (which does the best job), place about 1 ounce of batter in each individual mold.

Bake for 5 to 7 minutes, being sure to never open the oven door while your madeleines are baking. *Bon appétit!*

For more delicious French recipes, check out:

Chef Q in Paris: The Fall Collection
Chef Q in Paris: The Winter Collection

book club discussion guide

1. Amy was extremely lucky to find a home with Margaret in Paris. Some might say crazy lucky. But who do you think benefited the most from this arrangement—Amy or Margaret?

2. When Amy gets positive confirmation that she's pregnant, she takes numerous steps to contact William with the news (phone calls, email, texts, etc.) but he ignores all her attempts. Should she have tried harder? What else could she have done?

3. Six months after Kat's death Amy still misses her, though her grief is less acute than at first. Do you think Amy will always mourn Kat to some degree? How long do you think grieving generally lasts? When do the memories start to become sources of sweetness rather than pain?

4. At the beginning of the book Amy believes she has resolved all her food and body image issues. But what's your take? Could these problems reappear at some point in the future? What advice would you have for her?

5. When Amy and Sophie meet, they do not like each other (to say the least). What are the chances they will eventually become friends? Have you ever met someone whom you found really unpleasant at first and then later grew to like? Or are first impressions lasting impressions?

6. Amy is surprised by more than one person by the end of the novel. Do you think she was too gullible all along? Would you have been quicker to pick up on clues that Amy missed?

7. What are your thoughts about Amy's friendship with Manu as the story progresses? What does he bring to her life and her Parisian experience?

8. What role does money play in Amy's life and in her relationships with others? Is it important to her—why or why not?

9. When we first see Amy, she has been living in France for several months and is still definitely in the honeymoon period regarding the wonderfulness of Paris. Do you think her views of Paris will change and she'll become more cynical?

10. When we're in a completely different culture, our good sense that tells us something is wrong might not work as well. If you were in Amy's place would you have found yourself in similar situations? What are ways you use to avoid getting conned in an unfamiliar culture?

11. What do you think of the characters Madame and Monsieur? Do you believe, like Amy, that there are still kind, decent people in the world?

12. What do you think of the outcome of William and Amy's relationship? Were you happy or disappointed? Do you think their relationship will ever change?

THE Paris EFFECT

A NOVEL

K.S.R. BURNS

velvet morning press

I LEAVE THE HONDA parked in front of the Starbucks and walk over to Fifth Avenue, pausing in front of a jewelry store to scrutinize my profile in the reflection of a dusty plate glass window. This morning my jeans buttoned with difficulty, but they did button. Rule number five of the perpetual diet: Put on something a little tight in the morning, when you are at your thinnest, and you will be less likely to overeat during the day.

Of late, the rules have been swarming around in my brain like fire ants.

Fifth Avenue in Scottsdale is one tacky tourist shop after another, featuring objects I am embarrassed by—do visitors to our state think we all decorate our homes with bronze tabletop statuettes of bucking broncos and stylized pastels of Navajos wrapped in blankets? But two blocks later I halt in front of a different kind of window display. No bucking broncos here. No silver squash-blossom necklaces, no white ten-gallon cowboy hats, no green jars of prickly pear jelly. Just a single wooden easel bearing a single object: a three-foot-square watercolor of the Sacré-Coeur.

I know it's the Sacré-Coeur because I have read a ton of books about Paris. A passage from a guidebook pops into my head: "The basilica of Sacré-Coeur, set atop a hill in Montmartre, was built as penance for the crimes of the 1871 Paris Commune."

Which has always struck me as wrong. The penance part, not the crimes part. After all, look at it. Penitence was never on the minds of the people who built this building. It's jazzy and carefree. It's a wedding dress of a church, a frosted cupcake of a church, a Southern belle of a church. A party church. Not the least bit penitential.

Accordingly, the Sacré-Coeur painting in the window is not

only non-contrite but sassy. It vibrates, quivers, shimmers, twitches with joy. It yearns to jump up and do the cancan. Its rose window is askew, its Romanesque arches are lopsided, its smooth, round, shining white domes jig and jag. The sky above the domes is pulsating with pink and blue squiggles, like streamers being tossed from a celebrating heaven. This painter clearly grasped the party-church nature of the Sacré-Coeur.

In college Kat used to say, "Your eye for design rocks, you oughta be an artist." Five years later she was still at it. During chemo, when she should have been fretting about hair loss or fluid retention, she would nag me instead. "You should sign up for a watercolor class," she'd say, and I'd always counter, "Is fiber art not art?"

Because while books and words are my chief obsessions, I also sew, knit, crochet, even macramé. I like to make stuff. Step by step by step, until you have a physical and sometimes beautiful object you can hold in your hands. A real and solid thing that does not die and leave you.

One time Kat persisted. "You're not realizing your potential, Amy. You could do something more than make house-y crap," she said.

This was eighteen months ago, during the second chemo regimen. I shifted in my hard plastic visitor's chair and admired the regular twists of the French-blue shrug I'd crocheted for her during the first chemo regimen. I didn't want to argue so I said, "I'm a housewife, remember? A throwback. A dinosaur. One of the last of my kind. Woo-hoo."

"You loon." Kat heaved a pillow at me. "The minute the economy improves you'll get another job and forget all this domestic goddess bullshit."

Her eyes were bright and sparkling, which was so good to see that I strung her along. "I don't know. Maybe getting canned was the best thing that ever happened to me. Speaking of canned, do you think I should learn to put up jam? Tomatoes?"

"Maybe. But have you heard?" Kat said, wincing as she shifted the arm with the needle. "This is the twenty-first century, for shit's sake. Women have careers."

But I despised my old job. Human resources. Gag.

"Hello! Yoo hoo!" The Fifth Avenue art gallery woman is

holding the door open and waving. "Come on in! It's cool in here!"

I do not want to "come on in" and be the sole prey of a weekday-bored, fake-friendly, sales-starved store clerk. But it's a hundred-plus degrees out. My iced chai tea latte is melting all over my wrist, and the waistband of my too-snug jeans is sodden with sweat.

"Just looking?" the saleswoman asks, smiling brightly. She has lipstick on her teeth.

I nod and glance around the gallery. Yup, I am the only customer here. It's April, the winter tourist season is over, and summer is marching toward the unwary citizens of the Valley of the Sun with jack-booted feet. I set my chai on the concrete floor and flip through a stack of De Grazia greeting cards, grateful to the sound system for playing Billie Holiday singing "Mean to Me" and almost but not quite drowning out the labored breathing of the clerk.

Who is not so easily evaded. Who circles around a display of dream catchers and stands there until I am forced to look up at her. "Is there anything in particular you're interested in?"

"The Sacré-Coeur," I say. "The painting in the window."

Just like that. It pops out of my mouth just like that.

"Oh yes!" the clerk exclaims. "It's by Sarah Mae Hooter. Do you know her work?"

"Hooter? No. I do not," I say, keeping a straight face.

The saleswoman trots over to the display window, hikes up her pencil skirt, mounts a stepstool, hefts the painting from its easel, and props it on the edge of the dream catcher table. "Sarah Mae Hooter is one of our newest artists," she says, puffing. It's asthma. I'd know that wheeze anywhere. "Don't you love her palette?" she asks. "So joyous."

It is.

It's still joyous when I pay for it fifteen minutes later. The painting is not an original—it's a *giclée* print, seventy-five dollars without the frame and, with it, only two hundred. Which I have because ever since my layoff three years ago I've asked for ten dollars cash back at the grocery store and five dollars cash back at the dry cleaners every week. Being demoted from independent working woman to dependent unemployed spouse can freak out a person. If this happens to you, I recommend starting a collection of money. Cold cash, crispy green fives and tens, will make you feel less unmoored, less helpless. I always carry a couple hundred bucks with me.

As Kat would say, "You never know."

The delighted saleswoman helps slide the painting into the back of the Honda. I drive it straight home, get out the hammer and nails and level, and hang it in the downstairs guest bathroom, which William never uses. Not that he would object to the picture, or even notice it. Hell, he wouldn't register its presence if I hung it over our bed.

Because William is a numbers nerd, not a pictures nerd. I'm a word nerd, but I like lovely tangible objects, too, art and architecture and furniture. And clothes—I love clothes, maybe more than I should.

Dinner tonight is stracciatella, artichoke salad, sausage tortellini, and cannolis with homemade ricotta. Hard to believe that I can now produce a meal of this caliber and hardly break a sweat. It was all bearable, even funny, while Kat was alive. "What year does Will think this is, 1957?" she'd ask. "You two make Ward and June Cleaver look like the Ozzy Osbournes." She never questioned why I went along with it. She must have known that I was just looking for a regular life, a normal life, a solid life that would stick all the raggedy bits and pieces of me together, and keep my brain and my soul from flying apart in one big messy gooey bang.

"You've turned into a primo chef," William says now. Primo is William's highest praise, usually reserved for things like the latest killer app.

"Thanks," I say. I admire my plate, which is pretty much all I can do—I mean, it's not like I can eat this stuff, not until I reach my goal.

"I have news," he says, unfurling one of the blue pima cotton napkins I wash and iron every Monday. I adore ironing, especially napkins. I know, who irons napkins? But they are flat and square and simple and satisfying. William looks at me across the table and even smiles. "My trip plans have changed."

"Oh?"

He is scheduled to leave for New Jersey on Sunday, less than three days away. I have not forgotten.

"The prototype trials are going till Wednesday, not Friday," he says.

"Oh." I swallow a bite of artichoke heart from which I have scraped most of the vinaigrette. "You'll be gone for only two days then. Cool."

"No. Ten. I'm gonna have to stay the weekend."

I take a slice of Italian bread from Defalco's, slather butter on it, and stuff it into my mouth before I realize what I'm doing. Unbelievable. Ten days is exactly long enough for The Plan. Kat would die laughing. If she weren't already dead.

"What will you do here?" William asks, serving himself a second helping of tortellini. When we were first married he taught me how to make the pasta from scratch, rolling it out into thin, smooth translucent sheets, cutting out rounds, and folding them into perky little hats. Today I did it all single-handedly and had everything ready by the time William got home at six p.m. Rule number six of the perpetual diet: Eat regular meals. Regular meals are what set us apart from the animals.

"I'll be fine," I say. "No problem."

After dinner William retreats to the patio to smoke his cigarette, a habit he picked up in the military and has never been able to break. "The man smokes? For reals?" Kat said when she found out, not long after the wedding. I rushed to his defense, saying, "Just one a day. After dinner. It's his only vice."

I wonder if this is true. Inside, I polish the granite countertop with a microfiber cloth. Outside, William smokes and patrols the gravel landscaping. From time to time he leans down to pluck a white stone out of the black stones, or a black stone out of the white stones. How do they get mixed up in the first place? William could explain, using numbers. William says everything in our universe can be understood through math.

I wish that were true.

I look out at him one last time. His close-cropped head is tipped back to watch an airplane etch a fine white line across the Windex-blue sky. He's probably noting the model and altitude of the plane but, poised there, he looks like an actor waiting for his cue. I could end this impasse and go out and kiss him. I could wrap my arms around his annoyingly flat stomach and bury my face in his warm shoulder. Instead I slip off to the guest bathroom, lock the door, drape a towel over my head like a monk's cowl, and sit on the closed toilet lid, hugging my knees. I used to snuggle into myself like this when I was a little girl, when my mother went on the warpath, which was more or less regularly, and it was just all too much. I peer through a gap in my towel shroud. The only thing I can see, the only thing in my tight little circumscribed world, is the rocking-and-rolling Sacré-Coeur.

When I was six Dad gave me an old record player he picked up at a carport sale. I loved that thing—the hard rubber turntable, the chunky plastic dials, the dusty electrical smell. It came with half a dozen albums from the swing era, one of them "Ella Fitzgerald Sings the Cole Porter Songbook." My mother didn't listen to any music at all and Dad liked only fifties rock-and-roll, so to them the records were worthless.

But on Saturdays while they were out working in the yard, I would drop Ella onto the turntable, place the needle into the groove just right, so it didn't squawk, and play the record over and over. Sometimes I'd tie my old blue baby blanket around my waist and waltz around my bedroom.

My very favorite song from that album was "I Love Paris." Ella loved Paris in the springtime. She loved it in the fall. She loved it in the summer when it sizzles. She loved it in the winter when it drizzles.

At that age I didn't know if Paris was a where or a who or a what. Well, okay, I was pretty sure it was a where. What I was totally sure about, even at age six, was that every single note of that song is about yearning.

About desire.

Paris assumes that if you are not in Paris, whatever, whoever, wherever you are is legitimate cause for dissatisfaction. Because if you are not in Paris, you are nowhere worth being. Because— *mais oui!*—in Paris life is bigger, better, and more beautiful.

Most of all, you can be who you really are in Paris.

Unlike in Phoenix, Arizona, an ugly, makeshift, temporary place, a place that feels nailed together just yesterday, a place of lost losers, a place that has never felt like home. This knowledge felt like a secret and possibly shameful thing I wasn't meant to possess, insider information forbidden to obscure-ish people such as me and my parents, people living in a two-bedroom bungalow in central Phoenix, thousands and thousands and thousands of miles away from sizzling, drizzling Paris.

Eventually I realized how lame the whole thing was. Still, Ella Fitzgerald is the reason I defied conventional wisdom and studied French in high school and college instead of Spanish.

Now high school and college are long over and the faraway Sacré-Coeur quivers on my guest bathroom wall. Whispers, "The Plan."

Whispers, "It's not too late."

Find out what happens next… pick up a copy of *The Paris Effect* today!

about the author

K. S. R. Burns is the author of Amazon best-seller *The Paris Effect* (optioned for film and TV by Papazian-Hirsch Entertainment), its standalone sequel *Paris Ever After*, and *The Amazing Adventures of Working Girl: Real-Life Career Advice You Can Actually Use*. Burns has lived and worked in four countries and 22 cities, including Paris. No longer a wanderer, Burns now resides in the Pacific Northwest, where in addition to novels she writes a weekly career advice column for *The Seattle Times*.

She can also be found online at:

Newsletter: https://bit.ly/Parisaholic
Website: www.ksrburns.com
Facebook: KSRBurns
Twitter: @workinggirl

acknowledgements

Every book has many "godparents," and this one is no exception.

Huge thanks to Michelle Archer, Laurel Busch, Mary Casey, Oliver Ciborowski, Sarah Devine, Siobhan Ferguson, Tere Gidlof, Francoise Giovannangeli, Lynn Wiley Grant, Lora Hein, Tricia Law, Erika Mitchell, Gail Ward Olmstead, Mike Pope, Royce Roberts, Meredith Schorr, Tania Scutt, Joanne Shellan, Karen Story, and Samantha Vérant.

Some of you read the manuscript multiple times. Others helped with the French or the British or the timeline. (I am awful with timelines.) Still others offered insight into the intricacies of life in France or patiently listened to my fretting. (Novel-writing involves a lot of fretting.)

Deserving of special mention is my ever-patient husband, Steve Burns, who sat and listened while I read the entire manuscript to him out loud. Without your love and support I wouldn't have made it past page one.

I also owe a debt of gratitude to all the readers (especially the book groups) who read and reacted to this book's "prequel," *The Paris Effect*. Your questions, suggestions, remarks, criticisms, and complaints made *Paris Ever After* a better novel and me a more empathetic writer.

Of course, this book would never even have been born if it weren't for my amazing publisher, Velvet Morning Press. Adria Cimino and Vicki Lesage: You are the best "book midwives" ever! I can't express enough how wonderful you and your team have been to work with so I'll just say, *Merci mille fois*.

CPSIA information can be obtained
at www.ICGtesting.com
Printed in the USA
LVHW02s0022130618
580567LV00002B/172/P